THE BRAVEST GIRL
IN SHARPSBURG

Kathleen Ernst

WHITE MANE PUBLISHING COMPANY, INC.

This White Mane Publishing Company, Inc. publication was printed by
   Beidel Printing House, Inc.
   63 West Burd Street
   Shippensburg, PA 17257 USA

   In respect for the scholarship contained herein, the acid-free paper used in this book meets the guidelines for permanence and durability of the Committee on Production Guidelines for Book Longevity of the Council on Library Resources.

For a complete list of available publications please write

   White Mane Publishing Company, Inc.
   P.O. Box 152
   Shippensburg, PA 17257-0152 USA

Library of Congress Cataloging-in-Publication Data

Ernst, Kathleen, 1959–
   The bravest girl in Sharpsburg / Kathleen Ernst.
      p.   cm.
   Summary: In Civil War Maryland, the friendship of two girls is tested by their conflicting loyalties.
   ISBN 1-57249-083-7 (alk. paper)
   1. United States--History--Civil War, 1861–1865--Juvenile fiction.
   [1. United States--History--Civil War, 1861–1865--Fiction.
   2. Friendship--Fiction. 3. Maryland--Fiction.] I. Title.
   PZ7.E7315Br 1997
   [Fic]--dc21   97-28156
                                                                      CIP
                                                                       AC

PRINTED IN THE UNITED STATES OF AMERICA

Dedication

TO FOUR SPECIAL GIRLS
I DON'T SEE OFTEN ENOUGH:

ELIZABETH, LAURA, RUBY, AND LYDIA;
AND ALSO TO JIM.

TABLE OF CONTENTS

LIST OF ILLUSTRATIONS

*A*CKNOWLEDGMENTS

I'm grateful to the many people who helped make this book possible:

The ever-helpful staff at the Antietam National Battlefield, Regina and Lou Clark, Betty and Cal Fairbourn, and the preservation-minded citizens of Sharpsburg made research trips informative and enjoyable. Al Fiedler, Jr. generously shared his time, his information, and his research skills while tracking down details of the Kretzer and Miller families, helping the process immeasurably; and Georgeann Fiedler accompanied me on a wonderful day of discovery. Paul Chiles brought the Jacob Miller letters to my attention. Ted Alexander helped eliminate a number of errors from the manuscript. Jan and Ernie Wetterer, Mary Anna Munch, Marian Gale, Earl and Annabelle Roulette, and Maxine Campbell all shared their historic homes and/or family stories with me, and made me feel welcome. Linda Irvin-Craig, who shared her genealogical research about the Kretzer family, and John Frye, of the Washington County Free Library, also enriched the story. Doug Bast of the Boonsborough Museum of History kindly allowed me to use his photograph of Henry Kyd Douglas, and Paula Stoner Reed graciously gave permission to include her sketch of the Sharpsburg square.

Eileen Daily, Amy Laundrie, Julia Pferdehirt, and Gayle Rosengren provided encouragement and advice through multiple drafts. Marion Dane Bauer gave me early insight on point of view, and helped steer me in the right direction. Eileen Charbonneau took time from her own writing to read and comment on the manuscript.

As always, heartfelt thanks go to my greatest fans and supporters: my family. Barbara's proofing and promoting skills are especially appreciated.

I want to thank Meghan, who was so patient when most of my time was spent at the keyboard. And Scott, my husband, partner, and proofreader, thank you for giving me the freedom to write.

Main Characters

FOR THE UNION
The Kretzer Family:
  Mr. John Kretzer
  Mrs. Susan Kretzer
  Anne Kretzer
  Teresa Kretzer
  Aaron Kretzer
  Margaret Kretzer
  Elizabeth Kretzer
  Stephen Kretzer

Gideon Brummer

The McClintock Family*
  Reverend McClintock
  Mrs. McClintock
  Timothy McClintock
  Lucilla McClintock

Dr. Biggs

FOR THE CONFEDERACY
The Miller Family:
  Mr. Jacob Miller
  Samuel Miller
  Savilla Miller

Henry Kyd Douglas

Jeanette Blackford

Clara Brining

The McGraw Family:
  Mrs. McGraw
  Jacob McGraw
  Joseph McGraw

Bold type denotes characters based on real people. An asterisk* denotes characters based on real people whose names have been lost.

xi

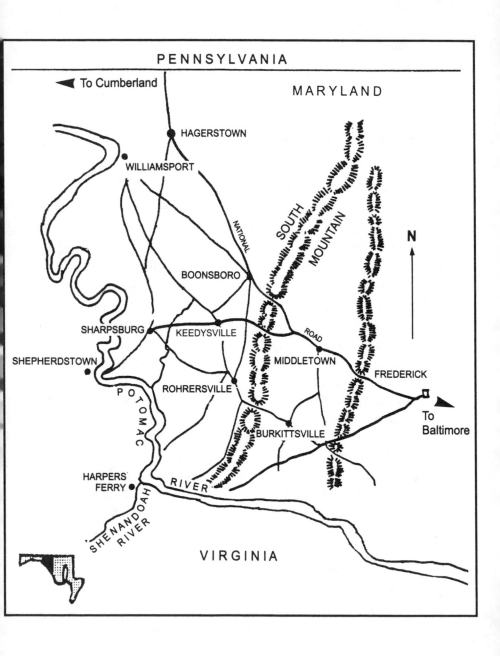

CHAPTER ONE

TERESA

I can't look back and point to a time when the trouble started. I'd already left school and started my millinery business when the war began in 1861, and angry talk had been peppering Sharpsburg for as long as I could remember. Jiggers! Local men tended to congregate in my father's blacksmith shop, so we heard it all. They shouted and argued about the idea of war long before it actually came. Some people in Sharpsburg were for the Union, and some were Rebels who wanted the South to leave and create a new country. Since Maryland bordered both the Union and the new Confederacy, nobody was quite certain for a time which side our state would be a part of.

I knew exactly where my loyalties lay: with the Union. My parents were among the most loyal Unionists in the village. I was mighty proud of that. Our family had come from Germany over a hundred years earlier, and the new country welcomed them. Kretzers raised their children to revere the Lutheran Bible and the American flag with equal respect.

Everyone in my family was a patriot. Two of my grandfathers died in the American Revolution which created our country. I had more kin who fought in the War of 1812. My father had captained a company of Maryland militia for a goodly number

This 1862 photograph of Sharpsburg shows Main Street, where the Kretzers and the Millers lived. Both houses are on the left side of the street; because of the camera angle, they are blocked from view.

of years. You can be sure my family wasn't about to watch a bunch of Rebels belittle everything my family had done to create and preserve the Union!

But Lord knows, it was a trying time. When the war between Northern and Southern states started, the country got torn in two. So did our little town, and families, and even best friends. I was right in the middle of it all.

When war was declared in 1861, President Lincoln issued a call for troops. The simmering kettle of arguments and harsh feelings boiled over. The men didn't take account of my opinions, but I had my own debates with Savilla Miller. She was my best friend, and her family was for the South.

I had hoped that me and Savilla could keep the politics aside. For a time we did. When some Unionists burned down a man's barn because he got engaged to a Virginia woman, I told Savilla I was ashamed of those arsonists. When the loyal residents of Sharpsburg erected a national flag in the public square, and someone stole the rope, Savilla declared it a cowardly act.

When another Union flag was raised, the pole was set on fire. That's when I decided to make my own big American flag, and hang it from my bedroom window. That's when me and Savilla finally parted ways. And that's when I started to take the war personal.

I heard the scrabbling outside one of the second-story bedroom windows just after dawn on a spring morning in 1861. Anne and I were shouldering each other before the single mirror, like we did each morning while trying to comb our hair. "Listen!" I said, cocking my head. Was someone trying to break in? "Margaret, hush!"

Margaret was at the chamber pot in a corner. "Can't help it!" she protested indignantly.

Anne had frozen like a wax figure in rag curls, her eyes open wide. "Oh Teresa, call Papa!"

That was just like Anne! I ignored her, as usual, and ran to look instead. I squashed my nose against the bubbled pane just in time to see Bobby McPherson pull my huge American flag from the rope draped beneath the window. I felt a curl of anger twist up inside. I stomped my foot and began wrassling with the heavy window.

"What is it?" Margaret pulled on a dressing gown and ran to the window. My youngest sister Bethie followed more slowly.

"My flag!" I couldn't get the iron pins free to raise the window sash, and I was ready to punch my fist through the glass. By this time the beautiful flag we'd hung from the windowsill the night before was lying in the dusty street like an old rag. Bobby was dancing a little jig. He stopped when I finally jerked the window open.

"Hey!" I hollered, leaning out so far I felt Bethie grab the back of my skirt. "You weaseling coward! You...you..." I couldn't find the right words.

Just then, I saw Savilla Miller and Jeanette Blackford walking down the street. Savilla was pointing at Bobby, laughing. Laughing! That wound was like a knife twisting in my heart. "And you dare laugh?" I yelled.

Savilla stopped laughing. She stared up at me and my sisters. I needed to confront them all face-to-face. "Teresa," I heard Anne protest, but I was already clattering down the stairs.

Bobby had run away by the time I got the front door open. Savilla stood still, although Jeanette was tugging on her arm. Jeanette was a Rebel too. In that moment, I felt the remnants of Savilla's friendship with me passing on to Jeanette. "You should be ashamed," I cried, but it rang in my own ears as more hurt than angry. Savilla gave me a long look before walking away.

I let her go. I scooped up the precious flag and tried to shake it out. My mother stepped outside, wiping her hands on a kitchen towel. "Teresa? What on earth?"

"Mama, look! Look what he did."

Mama's face crumpled with surprise. "Who? Who would do such a thing?"

"Bobby McPherson. And Savilla saw it and laughed!"

"Savilla laughed! But Savilla is...." Mama let her sentence die away. *Your best friend*, I think she was going to say. "Come inside, Teresa. Let's see the damage."

Anne hadn't come downstairs—Anne wasn't one to leave the bedroom until every curl was in place. Margaret and Beth weren't dressed yet, but they followed us into the dining room. We all spread the huge banner out on the table and brushed aside the dust. Thank goodness! The flag was still whole and glorious.

I felt a flush of reverence to see it. I looked at the blue and turkey red cloth, just the right shades, it had taken two trips to Hagerstown to find. I looked at the white appliquéd stars and saw the half-dozen I'd picked out and done over, making sure every point was even and sharp. I'd spent two weeks making that flag, working bleary-eyed every evening after I'd put my bonnets aside. My initials, "MTK" for "Maria Teresa Kretzer," were embroidered in one corner. Betsy Ross couldn't have been prouder.

Bethie touched it with a cautious finger. I'd let Bethie help with the straight seams, and she'd been good company. For the first time I noticed the stricken look on her face. I put my arm around her shoulders.

"It's fine," Mama said briskly. She kissed my cheek. "We'll see if your papa has any ideas about hanging it in a safer place. Meantime, you run on and finish with your hair. And you girls too, finish getting dressed. Breakfast is almost ready."

Upstairs, I plaited my long brown hair into a thick braid and coiled it in place. Bethie and Margaret pulled on drawers, chemises, light corsets, and day dresses as quick as they could. "Don't pull so hard, you'll pop a button," Anne complained. She made all of our dresses, and was a bit territorial. She was a dressmaker, and always after us to look our best for *her* sake. And to me, "Is the flag all right?"

"It will be, soon as I figure out how to hang it so the cursed Rebels don't pull it down."

"Teresa!"

I wouldn't shock Anne so often if it wasn't so much fun. Anne didn't have much sand. Instead of responding with any spirit, she tried to act more grown-up than the rest of us. It was a habit we all found highly annoying. "You're going to bring trouble to this house, Miss Headstrong," she said then.

"Oh, pish." I bolted back downstairs while Anne finished fiddling with her hair. Anne was only two years older than me. I never let her tell me what to do.

I headed toward the kitchen. There was always an immense lot of cooking to do. My father was a master blacksmith, the best in town, and he took pride in eating hearty. And there were eight in the Kretzer family.

Eight is only middling big, but we were a muddle of people. Some of my brothers and sisters were impossible to understand. Was every family so full of opposites? I often wondered.

I think my father explains it best. Because our cut-stone house on East Main is the largest in the village, we often had travelers stay with us. When a stranger sat down to dinner for the first time, my father introduced his children like this:

"My oldest daughter, Anne, is a fine dressmaker. She's the pretty one. Teresa, who comes next, is the bold one. She's got sand." This was high praise from my father, this business of having sand, and he always said it with a proud chuckle. He meant I had grit, and could take on anything and anyone. I felt like a candle got lit inside whenever he introduced me that way.

Then he'd continue. "My boy Aaron works as a clerk. Not a smith like I'd hoped, but he's the clever one. Margaret, now she can sing like a bird. She's the musical one. Bethie here, she's the quiet one. She doesn't say much. Bookish."

Bethie always studied the floor during these introductions. I suspicioned that she hated them. Fortunately for her the moment never lasted more than a pop, since there was one more in the Kretzer family. "And Stephen here, why, he's my young man." Stephen always put a smile on my father's face. He was eleven when the war began, and already cheerfully ducking school and working long days in my father's blacksmith shop. So, there we were, full of contradictions. Since mealtime was about all that brought us together in one place, Mama was used to setting a cluttered table.

Also, my brother Aaron, who was old enough to soon be starting a family of his own, was always bringing friends by. We had travelers like as not, and lots of neighbors came in and out too, so it was hard to predict just how many might sit down to any given meal. It might be ten. It might be twenty.

That morning, we'd no more than put the bacon, potatoes, and apple fritters on the table when Gideon Brummer walked in. He was a good friend of Aaron's. The Brummers farmed a pretty place east of town.

"Pull up and eat," my father gestured. He was pouring himself a huge mug of steaming coffee.

"Thanks," Gideon said easily, and pulled up a chair. Although he'd been born in Maryland, he spoke with a German accent because his parents had come from the Old Country. Anne passed him the plate of fritters, and he took two. "I thought to say good morning, then follow you to the shop if I may, Mr. Kretzer. I've got a plowshare with a cracked moldboard in the wagon. I'd be obliged if you'd take a look at it."

Farmers bore me. They're always bothered about the weather, hen worms, chinch bugs, or hoof rot. Talk of plows and such was enough to put me to sleep at the best of times. I stopped listening altogether.

I was still brooding about the flag. I was determined to get it flying, safe out of harm's way. That would show them all. Savilla had chosen her path—well, I had chosen mine too. I was determined—

Suddenly I felt a kick under the table. "You little snake," I hissed at Stephen, then noticed everyone looking at me. "What?" I demanded. Margaret pointed at my plate, snickering. I'd pulled a biscuit to crumbs.

"Appears likely you got something on your mind, Teresa," Gideon smiled.

"Doesn't she always?" Aaron snorted. I awarded him a practiced look of disdain.

Papa attacked a slab of bacon. "We ran into a spot of trouble this morning." In between bites, he told Gideon about it.

"Coward!" I added. "Skulking around before first light."

I thought I saw a hint of amusement in Gideon's eyes. I was about to explode, but his words gave me pause. "I have an idea for you."

"For me?" I asked cautiously. "What?"

"Well, the Rohrbachs across the street are Unionist too, aren't they? If you stretch a rope from one of your second-floor windows to one of theirs, and hang the flag from it—"

"Yes!" I cried, as the image came clear in my mind. "Oh, it's perfect. I can't imagine why I didn't think of it myself. Of course!

It will be too high for anyone to pull down, with no wall to lean a ladder against. And it will be over Main Street, for everyone to see! It's a perfect idea!"

Gideon did chuckle then, but I didn't even mind. I turned to my father. "Papa, let's talk to the Rohrbachs!"

He looked at me. "Teresa, can't it wait until—"

"Oh no, Papa, please!" As far as I was concerned, breakfast was over. "Please let's go hang the flag now. I want to know it's up, and safe, and that Bobby didn't win. I want to show him that. And Sa—well, anyway." And Savilla, I was going to say, but stopped. That thought hurt too much to say out loud.

My father laughed and pushed his plate aside. "Come along, Aaron, and Gideon," he said. "Let's find some rope and go talk to the Rohrbachs. We won't rest until Teresa sees her flag up."

As everyone pushed away from the table my mother put a hand on his arm. "John, is it safe?" she asked quietly.

"As long as the Union Army holds Maryland it is," he told her, then patted her hand. "Don't worry, Susan. It will be all right."

Mr. Rohrbach was pleased to let us use his window. It took some finagling, but finally the men got that rope stretched from house to house. A little crowd had gathered to watch by the time that flag was flying. Most of them cheered, although a few stood off to the side with folded arms, muttering to each other.

The sight of that glorious flag, fluttering over Main Street, took away some of the sting left from Savilla's laughter. "Let the whole Rebel Army come!" I cried. "I wouldn't give a fig if they did. I'd like to see someone try to rip my flag down now!" I was ready to take on anyone, *anyone*, who tried to harm my flag again.

"It is a beautiful sight," Gideon said softly. Mama was smiling. Papa put his hand on my shoulder, looking as proud as if his trotter had just won a blue ribbon at the agricultural fair.

Everyone was happy again. Then I noticed Bethie hanging back. Her face was troubled.

CHAPTER TWO

SAVILLA

Honestly, I hadn't been laughing at Teresa. I would never! When Jeanette and I came around the corner we saw Bobby McPherson dancing like some drunken puppet in the street. It would have put anyone to laughter! I didn't see the flag on the ground until after Teresa hollered. Having her screech like a banshee out her window at me, for all the village to hear, was hard to abide.

Jeanette practically pulled me away. "Come along," she muttered. "Don't mind her. She's always dipped her tongue in vinegar."

But it's usually not aimed at me! I wanted to say. Teresa had always been hot-tempered, that was certain. And stubborn. And easily excitable. But those were some of the things I liked about her.

Jeanette and I parted company at my front steps—which, incidentally, were just three doors up from the Kretzer place. Papa owned a farm but kept the little village house too. We had a small orchard beside the house, which was in flower. I was too vexed to even notice.

"Do come 'round to see Mrs. McGraw on Tuesday afternoon," Jeanette said. "We're organizing to knit socks for the Sharpsburg boys joining the Confederate Army.

"Yes," I murmured. Mrs. McGraw was a neighbor. Her son, Joseph, had joined a Confederate artillery unit.

Jeanette cocked her head. "What's the matter? Don't you want to support the cause?"

That question startled me. Not support the cause? How could I not? Everyone in my family was a patriot. We supported the Confederacy. The first Millers came from Germany in 1731, and the country welcomed them. They fought in the American Revolution, and the War of 1812. My father was a politician, and had fought to uphold citizens' rights. Millers knew the meaning of "Independence!" How could we not support the Southern states now fighting for their independence, when our own kin had fought to free America from British rule?

"I'll be there," I said firmly. There! Let Teresa do as she pleased. I had plenty of other friends. I waved as Jeanette walked away.

Inside, the house was still. "Auntie Mae?" I yelled, and then louder. "Auntie Mae!"

I found her in the kitchen, sound asleep in the rocking chair. I started to wake her, then stopped. The seamed black face looked peaceful, not pinched with frustration as it so often was. She couldn't hear well and was going blind. Her fingers were gnarled with rheumatism, and she couldn't tend to Squire Jacob Miller's family as she used to. No one was sure how old Auntie Mae really was, but I guessed over one hundred with supreme confidence.

I put the crock of butter she'd sent me for on the table and tiptoed back outside. I wasn't hungry anyway. I plopped on the step like a millhand, with nothing more to do than watch the world go by. The day yawned before me. Company would have been welcome.

Loneliness shouldn't have been a problem. I had more cousins than kernels on a cob. My own parents had eleven children, and all but two were living. But I was the youngest, born when Papa was almost sixty years old. Mama didn't live but a few days after birthing me, but Auntie Mae says she smiled like an angel when I was put in her arms. Maybe that's why God took her from us.

Papa married again, a kind widow who made a good step-mother, but she died in 1858. Now, although Papa kept his hand in, my brothers managed most of his business affairs, and the farms. My favorite cousin, DeWitt Clinton Rench, had moved to Hagerstown and started in law about the same time I finished school there and moved back to Sharpsburg. Everyone had a family of their own, or at least a job, except me.

The Kretzers had seemed like a second family to me. I had always envied Teresa, with all her brothers and sisters still under one roof. "We squabble like roosters!" she'd exclaimed, when I said as much to her. "Anne drives me to distraction. And Stephen is a constant trial—"

But I'd loved every hour spent in that noisy house. That's why it was so hurtful that she'd vented her anger my way.

I rested my chin in my hands, thinking about that morning. Drat that Bobby McPherson! I certainly didn't think kindly of him, even if he did proclaim to be for the Confederacy. He'd caused all the trouble, and it didn't surprise me at all. Bobby had reason to hate Teresa beyond politics. I wondered if that's what really brought her flag down.

Teresa and I came close to not being friends at all. My family attended the Christ Reformed Church, and the Kretzers were Lutheran. For most of my girlhood I was exiled away at Miss Elizabeth Carney's Insufferable School for Boring Young Ladies in Dreary Hagerstown. I came the twelve miles home just for weekends and holidays. Teresa's family couldn't afford to send her to boarding school.

But one autumn day, about six years before the war began, I was home for a weekend and saw a crowd of boys bunched in the village square. Fall harvesting was done and they were celebrating, noisy and rowdy. I thought at first they were watching a cock fight, and as I can't abide such bloody sport, I almost marched on by. Then I heard Teresa's voice, getting louder. "I said, you're wrong! Girls can be just as brave as boys."

"Who ever heard of such a thing!" Bobby hooted. He was strutting around like a sunrise cock, looking pleased with the other boys' encouragement. "I got two sisters, and they run squealing if I so much as say boo. I never met a girl brave enough to do half the things a boy can do. Ain't that right?" A few of the other boys clapped and whistled.

"Well, *I'm* brave as any boy," Teresa said stubbornly. I couldn't quite see her face, but her tone made me take notice. It was like nothing I'd heard at Miss Carney's!

The boys didn't take well to that. I didn't like the sound of their jeers. Without thinking, I pushed through the ring. "I'm brave as any boy, too."

Teresa stared at me, astonished. Bobby hadn't expected a second contender either. He paused, then changed direction. "Well, what do you know," he said to the crowd, swaggering back and forth. "Teresa Kretzer and Savilla Miller *both* say they're as brave as a boy. Well, I say we have a little contest. Let's see who the bravest girl in Sharpsburg really is."

That idea brought a burst of approval. I was startled but tried not to show it. I'd intended to come forward as Teresa's ally, and Bobby had turned us into adversaries! He was clever as he was mean. I started feeling angry then, and it stiffed up my spine.

Teresa opened her mouth but the boys swept on before she could speak. "Yes! A contest!"

Bobby was rubbing his cheek like a schoolmaster puzzling through a problem. "Let's see. A contest.... I know!" He beamed. "Widow Himebough's place. Teresa and Savilla have to walk down to Widow Himebough's cabin tonight. After dark. If they get that far, they have to go inside. The first one who skedaddles is the loser."

Well! Everyone knows Widow Himebough's place. It's the ruin of an old cabin on Shepherdstown Road, southwest of town. Nancy Himebough had run away from her family to marry her sweetheart, and they built the cabin together. But soon after, her husband marched off to fight in the Revolutionary War with a company of Sharpsburg men. He was killed. After Nancy got the news she went plumb mad with grief and hanged herself, right in the cabin.

Eighty years later, folks still talked of seeing Nancy watching for her husband, and of hearing her sobbing. They said Nancy was still waiting. No one traveled past her place after dark if they could help it. Only a few months earlier a canal worker had bolted down Shepherdstown Road into Sharpsburg one night on a lathered mule. He headed straight for Delaney's tavern. Only after tossing down a splash of rum was he able to tell of the ghostly figure and her mournful cries.

And Bobby McPherson had dared us to visit Widow Himebough's cabin! We considered, eyeing each other. After a moment Teresa nodded firmly. "I'll do it."

I looked her square in the eye. "I will too," I said, and the boys whooped and hollered. I took a deep breath. Well, this wasn't going to be a boring visit home! At least something exciting was happening. Of all the things in this world I couldn't abide, boredom ranked high.

All the boys, it seemed, wanted to go along and see which one of us was the bravest. "Hold the reins," someone finally broke in. "We can't have a whole crowd go. We might end up scaring Nancy Himebough off, instead of the other way around."

"I'll go with Teresa and Savilla," Bobby said quickly. "I'll be the witness. I'll see who's first to run." He gave each of us a look so smug I decided I'd face any haunt before giving him one more ounce of satisfaction.

Teresa, Bobby and I met in the public square that evening as planned. Dusk was spreading over Sharpsburg, bluing the outline of South Mountain to the east. Several men were hurrying to a meeting of the new Masonic lodge, and a barefoot boy was driving several of the townsfolks' cows home from the fields where they spent their days. A stonemason trundled by with a handcart full of tools. Sharpsburg was settling down for the night.

"I wasn't sure you'd come," Bobby said. His hands were stuffed in the pockets of his wool trousers, his vest buttoned against the evening chill. A low felt hat made him look older than he really was. Light from a glass-paned candle-lantern cast odd shadows on his face.

"I said I'd be here," I said.

"Me too," Teresa said quickly.

"Let's go, then." Bobby set off first, carrying the lantern.

We set a good pace down Main Street, out of town, and past a farm or two. I pulled my shawl snug. I was cool, but only from the autumn air. To keep from getting nervy I repeated Bobby's cutting words in my mind. Feeling angry, I thought, was better than feeling spooked.

I glanced at Teresa. She kept pace easily, her eyes focused front. She didn't spare a word for me, and I wondered if besting me was as important to her as besting Bobby McPherson. I didn't know Teresa well, but she didn't strike me as one to back down from a challenge.

Well—I wasn't planning to bolt from the cabin, no matter what happened. I'd wrassle the ghost of Nancy herself before losing that dare!

Closer to the river we left the farm fields behind. Once among the trees darkness settled down like a cloak. The night was clear, but the sickle-moon's light didn't push through the forest canopy. We slowed our pace, picking our way more carefully on the rutted road. Our footsteps sounded terribly loud. Every night creature's rustle seemed like a shot in the stillness. Once a whip-poor-will called and we all jumped like cracklings in a kettle of hot grease.

"Keep going," Bobby said after a moment, sounding more curt than cocky. "Come on."

We went another half mile. The Widow Himebough's cabin lay around the next bend. Something prickled along the back of my neck. Pure suggestion, I told myself firmly. Was Teresa's breathing getting more rapid? I thought so. Maybe the trial wouldn't last even to the cabin door.

Suddenly Bobby stopped. "I shouldn't be leading. You two go first," he ordered.

"But you have the only light!" I protested.

"Don't matter. I'll hold it up so you don't trip. Go on, now. I need to keep my watch on you two."

"Watch away," Teresa snapped. "You won't see me run first."

"Well, me either," I said. For a moment we glared at each other. Then Bobby pushed us forward. We stumbled on, feeling our way.

The cabin's outline emerged slowly from the gloom, coal black against a deep gray-blue sky. I pictured the scene in daylight: a one-room shelter, with the roof caving in. A tangle of forgotten briar roses almost covered the front wall, left from a single slip Nancy had planted the day her husband marched away. An old scarlet oak towered by the front corner. The forest had claimed the meager garden and field space once painfully cleared by the young couple.

For a moment we stood on the road, staring. The dancing leaves whispered above, and some tree frogs buzzed in the distance. I strained my eyes. In the little clearing the shadows seemed different than in the forest. For a moment I thought I saw—

"Well, go on." Bobby was suddenly whispering. "I'll wait here."

"If you wait here, how will you be able to see which one of us comes out first?" Teresa demanded in the same hushed tone. "It's too dark. I'm not favorable to losing the title because you can't see."

"Well!" I folded my arms firmly, annoyed by her tone. "I agree. You have to come too. I want you to be able to testify that I stood my ground."

Teresa clenched her fists. "Testify, indeed! Isn't that just like a politician's daughter! Let's get moving. You too, Bobby."

I was fast developing a firm dislike of Miss Teresa Kretzer! But I didn't want to squabble with her in front of Bobby. I stomped on down the path. Acorns, too bitter for the squirrels, littered the ground beneath our feet. In the doorway we paused. The yawning space inside looked like black velvet.

The door was long gone, and the frame was narrow. To her credit, Teresa took a deep breath, lifted her chin, and stepped inside. I pushed right in too.

We stood for a moment, trying to make sense of the gloom. I saw a few stars blinking through the roof. I was more afraid of tripping over fallen timbers than of finding Nancy Himebough.

"You coming in or not?" Teresa called to Bobby, sounding impatient. "I need the candle."

"I'll wait out here."

His voice was strained. Suspicion jiggled my brain. "What's the matter? You too scared to come inside with us?"

"Course not!" he protested. But a moment passed before he actually planted himself just inside the doorway. He held the lantern near his knees.

I wondered if his hands were shaking too badly to raise it higher. "Give me the lantern," I demanded, reaching for it. Bobby shook his head.

"Look, this is silly," Teresa snapped. "It's obvious that—oh!" She grabbed my hand. "Someone just tapped me on the shoulder!"

Bobby shifted from one foot to the other. "Look, you girls can both run at the same time. I won't tell—what's that? Did you hear something?"

I heard the faint skittering noise at the same moment. It came from the floor, and I pictured a mouse about to run over my boots. "Come over this way," Teresa said to me, pulling me aside.

I felt knobs of something cool, damp and smooth hit my face. A woody finger scratched my cheek. Later, neither Teresa nor I could remember who shrieked—maybe both of us.

Then came another spine-tingling wail: "Aaaaaaahhhhh...." Bobby's lantern crashed to the floor with a racket of shattering glass. The candle snuffed out. The sound diminished as he bolted from the cabin, yelling all the while.

I might have followed if a faint whiff of scent hadn't pierced my senses. "Grapes!" I gasped. I took a deep breath, feeling my heart thudding. Teresa hadn't run but was clutching my hand so hard it hurt. "Teresa, it's a grapevine!"

"Wait a minute. Let me—just let go for a minute."

I guess I'd been clutching hers too! I let go. Teresa scrabbled in her apron pocket and found a little tin of Lucifers. She scraped one of the matches on the floor until it sputtered to life. I fished Bobby's candle from the wreckage and held the wick to the flame until it caught.

"Jiggers!" Teresa held the candle high enough to see a thick tangle of grapevines flowing through the gaping hole in the roof.

"They must have twined all the way up and over the cabin wall." Clusters of grapes hung thick on the vines. We had walked into a cascade of grapevines.

"And there are acorns on the floor," Teresa observed. "That must be what hit me—a falling acorn."

I felt the last shreds of panic slide away. After a moment of silence Teresa giggled. The giggle turned into a laugh. Soon we were both whooping and roaring.

"I wish I could have seen Bobby's face when we yelled," Teresa gasped, wiping away tears.

"Me too! Oh, I wonder if he's still running." I clutched my side, weak from laughter.

"He probably thought Nancy Himebough was chasing him all the way into town!"

"He probably did!"

We walked back to Sharpsburg arm-in-arm that night. It took a long time, since without the lantern we had to move slowly so the candle didn't snuff. We didn't mind, though. We chattered like magpies the whole way. That's how we got to be best friends.

Papa drove me back to Miss Carney's after church the next day. Lessons in deportment and such were more tiresome than ever, and I was in a rare mood until I got a letter from Teresa:

> Dear Savilla, I surely wish you could have come to the village on Monday, after our adventure. Bless your soul! Everyone at school the next morning wanted to hear all about the contest. I told the tale and you and I were named the _two_ bravest girls in Sharpsburg. The boys tormented Bobby something merciless since _he_ was the one who skedaddled, while we stayed put. Whoever gets grapes or grape pie or grape jam in their lunch pail looks at him and snickers. Next time you come home why not come by for supper?
>
> Your friend Teresa Kretzer

Teresa and I gloried in our adventure. After that, I couldn't wait for visits home. Time spent with Teresa was never boring.

And I liked her family too, even if Stephen *was* at times a trial. I was especially fond of Bethie. Her face lit up like a candle first time she saw my papa's collection of books. It took up most of one wall, and her eyes went wide like she was staring at one of the Seven Wonders. Papa welcomed her visits, and let her borrow books, and she was so sweet I sometimes pretended she was my own little sister....

I don't know how long I sat on the step that morning. Thinking about it all, I felt partly sad and partly angry that the war was pushing me and Teresa apart. Our misunderstanding about Bobby and the flag that morning seemed silly. No doubt, I figured, Teresa was feeling badly about it too.

But just as I stood, about to walk back and sort things out, I saw a little crowd gathering in the street in front of the Kretzer house. There was some yelling and commotion. Then I saw Teresa's big American flag being hoisted on a rope stretched between her house and the Rohrbachs', high over the dirt street. Folks began to cheer.

I felt like I'd been slapped. What had happened to respecting other people's choices, and all the other vows we'd made? Teresa had every right to hang her flag from her own home. She didn't have the same right to hang it over Sharpsburg's main street! Many of her neighbors had chosen to follow the Confederacy, to follow a different flag. For most, it was a hard choice. Teresa's big flag, commanding the whole village, seemed to say she'd made a decision for every one of us. I mean, really!

I didn't feel like going to make peace with her any longer. I turned around and went back in the house.

CHAPTER THREE

BETHIE

I recollect that trip Teresa and Savilla took to Widow Himebough's cabin like it happened yesterday. Margaret and I were with Teresa in the square, heading home from the market, when she tangled with Bobby McPherson. I remember tugging Margaret's sleeve when Bobby threw that dare at them. "Margaret, I don't think she should," I whispered. I didn't like seeing Teresa taunted. "Stop her."

"Hush," Margaret hissed back. "I couldn't stop Teresa if I tried, and you know it."

I did know it. Mama could give Teresa pause by talking quiet, and Papa could give Teresa pause by bellowing. I wasn't certain anyone could truly stop Teresa once she had her mind set.

That afternoon, walking home, Teresa could tell I was worried. "I'm going, and that's that," she said briskly. "Everything will be fine." She was walking very quickly, swinging the market basket, but suddenly stopped. "And you're not to say a word to Mama or Papa, either one of you!" she ordered Margaret and me.

I wanted to disobey her. I wanted Papa to lock her in our bedroom. But even then, a special thread seemed to bind us together, like the fine silk thread Teresa used to join flowers on her bonnets. Maybe it was spun on my first day of school, when she had shouldered some of my burden. "My sister doesn't talk much. Please don't ask her to recite," she told Mr. Rubins when I was called on, so firm that he actually let me be. And later, when some of the younger boys were taunting my shyness, she turned on them something fierce. "You leave my sister alone or you'll have me to deal with," she cried, and they let me be too.

So I held my tongue at home that evening. After supper Teresa said something about visiting her new friend Savilla. I saw her slip a little tin of Lucifers in her apron pocket before leaving the house. Small comfort against a ghost, I thought. I went to bed and curled up under a rose appliqué quilt my mama had made, certain I'd never see Teresa alive again.

I did, of course—and heard the story. We all did! Papa took particular pride. "My girl Teresa's got sand," he told his customers, grinning each time. As the story snaked through town, even adults sometimes greeted Teresa and Savilla as "the bravest girls in Sharpsburg." I wished I could be just like them.

I loved visiting Savilla, most especially curling up in the study with a book. She never put on airs, even though over the years her papa had owned farms and mills and a weaving business. He'd served in the state legislature, too. Their village house is small, but nice. Auntie Mae baked gingersnaps, like as not, when Savilla had company.

Papa may be a blacksmith, with coal dust under his fingernails even on Sundays, but our house is fine by any standard. Even the family bedrooms, which guests never see, are pretty. My mama and Anne and Teresa have stitched bright quilts for each of the beds, and Anne has hung fashion prints from *Godey's Lady's Book* in our room. In the parlor downstairs is Margaret's new melodeon, walnut furniture with horsehair upholstery Papa special ordered from Hagerstown, and three oil lamps with etched-glass chimneys that never get carried from room to room. Down another flight of stairs is the huge cellar. It's dark and damp, and it's my favorite place in the house.

It's kept 'specially cool by the spring that runs right through, in one wall and out another. It's so big we have separate rooms for fruit and meat and dairy and vegetables. Every autumn we haul baskets of potatoes and cabbage and kohlrabi down to pack away in barrels. Big crocks of my mama's best pickles line the wall beneath shelves filled with tumblers of jams and preserves. When I was a little girl I'd often slip downstairs and crouch between two barrels in the dim still. I could hear the babble of my family's voices through the floorboards above, but only faintly. I could hear their footsteps, Mama's brisk back-and-forth in particular, but I felt far away. It was quiet. Peaceful. I liked that.

Once, I had quite a start down there. I'd been sent to fetch some potatoes for supper. When I heard a tiny noise I raised the candle, thinking it might be a mouse. Instead I saw a skinny young boy, crouched behind the vinegar barrel. His skin was the color of coffee.

I almost dropped the candle. I was about to scurry upstairs for help when I saw his eyes. They were huge, and full of fear. I realized he was trembling. The poor boy was more terrified than I was! I couldn't recall ever seeing anyone who looked more frightened than I sometimes felt.

Was he a runaway slave? He seemed too young to be a runaway, all on his own. Perhaps a local boy who'd gotten into trouble with his master, or with some of the white boys?

Suddenly it didn't seem to matter. Someone else had found shelter in my cellar. I can't explain why, but I found that a comfort. I knew from those eyes that he meant us no harm. I nodded to the boy: *You're safe here.* Then I slowly filled my apron with potatoes and tiptoed upstairs. I never saw the boy again.

Mama didn't mind me playing in the cellar sometimes, but when she caught me there with a candle and my schoolbooks, she ordered me away. "The cellar is not for studying," she said firmly. "It's the only quiet place," I tried to explain, but she herded me back upstairs like a stray calf. She did, though, give to me the weekly chore of checking every sealed crock and jar for signs of spoilage.

About a week after Teresa's flag was hung over the street, I went down to fetch a crock of spiced currants. A traveling book peddler named Amos Hicklin had just showed up at our door, looking for lodging. He stayed with us whenever he passed through Sharpsburg, and told Mama her spiced currants kept bringing him back. He was a weedy little fellow with a big laugh that echoed through the floorboards.

I hurried back up for once, because Mr. Hicklin sometimes let me borrow one of his books for the evening when he stayed over. Unfortunately, it didn't turn out to be a good night for reading.

We had a fair crowd for supper. Besides us and Mr. Hicklin, Aaron's good friend Gideon Brummer came by. He visited often, sometime when he had business in the village, sometimes just to play draughts with Aaron. I liked him. He always greeted each one of us individual. Even me.

Then Dr. Biggs, who lived just down the street, walked in. "I saw Amos turn in," he said, "and came to get the news." I scurried to get another place set.

Mr. Hicklin grinned. "Well, I've got news to tell," he admitted. "I've come from Hagerstown, and I saw—Oh, Mrs. Kretzer, you're an angel to be sure." He licked his lips as a well-laden plate was passed his way. "There's Union troops in Hagerstown."

That announcement brought a clamor. Stephen was the only one pleased with that news. "Is there going to be fighting? Can we go see?"

"Why are they in Hagerstown?" Margaret asked. "Are the Rebels coming?"

Papa nodded, as if this was expected news. "I'm sure the Union troops were sent here because they know the Rebels might come through Washington County if they invade Pennsylvania."

"Sure enough," Mr. Hicklin said. "Right now they're camped at the female seminary, but word is more are on their way."

When Virginia and the other Southern states left the Union, and war was declared, we had studied the map in school and seen Washington County squished smack dab between the Union and the new Confederacy. "A man could eat breakfast on the Virginia border and lunch in Pennsylvania," our teacher Mr. Rubins said. He rubbed his cheeks, looking pensive. Now I remembered that geography lesson and felt something uneasy ball up in my stomach. Virginia just south of us, Pennsylvania just north. It gave me the spooks.

"There's more news," Mr. Hicklin said through a mouthful of fried chicken. "Loyal folks in Western Maryland are organizing a regiment to protect our local borders. The Potomac Home Brigade, they're calling it. They want to make sure the Potomac is patrolled, and the railroads. That sort of thing. It's too easy for the Rebels to slip across the river and do mischief."

"I doubt the Confederate Army will cross the river," Aaron said. "Their war is about states' rights. Everything I've read claims they're fighting a defensive war, not aggressive."

Mr. Hicklin was not convinced. "Well, mebbe so. If they took Washington or New York it would end things quick, though. And Washington County could be back door to either. I think the Potomac Home Brigade sounds like a good idea." He winked. "Besides, it will give some local boys a chance to serve without having to march south. You boys may want to look into it. Don't want the war to pass you by!" He helped himself to another piece of cornbread, nodding at Aaron and Gideon.

The conversation paused. Aaron cut up a chicken breast like a master carpenter doing scrollwork. Then Gideon smiled, real gentle. "I'm a Dunker, Mr. Hicklin," he said. "We're pacifists. We don't hold with war." The Brummers attended the small Dunker church near the Mummas' farm.

"What about you, Aaron?" Teresa asked. "We're not Dunkers."

Everyone waited. Mama's lips were pressed in a thin, tight line. "At this time I have no plans to enlist," Aaron said slowly.

I dared a glance at Papa. Like me, Aaron didn't rest easy in Papa's eyes. After years of stormy apprenticeship, Aaron had finally told Papa he hated blacksmithing and was going to clerk at Gunnison's store. There was a terrible row but Aaron, quiet and stubborn, held his ground. My father thought Aaron didn't have sand.

I thought Aaron had immense sand, myself. He'd stood up to Papa! I'd only tried once to change Papa's ways, and hadn't gotten far. My family calls me "Bethie," which I don't like. I once tried to tell my father so: "I prefer *Elizabeth*, Papa." He'd nodded absently and gone right on calling me "Bethie," setting the path for everyone else. I'd never had the gumption to bring it up again.

That morning, to my surprise, Papa didn't say anything about Aaron's view. He took a huge second helping of bean salad instead, real deliberate, like nothing of importance was going on.

Stephen was not as restrained. "I could enlist," he offered hopefully.

"You can't fight," Anne said, in her most annoying manner. "You're only eleven."

"Well, I'd go if I could." He sounded sulky.

"I'd go too, if they'd take me," Teresa said. "In a minute."

Stephen scoffed. "They wouldn't take a girl."

"Well, maybe they should take girls, if the men won't fight," she snapped. "If I could—"

Mama's voice cut through the talk like a knife through lard. "That's enough of this. Aaron can make his own decisions."

That brought everyone up short. My mama didn't speak in that tone often.

"Your mother is a wise woman," Dr. Biggs said, covering the awkward moment. "In my profession, I have reason to look beyond the flags and parades. I hope this country isn't plunging into a war we're not ready to fight."

"Our fathers and grandfathers fought to create this country," Papa said. "I can't see letting the Confederates rip the country apart if there's a way to stop them. This family supports the Union."

Nobody had much more to say. I helped Mama clear and pour coffee, but even her first rhubarb pie of the season didn't coax smiles from anyone. After dinner the men retreated to the back porch to smoke and discuss more politics. I helped Mama wash up. From the parlor I heard Anne scolding Teresa for causing trouble. "Don't tell me what to do," Teresa flared back. Then Margaret and Stephen started bickering too. Everyone seemed in a temper.

By the time the last skillet was seasoned, and the last tin cup was tipped upside down on the stove to dry, I was ready to escape. "Mama, may I go visit the McClintocks?" I asked.

"Poor Bethie." She tipped her head, regarding me with a tiny smile. I had moments of believing Mama knew every thought in my head. "Yes, of course. Take some leftover pie with you. And there's a scrap of *blanc mange* in the pantry. It might set well with Lucilla." Lucilla was a sickly baby, and cause for considerable concern. I hoped Mama's *blanc mange*—a custard considered easy on the digestion—would go down well.

Gideon poked his head in the kitchen while I was wrapping up the pie. "Mrs. Kretzer, I am obliged for your hospitality. It was a fine meal."

Mama regarded him fondly. "You're like one of the family, Gideon. You're welcome at this table any time."

Gideon and I left the house together. "You're heading to the McClintocks'? I'll walk with you," he offered. I didn't mind.

Sharpsburg is a small village, surrounded by rolling hills. Before the war, farm families nearby raised wheat and rye enough to keep the sound of flails, thumping the threshing barn floors, echoing most all winter. They raised hay enough to scent the air with cuttings all summer, potatoes and wool and butter and honey enough to sell in Hagerstown for good prices. They raised geese and sheep, which milled about the rutted farm lanes when being driven to market or pasture. There were orchards, too, where boys tried to filch apples on their way to school on fall mornings.

The village was prosperous, too. The Potomac River flows just three miles away, with a good ford to Virginia. We had our own fire company. A town newspaper had been established so people didn't have to count on getting the news from Hagerstown. We even had an Independent Order of Odd Fellows Lodge, of which my papa was a founding member.

It was a pleasant evening. Mrs. Ward, a neighbor, was tending her back-lot garden. A hog wandered down Main Street, snuffling and snorting at every scrap of trash. We heard shouts from the public square, which was half a block from our house: probably a group of boys squabbling over a game of jackknife. Everything seemed normal, as it should be...except for the flags. Several houses had American flags draped from windows. A few had smaller Confederate flags, tucked securely behind second-story windows. And Teresa's huge flag commanded the village from its rope high above the street.

Gideon saw my gaze. "It's quite a banner," he agreed.

I looked up at him. He was one of the few people I felt comfortable enough with to talk to. "It was kind of you to help Teresa. She was in a state."

"Oh, I have no doubt she'd have managed all by herself." Gideon smiled. "I'm sorry I wasn't here to see Teresa take on that prankster. She has backbone, that girl."

"My papa calls it sand. But it gets her in trouble, sometimes." I remembered Aaron's face at the dinner table.

Gideon patted my shoulder. "Well, the people who love her best know she doesn't mean any harm. You know that if anyone does."

"I hate it when people think harsh of her."

"It just means they don't understand her. Teresa doesn't understand herself yet, I don't believe. I think she will one day."

In truth, I had no idea what Gideon was speaking about. I dared another sideways glance at him. His face was calm as ever. Come to think on it, I'd never seen Gideon agitated. That was probably one reason I enjoyed his company.

Suddenly a new thought danced through my head. Could Gideon be sweet on Teresa? I'd always thought of him simply as Aaron's friend. I chewed that idea over for the rest of my walk.

The McClintocks lived in a little place on the northern outskirts of Sharpsburg near Taylor's Landing Road. Gideon left me at the gate. "Give my regards to Reverend and the missus," he said, tipping his hat like I was a fine lady. "You take good care, Bethie. Ask Timothy to walk you back home." I was surprised and I reckon it showed. "These are harsh times," he said sadly, "and it's going to get worse before it gets better. Tempers are pulling thin. I'd rest better knowing you're not about alone after dark." I nodded and he went on his way. I watched until he disappeared before turning away.

Mrs. McClintock opened the door at my knock. "Elizabeth, dear, come in," she said with a warm smile. She took my hand and pulled me inside. The Reverend was reading his Bible by the fire. Timothy was sitting at the table whittling. They both smiled in welcome. I took a deep breath and felt something ease out inside.

It sounds strange, but there was a part of me that was more at home at the McClintocks' little house than at my own. It was small, just one room downstairs and two little bedrooms up. And the family was small: Reverend McClintock, his wife, my friend Timothy, and baby Lucilla. Because of all that smallness, everyone talked quietly. There were even long pauses where no one said anything at all. It was wondrous.

The McClintocks also took me as I was. Their acceptance began my first year in school, when I was struggling so with the terrible newness of it all. Timothy shared my desk. He was part of that newness, because he had bright red hair and more freckles than there are stars in the sky.

But he shared his lunch with me one day when I'd forgotten my own. And if he saw me frowning over my numbers, he'd help. "If you come home with me after school, we can work on it together," he offered one day. "You don't have to talk if you don't want to." I went, and he was right. I visited half a dozen times before I managed to find my tongue, and no one seemed to mind.

The McClintocks also called me Elizabeth, every time.

"My mama sends her regards, and some rhubarb pie." I handed over the basket. "And there's a bit of *blanc mange* in there too. She thought Lucilla might take to it."

"Your mama has a kind heart. Sit down, dear. I'm going to slice up some of this lovely pie."

I sat down next to Timothy. "What are you working on?"

"A teether for Lucilla." He smiled. "I'm glad you came by."

While we ate pie and drank tea, I told them Mr. Hicklin's news. "I shudder to think of soldiers here," Mrs. McClintock said sadly. Timothy had told me that she was a distant cousin of Robert E. Lee, a general in the Confederate Army. Yet the McClintocks were staunch Unionists, just like us. The war was doing horrible things to friends and kin.

"Papa, do you think the Confederate soldiers will come?" Timothy asked. He was fiddling with the wood shavings.

Reverend McClintock considered. "I think it very possible," he said finally. "Likely, perhaps. The question is simply when."

"My brother Aaron says the Rebels will fight to defend their homes and their states," I said. "He doesn't think they'll cross the river."

"We'll pray he's right." But Reverend McClintock didn't look convinced.

"I don't even understand why we have to have this war," I admitted after a few moments. "Why can't people just get along? I think I'd rather let the Southern states go than have a war."

"War is a very difficult thing to understand, child," Timothy's father said. He was a tall man with a long beard and kind eyes. "Everyone seems to have their own opinions about what it is all about. Some people think states should have more power than the federal government. Some people think the economy of the South and the North are so different they will never be able to work together as one country. And some people, a few anyway, believe the war is about slavery. Of the choices, that's the only cause I think noble enough to risk bloodshed over."

I considered that. There were some free Negroes in Sharpsburg, mostly farmhands, although one of the best stone-masons in the county was a Negro. Nonetheless, Maryland was a slave state. A smattering of people in and around Sharpsburg owned a few slaves. That number included Savilla's father, who used to own half a dozen but now just kept old Auntie Mae and her husband. But it also included Dr. Biggs, another staunch Union man, who owned several. I'd never heard a Confederate sympathizer mention slavery. My parents were true Unionists and I hadn't heard them mention slavery either.

It was all very confusing. Timothy did walk me home that evening and I was more quiet than usual, trying to sort it all out. Timothy, like always, sensed how I was feeling. "Are you all right?" he asked finally, as we turned onto Potomac Street.

"I hate this war more every day," I said. But I didn't want to talk about the war any more, and changed the subject. "I think Gideon Brummer is sweet on Teresa."

Timothy pondered that notion. "Well," he said finally, "Gideon's a good sort. I've heard my father speak of him with regard."

"Teresa and Gideon are like salt and sugar, though. I don't know much about it, but it seems folks should be more alike if they're going to make a match."

"Like you and me," Timothy said simply. I nodded. For me and Timothy, it was easy as that. I expected that in a few years he'd talk to Papa and we'd become betrothed. I wished everything were so simple.

There weren't many folks about that evening. We were almost to my house when we saw a lantern bobbing toward us. We all started to murmur a polite greeting when the other person stopped. "Bethie?"

I squinted beyond the light and recognized Savilla Miller. Even if I was a big talker, I wouldn't have known what to say.

For a moment it seemed she didn't either. Then, "Oh Bethie, I'm glad to see you."

I noticed a ribbon rosette pinned on her bodice. It was red and white. Confederate colors, to show her allegiance to their cause. I nodded.

"I wanted to tell you...well, you're still always welcome to visit. Anytime. Or borrow books. Really."

I wasn't sure what to make of that. Was the trouble a feud just between Savilla and Teresa? Or had Sharpsburg reached a place where politics was all that counted? "Well, maybe," I finally stammered.

Savilla nodded like she understood. She started to pass by, but suddenly turned back. "Tell Teresa I said hello," she said, then bit her lip like she wasn't sure if the words should have popped out, and hurried on by.

Timothy and I walked on to my house. "Will you tell Teresa what she said?" Timothy asked, as we stopped by the steps. The sound of Margaret's melodeon slid through the evening.

"I'll tell her. I don't know how much good it's going to do."

"All you can do is try." Timothy thrust his hands in his pockets. "Well, I'd best be going. My father's leaving again tomorrow, so I'll need to keep watch over Mother and Lucilla. If you want company, come back over."

Timothy's father wasn't minister of the Sharpsburg Lutheran Church my family attended, or the German Reformed Church down the street, or St. Paul's either. His father was a Methodist preacher charged with three tiny churches in remote valleys west of Sharpsburg. He was sometimes gone for a week or more at a time. I nodded.

Teresa sat up late that night, ruching ribbon to trim one of her bonnets. Zigzags of stitches were pulled to make neat, even points in the satin ribbon. She expected perfection from herself, which her customers appreciated, but it made for some late nights. I hoped to wait out the others, but Mama finally sent Margaret and me to bed. "Chores tomorrow, and school," she said briskly. "Off with you both." She folded us each into her arms for a tight squeeze before we went upstairs.

When I was a child I thought my mama never slept. She was working when I woke in the mornings, and working when I went to bed. Papa worked like an ox all day and often fell asleep soon after supper. Mama never seemed to stop. Everything about her was quick. That night I drifted off to the comforting sound of her footsteps below, as I had so many times.

It seemed much later when Teresa slipped into bed beside me. I could tell from their breathing that Anne and Margaret were both asleep in their bed. I forced myself awake. "Teresa?" I breathed.

"Hmm?" She sounded tired.

I whispered in her ear about meeting Savilla, and what she had said. I felt my sister's body go tense. For a long time I thought she wasn't going to respond. I was just drifting back to sleep when she heaved a mighty sigh. "Oh Bethie."

She sounded so sad I tried to reach out. "Can't you be friends again now? Maybe she's sorry. Maybe...well, anyway, she sent her regards. She must want to be friends."

"How can I? It's not just the flag. That just made me see how impossible everything is. The Union cause is terribly important to Papa and Mama. And to me as well. How can I be friends with Savilla now? Her father's one of the loudest Confederates in Sharpsburg."

I considered, trying to think of something helpful to say.

"And Aaron's not going to join the army. I don't want people to start questioning the Kretzers' loyalty. I can't bring any more dishonor to this family."

I thought on that for a moment. "I don't expect loyal people think poorly of us," I whispered finally. "Not with your flag hanging out for all creation to see."

"Besides," Teresa said, like she hadn't even heard me. "Savilla's wrong, Bethie. I believe in the Union. Men are going to die for our cause. I thought we could be friends despite it all. I don't think that way any more. I believe—"

"Would you two hush?" Anne mumbled crossly.

Teresa rolled on her side then. I tried to go back to sleep. It took a while. Trying to still my thoughts was like trying to herd cats. That's why I heard Teresa's whisper, so faint I guessed it was intended more for her own ears than for mine. "But I sure miss her something fierce."

CHAPTER FOUR

TERESA

What Bethie said about Savilla settled on my mind like fog on the river. Jiggers! It was unnerving. Sometimes I figured I should just march right over to the Miller house and put things to right. Then I'd hear my father's voice: "*This family supports the Union.*" I stayed put.

In the weeks that followed, there was plenty to remind me of my loyalties. Mr. Hicklin was right. There were more troops on their way to Washington County. The first arrived on a Sunday afternoon, when we were all at home after church. We ran to the front walk and watched the soldiers tramp past. Gracious! It was a sight to behold. They were in a ragged column, uniforms coated with dust. Their footsteps echoed on the road, and some of 'em had cups and things hung about which made an odd jingling noise.

"Give 'em Hades!" I yelled, waving my handkerchief. "Give 'em—"

"*Teresa!*" Mama's fingers dug into my shoulder. "I will not have blasphemy, most especially on a Sunday."

I nodded. "We're with you!" I yelled instead, my eyes never leaving the troops.

"You're a disgrace," Anne sniffed.

"Besides, I don't expect they're marching into battle this very moment," Margaret added.

I hardly noticed their disapproval. I was focused on the soldiers. *Our* soldiers! We had heard that the Confederate soldiers wore gray—a dismal color to be sure! Our Union boys wore flag blue.

The line seemed to go on forever. "Surely it's the entire Union Army," Stephen said with wonder. We heard later it was a regiment of Rhode Island troops.

Sharpsburg is a little village, but five roads come together here, so it's an easy passing point for just about anyone trying to get from one place to another in Western Maryland. By summer, soldiers were commonplace in town. We watched them marching back and forth. They bought out Gunnison's store, where Aaron worked, and clamored for more of everything: sweets, shirts, writing paper, buttons, tobacco. We heard their wagons creaking by the window at night; heard the men hoot and holler through the tavern windows; heard the gunfire from their drills. Even on Sundays, the Reverend couldn't get through his prayers without the sound of volleys echoing through church.

Like the town, my family reacted to the soldiers in different ways. My parents seemed glad to see them, but went about their business. Anne and Margaret fretted about the war only when troop movement delayed the mail coach—as if the latest fashion magazine or sheet music was more important than anything else! Aaron went to work at Gunnison's store every day, evidently waiting on soldiers without a lick of shame. And all those strange men toting guns and talking big made Bethie skittery, poor thing. Once school let out for the summer, except for visiting the McClintocks, she mostly stayed put at home.

The only person excited by it all, like me, was Stephen. I recall an afternoon when Anne and I were working in the parlor. She was cutting dress pieces from a bolt of black alpaca wool for Mrs. Kittering, who'd lost her soldier-son to influenza in one of the training camps in Washington D.C., and was going into mourning. I was shaping buckram, a starched-stiff heavy fabric, into bonnet forms. But I wasn't making much progress.

That confounded stuff puckered and buckled just like my thoughts. Finally I jumped up. "I'm going for a walk."

Anne frowned. "It's the middle of the afternoon," she mumbled. She was pinching several pins between her lips, and took the time to place each one in the fabric before continuing. "A customer might stop by."

"Well, take an order!"

"You're not helping your business by being flighty. We're both out of school now, Teresa. We have an obligation to help out."

I curled my fingers into a fist behind my back. "I do my part." It was true. I took in good business, and was happy to turn most of my income over to Mama. My bonnets were beautifully made, everyone said so. I took immense pride in them. But that couldn't cover the tedium of making them.

For a moment I regarded Anne. Did she truly feel nothing inside but duty and obligation? "Thunderation, Anne, everything's turning upside-down outside our very window! Don't you want to go see it? Be in the middle of it all? Does everything come down to twelve stitches to the inch for you?"

She regarded me with a look so blank I let her be. "I'll be back in an hour or so," I said, and escaped the house before she could say anything further.

Truth was, I wanted to go visit that army camp. I also was in the mood for company. I thought about asking Bethie, but didn't have the heart. Visiting the camp was more of an adventure than she'd be easy with.

Savilla would have gone with you. The thought popped into my head unbidden. She probably would have suggested some great dare, like bluffing our way past the sentries to get a closer look at what was really going on. It would have been a lark—

I waved that thought away like a pesky fly. Ignoring everyone else on the street I stomped around the corner in search of better—loyal—companionship. I wished I had more options. Truth is, I'd never had many friends, excepting Savilla and Bethie.

I ended up at my father's shop. It was a place I had once known well.

My father was a fine blacksmith, a rare craftsman who could shoe an ox in the morning and fashion a delicate ivy wreath crown for an iron gate in the afternoon. His shop gave proof. The nail where he stuck orders was always full. The room was always cluttered with broken pieces of farming equipment or other hardware customers left for him to repair. That day there were a sulky plow and two spare wagon wheels in front of the shop. Inside, a fanning mill and a small treadmill were jammed beside the portable forge in one corner. A decorative iron garden seat was waiting for pick-up. Horseshoes and oxshoes hung in a row across one of the ceiling beams, silently advertising my father's skill as a farrier as well as a smith.

The big double doors, covered as always with broadsides and handbills, were pushed open. I could see my father bending over the anvil; hear the clanging dance of his huge hammer hitting first the orange-hot metal rod he was forming and then the anvil itself, more lightly, to scatter stray bits of metal. When the rod had cooled to a dull gray he thrust it back into the coals of his open, raised hearth. He nodded and I heard the bellows' thump and wheeze as Stephen eagerly plied the handle.

And against my will I remembered the time when I was the one running from school to my father's shop, as Stephen did now. He had once let me pump the bellows, too. I loved listening to the men who congregated there, loved hearing them argue about politics and ask my father's advice. My father, obviously, was the most important man in Sharpsburg.

One day, someone said how nice it was that Kretzer's little girl liked keeping her papa company in his dirty shop. "Oh, I don't mind the dirt," I said enthusiastically. "I'm going to be a blacksmith too, like my papa."

Roars of laughter rattled the shop. "Ain't she a piece of work?" my father said, sounding proud, but he was laughing too.

I had been totally unprepared for that reaction, and ran home like the devil was after me. Mama found me standing by the stream in our back yard, heaving rocks into the water. "Mama, can't I be a blacksmith if I want to?" I asked, still bewildered.

"No, darling, you can't." She tried to explain how God had intended different paths for girls and boys. "You should practice your sewing, not blacksmithing," she said, and I ran away from her, too. I heaved my sewing basket in the creek, and ran off to watch for boats on the C & O Canal nearby, dreaming of riding one to far away places. I didn't come home until long after supper. I found my sewing basket, damp and waterstained, in my bedroom—although most of the spools, and all of the pins, were gone. My mother never mentioned that afternoon again. Neither did Papa. But I quit hanging around the shop after that.

I shrugged those cobwebs of memory away and went inside. Papa looked surprised to see me. "Teresa? Is something wrong?"

"No. I was looking for Stephen, actually."

"What for?" my brother asked suspiciously. "Papa, you said I could work here with you today—"

"I wondered if you wanted to walk out to the army camp with me. I want to look around. I could use some company."

Stephen instantly swallowed his whine. "Hey, sure!" he cried eagerly. "Papa? Do you mind?"

"Go on with you," our father said indulgently. "I can manage."

"Just wash first," I ordered Stephen. He was grimier than a chimney sweep.

Stephen hauled a clean bucket from the well outside and began splashing. Papa pulled his rod back from the fire and tamed it again on the anvil. It became a fire poker. Then, with a satisfying sizzle, he thrust it into a cooling tub of water.

"Keep an eye on Stephen, now," he told me then. "Don't let him pester the soldiers."

"I won't, Papa," I promised, and we set off. One thing I'll say for my father, he didn't wonder why we wanted to go, or try to keep us away. Some things he understood.

The army camp was just outside of the village. They'd taken over a big field beside a little grove of trees. It was odd to see the rows of wedge-shaped canvas tents blooming where clover had blossomed the year before. A few larger wall tents—the officers', I guessed—were in a tidy row beside the trees.

As we approached, a courier pounded down the lane toward the camp on horseback. A string of restless horses was picketed by the road. Men were bustling back and forth, busy as porters at a train depot. Across the road, in another hayfield, several officers were shouting at ragged squads of soldiers dutifully tromping back and forth. It was exciting just to be there. I felt my spirits rise.

"Let's go watch them drill," I suggested. Stephen nodded. I led him along the tree line, wanting to see without getting in the way. Farther along I saw a clump of girls about my own age, all belled up and toting parasols, clustered like toadstools beneath the trees. I steered clear of them, too.

The officers didn't seem to mind the onlookers. Their hoarse commands drifted to our ears while the privates scrambled to keep up: "Company, right face!" or "Left wheel!" On that last command a line of men swung around like a closing door, with the man on one end practically marching in place and the man on the other running like thunder to keep up.

"Some of them drill lines are a mite wavery," Stephen observed, sounding surprised. "And say, Teresa, look there. Some of those boys don't seem quite certain of their left from their right."

I scarcely heard. Those are our boys! I thought. Our hope and pride! It made me feel quivery inside to see them. I strained to see everything, trying to memorize the commands and responses.

One of the groups was dismissed, and paused to visit with the young ladies a short distance away. Stephen and I were watching the soldiers still on the field when a few of the first group drifted by.

"Say there, you sure are pretty!" one of them called. But before I could decide whether to feel pleased about that, he ruined it all. "Did you bring us cakes too?"

"No," I answered.

He looked disappointed, and trudged on toward camp. "That's too bad. Those other girls brought some molasses cakes that were first rate. You could bring some sweets 'round tomorrow, hear?"

"We need you girls to stand by us, now," one of his companions echoed. "To do your part."

"Do my part?" I sputtered. I didn't know yet what "my part" was going to be, but it most decidedly wasn't going to involve baking cakes! "I'd be marching with you if I could."

"Hey, that's ripe!" the boy crowed. He thought I'd made a joke.

I felt anger steam up inside. "Well, if I was given a chance—"

"Come on, Teresa," Stephen said abruptly. He tugged my hand. "They don't mean nothin'."

"Well...." I considered, and decided—generously, I thought—to let the matter rest. "I reckon it's time to head back anyway."

Stephen resisted for a moment, eyes fixed on the drilling soldiers. "They'll shape right up, I believe," he said slowly, like some veteran campaigner. "They're rough. But they'll come along." Then he looked at me, his eyes wistful. "Teresa? I sure wish I could join up."

"Me too," I said. Stephen nodded. I stared at him. I felt like I was seeing something—someone—I'd never seen before. I could have hugged him.

I left Stephen at the shop with Papa and walked home. I wasn't in the mood to go inside yet, and since it was almost milking time, I went around to the backlot instead. Like most folks in town, we tended a big garden and smoked our own meat. We also kept a few chickens, and a couple of cows. If Stephen was busy with Papa, we paid a neighbor boy a penny a day to walk them out to pasture each morning, and back each afternoon. Although the boys helped muck out the stable, me and Mama took care of the milking twice a day.

Since it was getting toward time for second milking, I fetched clean pails from the back porch and slipped inside the stable. "Sukie? Bess? Milking time."

Our stable had four stalls, two for cows, one for our horse, and one empty. I was about to squeeze beside one of the little cows when I heard an odd noise from the empty stall.

"Who's there?" I demanded. It didn't sound like a mouse. There'd been several stables and such burned to the ground, since all the trouble started, so when I got no answer I grabbed a pitchfork and marched back to take a look-see for myself. "Come out, you—"

"It's just me," Bethie said, her voice all teary-like. At the same time my eyes found her in the gloom, crouched in the corner.

"Bethie! What's wrong?" I dropped the pitchfork and hurried to her side. I could tell she'd been crying. Then I noticed she had been trying to wash something out in a tin washtub. Her apron, and...her shawl. "Bethie? What on earth are you doing?"

"It doesn't matter," she sniffled. "It's just eggs. And they weren't even rotten." She ducked her head, sloshing her apron again in the tub.

"Eggs...." I was trying to figure out if she'd dropped them when suddenly I noticed a shiny streak in her hair. I touched it and felt the slimy trail.

I was suddenly so angry I could hardly speak. "Who did this to you? I'll pound them. Who did this?"

"Some—some boys. I was walking home from Timothy's and they came out of the alley. I didn't pay any heed until I got hit with the first egg."

I didn't know whether to comfort Bethie or charge out on the street to find the cursed devils. "Who? Who was it? Was it Bobby McPherson?"

"It might have been. I thought I heard his voice. But I didn't see anyone. I had my shawl pulled over my head."

I could picture the scene. Bethie always kept her gaze on the ground, when she ventured out alone, instinctively avoiding trouble. She was an easy target for cowards and rogues. My own hands were shaking as much as hers, I was so angry. "But why?" I wondered out loud. "Why would anyone do such a thing to you?" Why hurt my sweet little sister?

Bethie rubbed her apron with trembling hands. "They kept yelling, 'These are Federal eggs! We don't want 'em!' And other things about Southern rights and such. I didn't listen. I just started running for home. I didn't know what else to do."

Her voice started shaking. For the moment I gave up on the spineless cowards who did this and put my arms around my sister instead. "Bethie, let's go inside. Mama can get this all cleaned up—"

"No! No. Please. I'm not hurt. I don't want anyone else to know. Promise?"

"But why?"

"Because...I just ran away! I'm not brave like you, Teresa. Besides, I don't want everyone all riled up. It will only lead to more trouble. I couldn't bear to have everyone fuss. Please, just help me wash this out. I just want to forget about it."

In the end I sat her down and washed out the clothes myself. I almost rubbed holes in them because I kept thinking about Bethie's tormentors. Rebel rabble!

Bethie managed to appear for dinner without sign of her troubling afternoon. She didn't say much—but then, she never did. No one paid her any mind in particular.

After supper that evening we sat in the parlor. Bethie hid behind a book. Margaret was practicing her melodeon, stumbling through a new piece, and the chords jangled my nerves. "Must you do that right now?" I finally snapped.

"Yes!" she huffed, and Mama gave me a look. I sighed loudly and turned back to my sewing. I was working on a mauve bonnet the preacher's wife had ordered.

I was feeling mighty out of sorts. It was hard to keep my anger inside. The war was tearing everything apart, and all I had been asked to do was bake cakes. The satin roses I fashioned mocked me with every stitch. Satin roses and molasses cakes! Was that all I was good for?

It didn't help that Aaron was sitting calmly in the corner, playing draughts with Gideon Brummer. I glanced in their direction. How could they be so serene, when boys their own age were camped nearby right this moment, defending the Union? It was beyond my understanding. The only way to end the growing troubles in Sharpsburg was to end the war. I had to resist the urge to shake Aaron whenever I saw him, these days.

The pounding on the door was so unexpected that I pricked my finger. "Gracious, I hope it's not travelers out at this hour," Mama said. She hurried into the hall. A moment later we heard her call, in a different voice, "John? John!"

Papa was snoring over the newspaper. Aaron frowned and hurried out after Mama. At least he had that much sand, I thought grudgingly. Anne put her sewing aside, and Margaret's tune died away. Gideon leaned over and shook my father's shoulder.

Then Mama and Aaron reappeared. To my surprise a soldier was with them, a tall man with ginger-colored whiskers and officer's straps on the shoulders of his uniform. My father rubbed his eyes, saw the soldier, and jumped to his feet. "Uh—good evening. I'm John Kretzer. Are you looking for a room?"

Mama gestured at me. "He's here to see Teresa."

I felt my eyebrows raise in surprise as every head turned my way. "*Teresa?*" Stephen gawked with disbelief, and envy.

I had been sucking the blood drop on my finger, and quickly thrust my hands behind my back as I stood up. "Yes?"

The man tucked his hat under his arm. "Forgive me for interrupting. I'm Captain Markham. I understand you made the flag hanging above the street outside?"

Pride bubbled up inside like a spring. "Yes. I did."

"It's beautifully made. We've all remarked upon it. Would you be willing to make more of them? They don't have to be that large. But the provost guard is interested in acquiring a number of American flags to hang about town. Good for morale, that sort of thing."

I didn't have to ponder that at all. "Yes sir! I'd be honored!" I couldn't hold back a very unladylike grin. By stars! I did have more to do than make ribbon roses. I could sew flags for the army! Who'd have thought the detested sewing would bring an army captain to my door?

Captain Markham told me where to bring the flags as I finished them. He started to back out the door, but got pestered into sitting for a spell. My father wanted news of the war. Mama scurried to get a bottle of her finest cherry wine. Margaret launched, unasked, into a determined rendition of "The First Gun Is Fired! May God Protect the Right" on her melodeon. Anne pretended indifference but I saw her pinch her cheeks, when she thought no one was looking, to bring out their color. Stephen hung by the captain's chair, offering to run errands or curry the officers' horses or anything else he could think of, until Mama frowned him away.

After Captain Markham escaped, Gideon said good-night as well. I was figuring yardage in my head and scarce noticed. I was startled when he stopped by my chair. "Perhaps you've found your way," he said softly.

Margaret was still hammering away at the keyboard, and for a moment I thought I'd misheard. "What's that?"

But he just smiled and nodded good-night.

I stared after Gideon for a moment. He was a nice enough fellow, I supposed. I'd never held him in particular esteem, because he struck me as mealy. Like Aaron. I don't have much tolerance for mealy men.

But it was easy enough to push Gideon and Aaron both from my mind. I had too much to do. The preacher's wife could take her bonnet without roses, or bide a while. The Murphy baby might just have to get baptized without a christening bonnet, and everyone else would have to wait too. The United States Army had come calling, and I had some flags to sew.

CHAPTER FIVE

SAVILLA

I was helping Auntie Mae fry chicken when the Union soldiers came to our house. We were expecting my brother Samuel for dinner, and Auntie Mae always fussed over the meal when one of my brothers came by. The pounding on the door was loud enough to hear over the sizzling grease.

"Oh stars!" I said, vexed with the interruption, then raised my voice for the old woman's benefit. "Auntie Mae, someone's at the door! I have to go answer the door!"

She nodded. "You go on. I don't need your help for this, nohow."

That was debatable. Her arms trembled when she tried to move the heavy iron skillet, and her gnarled fingers could scarcely hold a fork. I hesitated, afraid she might burn herself, but the pounding came again.

"I'm coming!" I hollered. It was probably someone peddling tinware, or patent bitters, or some such—I couldn't think who else would knock.

I tried to take my apron off as I went but I got to the door before my fingers mastered the stubborn knot. I was still fumbling with it when I opened the door. I felt my breath catch in my throat. There were four men crowding the front step, so

43

close I could smell the odors of horse and smoke and sweat that clung to their uniforms. Their *blue* uniforms.

Instinctively, I blocked the doorway with my body. "Can I help you?" I kept my voice calm, but cool. I wasn't nervous, just ashamed to be seen in a grease-spattered apron by these Union soldiers.

"Is this the Jacob Miller household?" The one who spoke was a tall man, with ginger-colored whiskers and officer's straps on the shoulders of his uniform. A bundle was tucked under his arm.

"It is."

"I'm Captain Markham. Is this a Union house?"

Well, I didn't know what to say to that! I wasn't ashamed of our loyalties, but I also didn't want to land my father in jail. Finally I said, "I think politics are best discussed with my father, sir. He's not at home."

"Doesn't matter," the captain said. "Miss Miller, we've noticed that you're not flying a flag." He pulled out his bundle and began unfolding it.

I saw red and white stripes, then a blue field with white stars. I stared like he'd pulled out a snake. Then I felt anger spurt up inside. My family hadn't caused any trouble! I had a couple of cousins in the Confederate Army, but none of my brothers had left home. We weren't even flying a Confederate flag! Why would these men harass us? I decided to simply refuse it.

But the captain decided things for me. "We'll be hanging this for you, Miss Miller." He nodded to his men. One was carrying a hammer.

"Wait a minute!" I sputtered. "This is private property! You can't just—"

"Are you refusing to allow this flag to fly?" Captain Markham asked. His tone was even. But I saw something in his eyes I didn't like. I couldn't find an answer, and he nodded again to his men. "Miss Miller, I suggest you stand aside. I would hate to see someone get hurt."

That was too much to allow. "Are you threatening me?" I gasped, furious. "Why—"

"Miss Miller, *stand aside.*"

It was beneath my dignity to brawl with these mannerless Yankees. I stood beside the front step like I was made of stone, arms crossed, and watched while they hung the American flag beside our door.

It only took a moment. "We will be watching this house," the captain said then. "Do not take the flag down, Miss Miller, or allow it to be harmed in any way. Do I make myself clear?"

I looked him in the eye, refusing to answer. And I won a small victory, for he looked away first. He turned and marched back to the street. His men followed like obedient puppies.

After they'd disappeared down the street, I stared at the flag like I'd never seen one before. I felt a little sick inside. I'd grown up saluting that flag! Just because my family chose to follow a different flag when the war began didn't mean we hated the stars and stripes. But now, these Union Army men had turned the American flag into something ugly. They'd forced it upon our house to shame us. The patriots who first designed and followed that flag had never intended it to be so used.

I was about to go inside when another thought struck. I hadn't even noticed at first, but the flag was exquisitely made. Reluctantly, I stepped closer for a better look. The stitches were tiny and even. The stars were appliquéd beautifully, with perfect points. I picked up a corner of the flag and squinted. Barely visible, red thread on red fabric, was a tiny embroidered insignia: MTK. Maria Teresa Kretzer.

Teresa had done this. Teresa had made this flag and sent it over with the provost guard to humiliate my family.

I was so angry it was hard to breathe. Dropping the fabric like it scorched my fingers, I stormed inside and slammed the door.

My brother Samuel stomped in half an hour later and demanded, "Where did that flag come from?" I told him the story. Two minutes later my father got home, and I had to tell it all over again.

We were sitting around the kitchen table. "I'm sorry, Father," I said. Auntie Mae shuffled toward the table with the platter of fried chicken, and I jumped to take it from her. "It happened so fast. I just didn't know what else to do. What to say."

"Those Republicans," my father growled. "The Union party? I call them *dis-Unionists*. They're pulling this country apart. Now they're pulling this village apart, and insulting my daughter. And my house."

People sometimes mistook my father for my grandfather. But no one could listen to him for more than a moment and think of him as old, or frail. No one who knew him, I don't think, was surprised that he sired a child so late. He always did the work of three men. In his life he managed several farms, a gristmill, a sawmill, and a flour mill. He traveled to Pennsylvania to learn weaving, then built a weaving shop in Sharpsburg which operated a dozen looms. He also found time to serve as a judge and county commissioner, and even served one term in the state legislature.

The past few years had been hard on Father. He'd become a widower for the second time, and suffered some financial losses. But he'd never lost his spirit. Once he got going on something, it was hard to get him stopped.

"You couldn't have done anything different," Samuel told me quietly, while Father muttered. "Not with a provost guard. We're under martial law."

I gave him a look of gratitude. I'd been sorry when Samuel, the brother nearest to me in age, moved out of our house. He managed a farm and also ran a canalboat operation with two more brothers, Andrew Rench and Morgan, on the C & O Canal nearby. He came by when he could, but I missed him.

Father still had up a good head of steam. "Scoundrels! It's those rowdies, the boys who spend their day on the square looking for trouble instead of doing an honest day's work. I knew they would stir things up. I knew those rowdies would point fingers at us when the troops came to town."

Anger flickered up inside like a flame from dry tinder. I wasn't in the mood to tell Father that it wasn't the Unionist boys who'd pointed a finger at our house, but Teresa Kretzer. I picked up a chicken leg, then put it back on my plate. I wasn't hungry.

Suddenly, Father threw his napkin on the table. "Well, I won't allow it! I will not allow those scoundrels to call the tune. That flag is not going to fly at this house for one more minute!" He was already on his way out of the room.

Samuel jumped up and went after him. "Father, don't! Don't do it. You'll be arrested—"

"I'm not afraid of being arrested! Come help me, Savilla, if your brother won't."

"Father, listen to me," Samuel said more forcefully, grabbing his arm. "That's what they want, don't you see? That's exactly what they want. Half a dozen men in this village have already been arrested because of Southern sympathies. More in Funkstown and Keedysville."

"All the more reason—"

"We can do more good here," Samuel said. "Think about it. If we swallow this, they won't have any more than hints and rumors to hold over us. It means we can go about our other business. That's more important, Father. It is. At least right now."

Father hesitated. I looked at the familiar face, wondering if he could survive prison. He was too old for rough treatment. His welfare seemed more important, at that moment, than politics. "Father, come back to the table," I said, and it was Samuel's turn to give me a look of gratitude. "You'll upset Auntie Mae if you don't finish your dinner."

Father straightened his vest with great dignity. "The flag will stay for the time being," he said. "That's all I'll promise."

We finished our dinner in peace, all of us trying to forget that galling flag hanging beside our front door. But that evening, after Samuel had gone, Father called me into the study.

It wasn't a room I visited often. I'm sorry to say that my years at Miss Carney's school didn't instill in me a particular love of books. Besides, the room reminded me of Bethie Kretzer. How many times had she lingered at the shelves, running a finger over leather spines, a look of awe on her face? The memories made me realize that angry as I was at her mule-headed sister, I missed Bethie.

Father was seated at his desk, some papers spread before him. He came straight to the point. "Savilla, there's some things you need to know in case something happens to me."

His words made me uneasy. "Father! Don't talk like that. You're fit as a spring calf."

"I'm a cranky old man who's too stubborn to keep from drawing trouble. Heed me, now. You know we don't have as much money as we once did."

I nodded. Father had lost money in some mix-up regarding my step-mother's estate three years earlier.

"I have enough set aside to meet your needs. Besides, any of your brothers or sisters would be happy to take you in."

I nodded again.

"But you must protect Auntie Mae and Uncle Bob. If there are any debts, any confusion with my affairs after I'm gone, the law might try to take them." His voice was bitter. In the troubles three years earlier, creditors had ordered the sheriff to seize my father's other five slaves, and sell them south. It had been a terrible time.

"Father, I promise. I'll always take care of Auntie Mae and Uncle Bob. We all will." It was an easy promise to make. I knew my brothers felt the same way I did. Auntie Mae still felt useful at the village house, and Uncle Bob was helping at the farm. But they'd always have a home with us, no matter what happened.

That satisfied him, but he still regarded me somewhat sadly. "Savilla, my last child. And what of you, my dear? What does your future hold?"

I knew what he was thinking. He was worried that I had finished school, and come back home, but had no prospects for marriage. What was I going to do with my life? "I don't know," I finally answered, because it was the only answer I could find.

He patted my hand. "Well, your brothers will always protect you," he said, and it seemed to ease his mind.

It didn't do as much for mine. I knew my brothers would always take care of me, but I wanted a home and family of my own. I went to bed that night feeling very lonely.

We got used to the flag hanging by our door, and sometimes I was even able to forget who had made it. It was bitter to see Teresa's big flag hanging over Main Street day after day, but I got practiced at ignoring it. Aside from some name calling, and one episode when some Unionist boys pelted my father with eggs, we were left alone. I was glad the war was staying away from us.

But it didn't stay away from us for long. Dr. Biggs brought the news, one evening while Father was reading the newspaper and I was baking gingerbread. I was surprised to see him, for although he and Father had once been good friends, politics and the war had come between them. One look at his face and I knew there was trouble.

"Jacob, Miss Savilla, I'm sorry to intrude," Dr. Biggs said. "But a rider just came into town with news, and I didn't want you to hear it on the streets. This fellow was just in from Williamsport. It seems Clinton Rench was there this afternoon. He was on, ah, some kind of...business for his father. He has been shot."

"Shot!" I gasped. I felt like pins were pricking me, all over. Clinton Rench was the son of my mother's brother, and my favorite cousin.

My father's jaw moved before the words came out. "Is the boy dead?"

Dr. Biggs nodded gravely. "I'm afraid so."

I felt tears burning my eyes and I wiped them away angrily, still struggling to understand. "But...what happened? Some kind of accident?"

"No," Dr. Biggs said evenly. "There was trouble. A scuffle with some of the boys in town. He was shot deliberately."

I don't remember too clearly what happened next. I recall my father saying "murdered," more than once, while he listened to the few details Dr. Biggs knew. Then Father thanked him for coming. All I could see was my cousin's face. It was full of life, the way I always thought of him. Clint wasn't afraid of anything. He brimmed with such energy I'd once fancied he'd make a fine partner for Teresa. In my mind he was so vivid I couldn't believe he was truly gone.

It took some time to piece together the story. Clint had ridden into Williamsport. Some Unionist boys in that town had recognized him and given trouble. Soon Clint's horse was surrounded. Ugly words passed back and forth. Someone started throwing stones. Finally Clint pulled his pistol and fired into the air, over everyone's head. One or more of them shot him down. He died within minutes. Someone sent word to his father.

"Do you know what they said?" Clint's father said bitterly, the day of funeral. "They said I could collect my boy's body *if* I didn't say anything about what happened. As if I would agree to such a demand! Like a hundred people didn't witness my boy's murder! The Williamsport *Ledger* even published a story!"

That day was something to be endured. I wore the black dress Anne Kretzer had made for my stepmother's funeral. I refused to wear my own mourning bonnet with the almost-invisible "MTK" stitched near the bottom ruffle. I was ready to scandalize the village, not to mention the family, by going without. At the last minute Jeanette Blackford loaned me hers. She'd bought it in Hagerstown.

We were in my bedroom, and I was putting it on, when we heard someone knocking at the door downstairs. "I need to see to that," I said wearily. My father had already left, and I knew Auntie Mae probably hadn't heard.

"You stay here. I'll see who it is," Jeanette said, and gave me a hug.

I was grateful. Clint's death had hit me hard. The ugliness of his death soured my grief.

Jeanette was back before I'd gotten the bow properly tied. "Well! You'll never guess who that was! Teresa Kretzer, can you believe it?"

I darted to the window and pulled aside the lace curtain. Teresa was marching away so fast I barely caught a glimpse before she disappeared. Bethie trotted along beside her.

Stunned, I sank down on the bed. "What did she want?"

"To gloat! Don't worry, she's gone." Jeanette sniffed. "I told her you'd seen her coming, and wanted nothing to do with her."

I felt my jaw drop. "I never told you to say such!"

Jeanette looked surprised. "But you don't, do you?"

"What I want...." My voice trailed away. I didn't know what to say. I was angry and lonesome, all tumbled together. What I really wanted was to go back in time, before the war tore everything apart. I wanted Clinton alive, and Teresa to be my friend. I shrugged, too tired to explain. "Let's go."

We went downstairs, but I stopped when we reached the front door. I could see the American flag, drooping in the sultry heat. Teresa had stitched every proud stripe, every scornful star. It seemed a symbol of the forces that had killed Clint. "Let's go out the back door," I said to Jeanette, and turned away.

If nothing else, we learned who our friends were that day. In truth, a few Unionist folks came, out of respect. Dr. Biggs, for one. But mostly, the mourners were Confederates: the Blackfords, the Groves, the McGraws, the Brinings, the Harts... and of course the huge family clan. It was more than I'd expected, in this time of occupation, and the numbers gave me strength.

I even saw an old friend. Henry Kyd Douglas lived in a big house named Ferry Hill, near Sharpsburg on the bluffs above the Potomac River—at least he had, before going away to law school, where he and Clint had been roommates. I hadn't seen him in over a year. I'd heard he'd enlisted in the Confederate Army, and was surprised to notice him across the churchyard. In fact, I almost forgot where I was for a moment. Henry Kyd looked more handsome than I remembered. I imagined him in his Confederate uniform—he didn't dare wear it in Maryland— and was even more impressed.

Later, at Clint's parents' farm where the supper was spread, Henry Kyd sought me out. "I was so sorry to hear about your cousin. My condolences."

"Yes," I murmured, as I had so many times that day. "And to you as well."

"Clint was my closest friend. His murder was a coward's act," Henry Kyd said, and although his voice was flat, I caught a glimpse of hurt and rage in his eyes. "I saw Clint just a couple of days before he was murdered. He came across the Potomac, and visited me in camp. He'd been wanting to join us, and this time he promised he would soon cross the river for good."

"I didn't know that," I said, although I wasn't surprised. Clinton Rench wasn't one to sit out a war!

Henry Kyd plucked a blade of grass and crushed it between his fingers, staining his gloves. He didn't seem to notice. "A large body of my regiment was wild for revenge. Had it not been for the vigilance of the officers, the gun and torch would have visited Williamsport to demand the murderers of Clinton Rench."

That painted an ugly picture. "I'm glad they were stopped," I managed. "An angry mob can't find any justice."

"No," Henry Kyd agreed soberly.

I didn't want to talk about Clinton anymore. It was too hurtful. "It's good to see you," I said instead, when the silence was about to get awkward. "I heard you're with General Jackson." Confederate General Thomas Jackson was making a name for himself.

Henry Kyd Douglas
Courtesy of Doug Bast,
Boonsborough Museum of History

"I'm on his staff," Henry Kyd said modestly. And then, as if sensing what I needed, he began telling me stories about the war. Not vainglorious, not frightening or sad, but humorous tales of life in the army. We sat on a bench eating pickled cherries and biscuits and ham, and for a little while, I forgot about Clint.

I don't know how long we sat before my brother Samuel found us. "Henry Kyd, it's good to see you," he said, shaking the younger man's hand. "It was kind of you to come."

"I was able to get leave. My regiment is just across the river. I'm glad I could be here."

Samuel looked at me. "I came to see how you were making on, Savilla."

"I'm managing," I said stoutly. If Henry Kyd could be lighthearted about the war, I could put on a brave face too.

Samuel sat down. "Well, I wanted to talk to you about something. No, Henry, don't leave."

"What did you want to talk about?" I frowned. Not more trouble, I hoped. Not today.

"Well, I wasn't sure if you'd been hearing talk, rumors...." He looked me straight in the eye. "Or even if Clint himself had talked to you, or written. Did you know he wanted to join the army?"

I shook my head. "Henry Kyd just told me. I'm not surprised."

"His father was against it. They had terrible rows about it. Anyway, Clint settled into something else. Since last spring, he'd been carrying goods and information to the Confederate Army, across the lines."

I raised my eyebrows. "Dangerous business."

"It can be." Samuel nodded evenly.

I eyed my brother suspiciously. "How do you know so much?"

"Because Clinton was working with me." He paused to let that news get through. "It's not as dangerous as it might sound, Savilla. I think Clint got into trouble because he couldn't keep his mouth shut. He was too proud of his adventures."

I thought about Clint. Yes, that was possible. Then I remembered another conversation, the day the provost guard had forced Teresa's flag on us. Samuel had talked my father out of making trouble: *We can do more good here.... If we swallow this, they won't have any more than hints and rumors to hold over us. It means we can go about our other business. That's more important. Father. It is. At least right now.*

"Father's in on this too, isn't he," I said to Samuel. It wasn't really a question.

"Yes. And Morgan, and Andrew." Those were the two brothers who shared Samuel's canalboat business. Samuel cocked his head. "How about you? We've tried to protect you, Savilla, by leaving you out of it. But I think Clinton's death has changed things. You have a right to make your own choices. Are you in?"

I looked at Henry Kyd. The corners of his mouth hinted at a tiny, proud smile. I thought about Clint, shot down like a rabid dog. I thought of Teresa, who was already finding ways, hateful as they were, to help her cause.

"Yes," I told Samuel. "I'm in."

CHAPTER SIX

BETHIE

When Clinton Rench was killed, the rope choking Savilla and Teresa's friendship got pulled tighter.

Teresa, to her credit, did her best. "Oh Lordy be," she exclaimed, when Aaron brought home the news. "Savilla thought the world of Clint." On the day of the funeral, she put on her best dress. "Bethie, come with me?" she asked. "I want to express my regrets to Savilla. She's always liked you. It might make things...easier if you come too."

So I went. Teresa marched right up to the front door, which took a certain amount of sand in itself, I thought. Her flag was hanging there for all to see, which was another sticky spot. Captain Markham hadn't told her about forcing Confederate sympathizers to fly her flags, and she felt she'd been ill-used. She wasn't making any more for the provost guard.

When Jeanette opened the door, the hatred in her eyes was like a slap. "What are you doing here?" she demanded.

Teresa didn't back down. "I came to express my regrets to Savilla."

"She saw you coming. And she asked me to tell you she wants nothing to do with you."

"Well," Teresa began, but the door slammed in her face.

I gaped, plumb shocked. For a moment I thought Teresa was going to barge right on in the Miller house and have it out with Savilla. Then she turned on her heel and stamped off, mad enough to spit. It took all I had to catch up with her.

There was nothing I could say to calm her down. In the end I let her be and fled to the cellar, where I could sit in peace and fret about life, which was surely coming apart.

In July, Teresa and a couple of ladies from church decided to convene a Relief Society, for the express purpose of providing aid to the Federal soldiers. They duly scheduled a meeting in the church basement, and invited every loyal lady in town.

When the day came, Teresa was fit to be tied to find that all of the Kretzer ladies wouldn't be there. Mama had a house full of travelers, and couldn't spare the afternoon. Anne had a fitting scheduled with one of her best customers. Margaret, who'd been asked to play and sing "Brave Boys Are They!" at an upcoming patriotic rally, said she needed to practice.

"We've already heard your rendition of the blasted song with a frequency that's like to drive us to a frenzy!" Teresa observed. Margaret opened her mouth. Before she could squall Teresa quickly turned to me.

That's how I ended up lacing on my fullest hoopskirt and best polished-cotton dress, packing up my sewing basket, and heading off with her that afternoon. "I'm not much with a needle," I reminded her.

"Doesn't matter." She was happy again. "There will be plenty of work for everyone."

She was right. The older ladies decided to make flannel shirts for the Sharpsburg boys who'd enlisted. Soon a line of women was tracing patterns and snipping pieces with fierce intensity. The less able were set at another table to scrape lint. I scraped.

"The army surgeons are pleading for lint," Mrs. Collins informed us, plopping a big pile of heirloom linen tablecloths and sheets on the table. We stretched them taut over up-turned plates and scraped them with knives until they disintegrated into shreds of fluffy fiber. The piles were carefully tucked into cloth bags, to be sent to the army surgeons. Wadded inside strips of linen, the lint would make nice absorbent bandages.

It was a tiresome job. My fingers cramped and twice I scraped my own knuckles bloody. I'd been given a beautiful damask tablecloth to destroy. I stared at the slowly growing pile of sweet, clean fluff and imagined it soaking up blood and pus from battle wounds. It gave me the quivers.

To keep from thinking about that I tried to listen to the older women's conversation. Most of it was about the glory of our Federal boys, with a bit of bickering about stitch lengths and such. Toward the end of the afternoon, though, it got more interesting.

"The Confederate women in town are organizing as well, I hear," Gussie Rohrbach said.

That brought a flurry of exclamations. "How do you know?" someone demanded.

"A body hears things," Gussie said defensively.

"I've heard even more," Mrs. Collins said. She was a gossip. She also drove Teresa to distraction by asking to have the same, tired bonnet made over every six months. "I've heard that certain Rebel ladies are smuggling goods across the Potomac under their skirts. Quinine and woolens and such."

"They couldn't possibly!" Mrs. Ward exclaimed. "The river is being patrolled. Anyone crossing has to pass through the sentries."

Mrs. Collins leaned closer. I strained to hear. "Well, it's true. I know for a fact that Miss Savilla Miller has already made two trips. The second time with a pair of pistols in a bag stitched to her hoopskirt."

"They should have searched her clothing," someone muttered.

"Oh! They wouldn't dare!"

"Can you imagine walking up to enemy soldiers with pistols hidden in your skirts?" Gussie breathed. "I'd be too rattled to speak straight. I hate the idea of goods going into Rebel hands. But I think Savilla is real brave to do it."

I realized Teresa hadn't said anything, and stole a look her way. She was bent over her work, stabbing a needle in and out of the flannel like *it* had Rebel sympathies. I could tell she was very angry. Whether at Savilla for doing it, or at Gussie for calling her brave, I didn't know.

The meeting lasted until late afternoon. Teresa didn't say much after we waved good-bye to the rest. We were almost home when a column of troops spilled onto Main Street from Mechanic Street. They were marching quick, raising little puffs of dust. Their line bristled with guns like some strange, huge caterpillar. A couple of boys jigged along in front of them. A black dog barked and nipped at the soldiers' ankles, much to their consternation.

Teresa and I stepped back to watch. Their young faces passed in a blur. "Oh Bethie, isn't it fine," Teresa breathed. "I'm so proud of them." She scrabbled in her pocket for her handkerchief to wave. "God keep the Union!" she cried, waving it over her head. "We're with you!"

The fellows grinned at each other and grinned at her. "Why don't you come along!" one of them called.

"I would if I could," Teresa yelled back.

The boy grinned wider. "Recruiting station's set up in Hagerstown!" he yelled, before being lost in the passing column.

"I would if I could." This time her voice was very quiet.

I didn't like her tone. "Teresa, let's go on."

She didn't move. "Bethie, do you ever wish you were a boy?"

"No!" I was dumbfounded by the very question.

"Sometimes I wish I were a boy. Don't you hate being trapped like we are? Having to wear these clothes? Not being able to choose a job?"

"I've never much thought on it," I admitted.

"I think on it all the time."

It was a queer moment. The tail end of the column passed. Teresa stared after them. But I had the feeling she saw something else altogether. "Let's go home," I said again. This time, looking reluctant, she followed.

Teresa was in a rare mood for several days. She offered Margaret a nickel if she'd stop playing the melodeon for a day, and Margaret flounced off in a huff—without even collecting the nickel. She invited Gussie Rohrbach over to work on soldiers' shirts, then got so frustrated with the project she heaved her own flannel in the fire. That Sunday night, when a storm blew in over the mountains, was the first time I saw her smile.

"Come on Bethie," she said impulsively. Everyone else had gone to bed; we had stayed up to work on a pretty spoon bonnet Teresa was anxious to finish. She had never been one to let the Sabbath slow her down. "Let's go watch the storm."

I looked up from her feather collection, where I'd been searching for a plume to match the ribbon trim she'd chosen. "Why?"

"Come on!" she cried, grabbing me by the wrist. "It's stifling in here." She pulled me outside after her.

We stood on the step for a moment, watching lightning glimmer in the eastern sky. Distant cracks of thunder, faint at first, moved closer. The day had been sultry, and the first fresh breezes did feel good. "I love summer storms," Teresa said. "So much energy and life. Aren't they wonderful?"

It seemed an odd notion, but I nodded. She smiled, and put her arm around my shoulders. "You are a sweet sister, Bethie. I've tried to make your way easier. I hope you know that."

"I do," I began, a might bewildered, but suddenly Teresa laughed and skipped out onto the front walk. The wind was picking up and she raised her arms above her head, turning 'round and 'round as if embracing the coming storm. When the lightning flickered I could see her plain, and couldn't help wondering if the neighbors did too.

The rain came hard and fast. Teresa stayed out on the walk, her head thrown back. I retreated to the entry, watching her glory in it all from the open door.

Finally she scampered back, dripping. "Lordy be, what a night!" she exulted in a hoarse whisper. "I feel wonderful. I'm alive, Bethie! I can't live any other way."

"We're all alive," I said, more intent on wiping up her puddles than trying to understand her words. I could tell her troubles had eased out somehow, and that's all that mattered to me.

Usually in the summer we did the laundry outside. But although the rain had stopped by morning, the yard near the tripod and cauldron was so muddy Mama moved the whole undertaking back to the kitchen. Margaret and I lugged half a dozen buckets of water in from the well, the mud squishing between our toes. I thought it felt good. Margaret squawked and squealed.

We washed with our own soap, made two or three times a year from lye water leached through wood ashes, and lard left from butchering. The mystery of that process befuddled my brain. How could ashes and lard, hardly two things you'd rub your face in, make such nice soap? Why did pig fat make hard soap, and chicken fat make soft?

I'll wager the answer is in a book, I thought that morning, as I shaved a bar of lye soap into one of the big tin washtubs. Books were so helpful. I wished my own family thought more highly of them. If I were rich I'd hire someone to do my laundry every Monday, and disappear into the cellar to read.

That image was as likely as Teresa's ideas about being a boy! I sighed and got back to business. "Give me the boys' things, Margaret."

Margaret rummaged. "I can only find Stephen's."

"It's not like Aaron to forget," Mama said. "Bethie, run upstairs and see if you can find them."

My brothers' room was dark and spare. I didn't find Aaron's extra shirt and trousers. Their loss didn't seem to lessen our labors, though. By midday the kitchen windows were steamed and so were we. Mama stopped long enough to fix plates of bread and cheese, and Margaret eagerly offered to take a basket 'round to the shop for Papa and Stephen, and another to Gunnison's store for Aaron. Mama called the older girls. "Where's Teresa?" she asked, when Anne appeared a moment later.

"Went to see a customer. Somewhere out to Keedsyville. Said she won't be back until late."

That was sorry news. I was bored with scrubbing and rinsing and wringing, and had hoped Teresa would leave her sewing and join us in the kitchen for a spell. Her spirits and whirlwind energy always made chores lighter.

Someone knocked on the front door as we were finishing our meal, and Anne scrambled to her feet. It was likely a customer of hers or Teresa's. Most folks we knew would have walked right in.

Anne was back in a shake. "Bethie? It's a Mrs. Sutherland, looking for Teresa. She says she'd made arrangements to pick up a collapsible bonnet two days from now, but was wondering if by chance it was done early. Teresa never bothers to keep me informed about her projects. Do you happen to know if it's ready, and where it might be?"

"I'll look." I followed her back into the parlor, where Mrs. Sutherland was waiting. I'd never met her before, but she looked pleasant, and I tried to smile.

"I'm sorry to trouble you," she said. "Your sister had told me it wouldn't be ready until Wednesday. But I just got word that my mother is ill in Baltimore, and I'm leaving this afternoon. I thought I'd see if it might have been completed early."

Teresa kept all of her projects in muslin bags, safe from dust. I quickly found the right one. I opened it and to my surprise, saw a folded piece of paper with "TO MY FAMILY" printed on it in Teresa's bold hand.

Mrs. Sutherland and Anne were hovering, and some instinct made me slip the note in my apron pocket. Then I pulled out the bonnet for inspection. The accordion-like wire form was completed, and covered neatly in russet silk. But there was no trim, no bonnet strings.

"I'm so sorry, Mrs. Sutherland," Anne said smoothly. "My sister's bonnets are in great demand, as you can imagine. I'm sure it will be ready on Wednesday, as she promised. Pleasing her customers is her first priority."

After seeing Mrs. Sutherland out, Anne went back to the kitchen. I lingered in the parlor and with nervous fingers pulled out Teresa's letter. Should I take it to Mama? I hesitated, uneasy, then unfolded the paper. After all, I was family too.

> Dear everyone,
>
> I'm sure by now you are worried, so I am leaving this to tell you not to be. I have left to do my part

in the war. I'll write when I can. Please don't worry.
You know I can take care of myself.

Tell Mrs. Sutherland I'm sorry her bonnet isn't
finished. All it needs is trim. Anne and Bethie can do
it between them. I have three other bonnets not done,
but the forms are done on them all, and that's the
sticky part.

Bethie, I am leaving my alpaca cape for you to
wear this winter. Anne can cut it down for you. I
know you always admired it.

My regards to you all, and God bless the Union.
Your loving daughter and sister, Teresa

My skin was prickling. I read the brief letter again, looking
for clues that weren't there. Then I stuffed the horrid thing
back in my pocket, trying to think.

Thank goodness for Mrs. Sutherland! At least Teresa's letter
had been found only hours after her departure, instead of days.
Maybe she hadn't gotten too far. Maybe Papa could find her, and
haul her back. Would she even come? Not if she didn't want to.
Besides, we had no way of knowing where she'd even gone....

Sudden images flashed through my mind, like shadows on
the wall at a magic lantern show. Teresa's face, angry and envious, when she heard about Savilla's adventures smuggling goods
across the Potomac. The passing column of soldiers, and the
boy yelling "Recruiting station's set up in Hagerstown!" Her ju-
bilance, dancing in the rain, and then coming in peaceful like
some decision had been made. Even Aaron's missing trousers
and shirt, that morning.

I knew where Teresa had gone. I started for the kitchen. My
first impulse was to tell Mama, then run get Papa. Papa could
ride out after her. I couldn't bear the thought of Teresa joining
the army.

But I stopped almost as quickly. Teresa would be furious if
I sent Papa to find her. She'd be humiliated. She'd probably run
off again, first chance she got. And she'd never forgive me.

Teresa hadn't even been missed yet. I had to get her back
before Mama and Papa found out. If I could find her, talk some
sense into her, none would be the wiser. But how?

I could ask Timothy for help...but I knew his papa was away on his rounds again, with the family's only horse.

Then I thought of someone else who would probably—gladly—help me find Teresa: Gideon Brummer. He was kind, and dependable. And he seemed to have a soft place in his heart for Teresa, prickly as she could be.

I heard Mama's footsteps, and quick slid the letter back in my pocket. "Bethie? We were wondering where you went. Are you well, child?"

"Yes, Mama, I...I was hoping I might be excused from the starching and ironing this afternoon." It was a tall request.

"What for?"

"Well, I was thinking on...visiting a friend. It's important."

"You want to go out to the McClintocks'?"

I'd been hoping she wouldn't ask quite so plain. I'd never lied to my mama before, and the word stuck in my throat. So I nodded.

She looked at me for a long moment. I was terrified she was going to refuse. Then, "All right, dear, since it's important. You may go."

I couldn't look her in the eye. Quick, before she could change her mind, I grabbed my straw hat and scuttled out the door.

The Brummers lived about two miles out of town. I'd never been there before but I knew where it was. I walked as fast as I could and my chemise was damp with sweat by the time I arrived. I hoped too much hadn't passed on through.

I paused in the drive, wishing Gideon would miraculously appear. It gave me a moment to look around the farm. Two fat geese were drinking from a puddle in the drive. A huge, tidy garden stretched to the left, surrounded by a woven scrap-limb fence. The farmhouse stood on the right, a small whitewashed half-timbered building with wattle-and-daub mortar. The stables and huge thatch-roofed threshing barn were behind it, and I could see acres of grain rippling beyond.

An old woman in a faded dress, with a kerchief tied under her chin, came around the back corner of the house. She was headed for the garden, but saw me and stopped. "*Ja?*"

I swallowed hard, working my fingers together. Gideon's mother grew impatient and walked closer. "*Ja*? What is it you want?"

I wanted to say, "Excuse me, please, is Gideon at home?" All I squeezed out was "Gideon?" The woman leaned closer, frowning and cupping a hand to her ear. "Gideon!" I managed, this time above a whisper.

She turned, with a gesture to me. I followed around the house to the back farmyard where three girls I took for Gideon's sisters were hanging laundry, and past the small animal barns and corncrib to the grain barn.

Mr. Brummer was sitting in a chair on the threshing floor with a huge pile of rye on his left side and a stack of neatly tied straw bundles on his right. He had a long gray beard hanging from the bottom of his chin, and the fingers which stamped and tied the grain bundles so expertly were gnarled. He stared as we approached, but didn't stop working.

Mrs. Brummer said something in German. The only word I made out was "Gideon." Mr. Brummer sized me up. "What do you want with Gideon?" he asked, in heavy English. His bushy brows made him look fierce. My skin grew clammy. Desperate as I was, no words came.

I was terrified he would shoo me off like a silly hen, but finally he put his tools aside. He led us out the drive-through, where a ladder was leaning against the back of the barn. I followed his gaze and saw Gideon on the roof, patching a hole in the thatch by sewing the rye bundles onto an exposed cross-piece with a two-foot wooden needle and twine. When his father called he waved, and carefully made his way back to the ladder.

"Bethie!" he said in surprise, as he jumped to the ground. His linen shirt was drenched, clinging to his chest, and I couldn't help thinking that Teresa could do much worse than think kindly on Gideon Brummer. "What are you doing here?" And to his parents, "She's a friend of mine. Beth Kretzer."

Satisfied, they went back to their chores. I fished the letter from my pocket and handed it to Gideon. "It's Teresa."

He scanned the page and drew a slow breath. "That girl...."

"I think she's gone to Hagerstown. To enlist."

"To enlist—"

"Can you help me find her? If we can fetch her home, my parents won't have to know."

"What makes you think she's gone to Hagerstown?" He smacked the letter against his palm, his mouth tight.

I quickly told him. "And I'd reckon she's been thinking on this for some time. She's been vexed so with Aaron...and she was furious when she heard about Savilla running the blockade.... I don't think she wants to *be* in the army as much as she wants to show them all up by enlisting. Will you help me?" I pleaded. "I didn't know where else to go for help."

He smiled a little, and put a hand on my shoulder. "You came to the right place, Bethie. Of course I'll help you. Come along."

He told his father he had to take me to town. Gideon spoke in English, and his father answered in German, so I had trouble following, but was relieved when Mr. Brummer nodded assent.

Gideon quickly led me to the horse barn, and harnessed a big gelding to a market wagon. "We're lucky," he said, handing me up to the high seat. "My father wanted to cut hay today, but it was too damp. A few new holes in the roof can wait a day, but if we'd been haying, I couldn't have been spared."

Gideon drove at a bone-rattling pace on the rutted farm lanes. We cut north near his Dunker church, then caught the Hagerstown Pike. I gripped the seat tightly, trying to keep from bouncing off. I felt a little better for sharing this trouble with Gideon. Now, I could only hope we'd find Teresa in time.

CHAPTER SEVEN

TERESA

I almost made it. Jiggers! I was in line with a handful of gangly boys, already signed up, ready to take the oath of allegiance and get mustered in. Then another officer came to look us over. He squinted at me long and hard, and almost moved on. I thought my heart was going to burst with excitement. But—"Sorry, lass. You'll have to step out," he finally said, with a faint smile. My heart dropped like a stone tossed down a well.

I hadn't brought much money, and I'd been so hungry by the time I got to Hagerstown I squandered most of that on a huckleberry pie a woman was hawking on the street. I'd figured the army would be supplying my next meal, so it hadn't worried me overmuch. Back in the crowded street outside the recruiting office, I shoved my hands in my pants pockets, considering.

Truth was, I hadn't given this plan much thought. All I wanted to do was join up. It had suddenly come over me that I had to do it, right away. After all, *I* was the bravest girl in Sharpsburg, but if someone had started counting recent adventures, well, Savilla just might come out on top. I figured enlisting would even things up. Besides, *someone* had to prove that the Kretzer family was for the Union.

I had figured that if I got recognized, I would just go someplace farther away, and try again. But this officer hadn't recognized me as Teresa Kretzer. He'd just spotted me as a girl. If he could tell, I figured the next officer would too. There wasn't much left to do but head for home.

I'd caught a ride to Hagerstown with an army teamster that morning, but my spirits were so low I headed out walking. A buggy or two passed, and the mail coach, and a passel of wagons driven by farmers eager to make a rare profit from the hungry soldiers in the city. But I didn't try to flag a ride. I didn't want to risk stumbling into someone I knew. I didn't feel much like conversation on any count.

By late afternoon a light rain began to fall, and I was still more than a few miles from home. I liked the freedom of wearing trousers, once I'd got used to it, even though the suspenders were all that held them up. But three pairs of socks weren't enough to make Aaron's brogans fit proper, and my feet were starting to smart rather powerful. His old felt hat was only middling defense against the rain. I ducked my head and slogged on, pretending I was in the army marching toward the enemy. Soldiers, after all, could handle 'most any hardship.

I was just passing Ground Squirrel Church when I heard someone calling my name. Looking up, I was plumb astonished to see Bethie and Gideon Brummer pulling up in a wagon. Little Bethie! She'd somehow figured me out. I was cold and hungry enough to be more than a bit relieved, if truth be known, but I didn't see the call to let on. I didn't even mind that she'd brought Gideon. Maybe, I thought, my trying to enlist would set a good example for him.

"Teresa!" Bethie scrambled down and just about squeezed the breath out of me. "Thank Heavens!"

Gideon waited on the seat while I hoisted Bethie back up and clambered on behind. What a marvel to wear trousers, I couldn't help thinking, and not have to worry about showing ankle! It was enough to give me a smile. Then I looked at Gideon. He wasn't smiling.

"Hello, Teresa," he said. Then he gave his attention back to the gelding, turned the wagon around, and headed for home.

"How'd you find me?" I asked Bethie.

She quickly told me about Mrs. Sutherland, and squeezed my hand. "What happened, Teresa? Did you change your mind?"

"No!" I sent a look at Gideon, who was staring ahead. "The recruiting officer picked me out for a girl. Sent me off."

"You didn't cut your hair, did you?" Bethie asked fearfully.

I pulled off Aaron's hat and showed her my fat braid, pinned up behind. "I didn't see any point in cutting it until I got to the army camp. I was ready to do it, though."

I told Bethie about the sights I'd seen in Hagerstown: the troops camped on the seminary lawn, yelling couriers spurring through the city, raw recruits trudging along with lap desks and spare brogans and volumes of poetry and all kinds of other truck sent along from home. Gideon smacked the gelding with the lines, and we were soon coming into the village.

I pulled Aaron's hat down low on my forehead. Wise little Bethie asked Gideon to stop a block away from our house. "We can walk from here," she told him, and to me: "You still might be able to sneak in the back way. I don't know that Mama's missed you yet."

It was worth a try, in my eyes. I figured I could handle Mama and Papa, but now that my adventure had gone bust, I wasn't much in the mood to.

Gideon handed Bethie down. "Do you mind if I speak to Teresa for a bit?" he asked.

She glanced at me, then shook her head. "No. I'll go on. I thank you, Gideon, for your help. I hope you can finish your roof tomorrow." Then, with her shawl pulled over her head to ward off the misting rain, she headed for home.

I scrambled down after her, and extended a hand to Gideon. "My thanks, too. For helping Bethie, I mean. I hope she didn't pull you away at a bad time."

He had dropped the reins in his lap, but he didn't take my hand. For the first time I wondered if he was angry. It was hard to tell. I was just about to shrug and turn away when he finally spoke. "Why'd you do it?"

"Someone has to prove the Unionists in this town will take as many risks as the Confederate sympathizers." I gave him my best scornful look. "But I don't expect you to understand. If you have to ask, I can't explain."

He ignored that, although I thought his muscles tensed. "Did you think at all about your family? That they'd be terribly worried?"

Who was he to meddle! "My parents know I can take care of myself—"

"I'm not just talking about your parents. What about her?" He nodded toward Bethie. "She looks to you."

That gave me pause, I admit. Didn't he know how special Bethie was to me? It took a moment to find an answer. "I know it," I said slowly. "But some things are bigger than...than family. And someone has to prove where my family stands. If Aaron won't do right by the Kretzers and enlist—"

"Teresa, you are a marvelous girl." Before I could do more than gawk he went on. "But the things I admire most about you also make me want to shake you! When are you going to see that this war is not a game?"

His words made my skin prickle. I wasn't sure why. "Game!" I flared, responding to the only thing he'd said that I understood. "I don't—"

"And it's not some kind of a dare. This is not the time to take foolish chances just to impress Savilla Miller." He stared down at me like I was a child.

I was too angry to speak. I smacked the gelding's rump, hard as I could. The wagon had rumbled past our house before Gideon got the lines sorted out.

I did manage to sneak into the house and change before anyone but Bethie was the wiser. I was still fuming at Gideon's brass, though, and lacing into my corset didn't improve my mood. Neither did spending the evening finishing Mrs. Sutherland's bonnet.

But late that night, when we'd all gone to bed, Bethie whispered, "I'm so glad they didn't take you. I'd miss you something terrible. Please don't try it again."

"Not much point, I guess," I whispered back.

"I'd never have the gumption to try." Bethie sounded discouraged. "I wish I had sand like you, Teresa."

"Never mind, goose," I whispered. "I like you just the way you are."

In a few minutes I heard her breathing slide into sleep. Tired as I was, it took me longer. I did feel better, though.

As for Savilla, well, I felt better about her too. She'd likely never know what I'd done that day. But if we ever had cause to compare, I could claim an adventure bold as any of hers. If need be, Bethie and Gideon could prove it. For the moment, it was enough.

Running away to enlist was my last big adventure for a while. But there was enough excitement to keep us all occupied. News of the war's first big battle, at a place called Bull Run, tapped over the telegraph wires in late July. I couldn't believe my ears when I heard tell of the big Rebel victory. The Rebels in town crowed over that news, you can be sure.

Still, that battlefield in eastern Virginia seemed far distant. To us, the war was a stone's toss away. The Rebels commenced skirmishing with Federal patrols along the border. The Potomac Home Brigade helped some Massachusetts troops patrol the river and fords. In September John Marrow, a member of the brigade, was accidentally killed by one of his comrades. Most everybody in town attended the funeral.

In December, rumors of a Confederate attack at Sharpsburg raced through the village like brush fires. Nothing came of it.

In the spring we got another scare with news of a big Confederate force chasing Union soldiers north through Virginia's Shenandoah Valley, headed straight at us. The roads were jammed with folks scrambling to get out of their way. They toted babies, and pushed carts and wheelbarrows piled crazily with baskets of food and prized china. Our house overflowed with travelers, and most of our neighbors took folks in, too. Other refugees just camped along the edge of the roads, or in farmers' fields.

One of the refugees was a war widow with four young children. "I was too afeared to stay," she whispered one night in our kitchen, while Mama and I warmed up some milk for the little ones. "My husband was one of the first to join the Union Army. He was real vocal about it. I've got Rebel neighbors who haven't forgotten some of those angry words. I'm afeard they'll turn the Rebel Army on me when they cross the river. I got to get the children away safe."

Those children were shivering and hollow-eyed. It broke my heart to see them. "Everything will be well in the end," Mama said, real soothing. We made sure they all got something warm to eat before bedding them down for the night. But when I passed Aaron on the stairs, I felt anger simmer up inside like a soup kettle left too long on the fire.

"How can you look these people in the eye?" I hissed. "You should be ashamed."

His mouth pinched in a tight line. "It's not your place to say."

"It is! I'm talking about defending your own home and state! That poor woman downstairs already lost her husband to the cause. When the Rebels cross the river—"

"You don't know everything, Teresa," Aaron said, and pushed past me. "I don't think the Confederate Army is going to cross the Potomac."

By stars! It chokes me to admit it, but Aaron was right. He was out of a job for a few days because Mr. Gunnison packed up his merchandise and fled to Pennsylvania. But within a week

Mr. Gunnison was back, restocking his shelves. The invasion scare was over. The refugees trudged back through Sharpsburg, heading for home.

I refused to speak to Aaron for a couple of weeks, but other than that, things quieted down. Gideon came around sometimes, and most of the time I didn't speak to him either. I watched them, deep in conversation, sitting on the front step or in a corner of the parlor, and my hand itched to smack them. I wished the Rebel Army *would* come, just to give my brother and his friend a real taste of the war.

Back then, of course, I was too foolish to know what I was wishing for.

CHAPTER EIGHT

SAVILLA

It wasn't long before stories snaked through the village about Teresa trying to enlist. Most folks just chuckled. "That Teresa Kretzer," they said, shaking their heads. "She's got sand."

The tale came up one afternoon when some of us girls—me and Jeanette, and Maggie Hart, Jennie Mumma, and Clara Brining—were making little sewing kits to send to the Southern troops. It was boring work, so we generally chattered to keep things lively. Clara brought the story about Teresa.

"Foolishness," Jeanette shrugged.

I didn't say anything. I didn't like talking about Teresa. Maybe it was because that whole flag business had been so hurtful. Or maybe because, much as I liked these girls, if truth be known I didn't find them as good company as Teresa had once been. None of them would have suggested trying to enlist! It sounded like a lark, the kind of adventure I once would have shared with Teresa. I didn't know whether to be envious or angry. I let it all stew inside, and held my tongue.

Our little group met once a week to sew or knit for the Confederate Army. Sometimes someone had received a tattered letter, and shared their news with the rest of us. And we talked like the Southern Army was invincible. Back then, we believed it. I think some of the Unionists in Sharpsburg trusted that the Confederate Army would never cross the Potomac and invade the North. We always knew in our hearts that they would, and we ached for the day.

Working on relief packages with the other Confederate girls gave me something useful to do, and helped pass the time while we waited. But working with my brothers and father did even more for my spirits.

When Samuel first talked to me about it, the day of my cousin Clinton's funeral, I had visions of carrying military secrets through the lines, dodging bullets, making breathless reports to grateful generals, and generally saving the South. Instead, several times I stitched little pouches of medicines to my hooped petticoat and carried a forged pass to the sentries guarding the Potomac River. They never so much as questioned my pass, and I smuggled the goods across. Once I got to carry a pair of pistols someone had donated to the cause, which was more exciting.

And every once in a while, if Samuel or my father couldn't get a Federal pass, Samuel rowed across the river himself, sneaking past the sentries. Sometimes he let me come, and those trips were thrilling.

"Don't speak. Don't even whisper," Samuel warned me, so we made each trip in silence. Samuel picked cloudy, moonless nights, and we waited until long after dark to set out. We slid the rowboat into the current from steep, brambled banks far removed from the usual fords, and muffled the oarlocks with rags. Samuel leaned into the oars while I crouched in the bow. Quickly we were lost in the night. I smelled the fresh cold Potomac. River breezes ruffled my hair and cloak. My muscles tensed with every dripping whisper of the oars. I always lost track of time, always wondered if Samuel was rowing in circles...and always had to fight the urge to laugh out loud. And soon enough we'd feel sand and gravel scrape beneath the hull: safe on Virginia soil. I never felt so alive as I did on those nights.

And when I was back home in Sharpsburg, no one the wiser, I glowed with my secrets. Teresa's flags, hanging by my front door and waving over Main Street, weren't as hurtful to see. The bravest girl in Sharpsburg! I'd once been content to share that crown, but no more. And in my eyes, the contest was over. Maybe Teresa had tried to enlist, but she hadn't gotten far. While she stitched flags for her Union cause, I was smuggling quinine and opium and sometimes even firearms for the Confederacy.

So, I managed to hold my head high during those long fifteen months of occupation. That summer of 1862, we held our breath with each new report of a Federal offensive against General Lee's Southern Army in Virginia. And then, in August, came the first rumors of what we'd been waiting to hear.

Samuel stopped by unexpectedly one hot evening. Father was writing a letter to one of my married sisters, who lived in Iowa. I was trying to write a letter to Henry Kyd Douglas. But I didn't have much news beyond the heat, which came down to infernal flies and moldy cheese and the discomfort of a chemise wet with sweat. After half an hour of considering, I hadn't gotten beyond "Dear Henry Kyd." The house was still, lonely. I welcomed Samuel's interruption.

He didn't waste time. "Word from Virginia is that the Southern Army is ready to invade the North."

"Really?" I squealed. I made a huge blot and didn't even care. They were coming!

Father capped the inkwell and wiped his pen dry with a look of calm satisfaction. "What have you heard?" he asked Samuel.

"Well sir, the time is ripe. The Union Army tried to seize Richmond, and failed. The Southern Army is ready to strike back. And besides," he added more soberly, "Virginia has been feeding the army for over a year. It's stripped bare. Our soldiers are starving, and if they stay in Virginia much longer, the farm families there will starve too. The Southern Army needs lots of fresh food, and the best place to get it is north of the Potomac."

I thought about that. When the war began, I'd thought the soldiers needed guns and ammunition most. Since then, I'd learned better. I pictured the farmland around Sharpsburg: orchards with dripping branches, endless fields of ripe corn, well-stocked root cellars.

"There is no famine in Maryland and Pennsylvania," Father said thoughtfully, nodding. "Besides, it's good politics. It's time the Confederacy took the offensive. If we can capture Washington, the war will end. What General Lee needs to do...."

I let Father talk on, mapping out the entire campaign with authority. My thoughts were tumbling like leaves in an autumn wind. Would Southern soldiers come to Western Maryland? Oh, it would be glorious! In my mind I could see the Union troops skedaddling, see Confederate flags hanging in place of the American banners. And maybe, just maybe, I'd even get a visit from a certain young officer on General Stonewall Jackson's staff....

I hadn't seen Henry Kyd Douglas since Clinton's funeral, over a year earlier. In that time I'd gotten three letters from him. Considering the war, the difficulty in getting mail across the lines, I was content with that number. I kept them all in my glove box upstairs, safe from curious eyes.

Henry Kyd wrote well, and I smiled over tales of army oddities. And through his eyes I saw battlefields like Malvern Hill and Slaughter Mountain—at least what was proper for a young lady to see. But mostly, I made better acquaintance with a young man who missed his friend Clinton Rench, and worried about his family. I wrote him letters filled with whatever news of home I could think of. I even made bold to call on his parents, Reverend and Mrs. Douglas, so I could write Henry that I'd seen them.

I'd been in love once before. Several years earlier, when my father still ran a flour mill, an itinerant grinder walked in one day, and offered to clean and edge the immense grindstones. He was a young man, but skilled, and my father gave him a chance. I'd been home from school for the summer, bored as usual, and lingered in the mill while he worked.

Something in him drew me. I watched his scarred hands lovingly re-shape the grinding edges, and listened to tales of the sights he'd seen wandering back roads from mill to mill. And I dreamed of wandering away with him to see what lay beyond the hills of my suddenly-small world. He'd winked at me and promised, when my father wasn't listening, to come back.

He never had. Now, I couldn't remember his name. Instead, I found myself hanging onto conversations of "our boys" at the front in hopes of hearing another name. And often enough it came, for Washington County Confederates were proud of Henry Kyd Douglas. He was the youngest member of General Jackson's staff, and already making a name for himself.

Once, I might have talked to Teresa about him. But now, there was no one I felt comfortable confiding in—not even Jeanette, who in her own way was a faithful friend. So I kept my secrets. But for the first time, when Father asked me about my future, I began to hope I might have one.

The Confederate Army commenced splashing across the Potomac River on Thursday, September 4, at several fords near Leesburg, Virginia. When we heard that news I begged Father to go watch. It was a smart distance from Sharpsburg—about twenty miles—but well worth it, to my mind.

"Don't dare," Father growled. "Everybody in town is on edge. I don't trust those scoundrels not to make us pay for this news. I mean to stay and protect my property." He patted the old revolver he'd taken to carrying.

We'd so far been spared anything worse than a Union flag, but some Confederates in town hadn't been so lucky. A few had burned barns and smokehouses as testament to their sympathies.

My brothers all begged off too. In the end I got mad and saddled Honey, Father's old mare, and set out for myself. I knew no one would miss me. With no mother, an elderly father, and brothers all out on their own, I had more freedom than most.

But by mid-day I had to turn back, still miles away from Poolesville, the nearest ford. The roads were jammed. The countryside was aflutter with the news. Unionists were stampeding north, heading for safe haven, just as fast as Southern sympathizers stampeded south for a look-see. I was forced to admit I'd never make it to Poolesville before dark, much less home again.

Still, knowing the Confederate Army was so close was a thrill. I imagined them wading to shore and hoped with all my might that some would come to Sharpsburg.

No one seemed to know just where the Confederate Army was headed. In the days that followed we heard talk of Washington, Philadelphia, even New York, but it was all speculation. The Union troops along the canal, we heard, got ready to scamper. We got word that the Southern Army descended upon Frederick, and then Hagerstown. They overjoyed some and panicked others and generally ate everything put in front of them.

That was all, though. General Lee hoped to win support in Maryland, maybe coax more young Maryland men to enlist and march away with his army. He issued strict orders against foraging, which were more-or-less obeyed. Unionist citizens, who'd been terrified of the Southern Army, sheepishly admitted that the soldiers were generally well behaved. They didn't come to pillage and plunder. They just didn't want to starve.

Then all telegraph wires were cut. The mail coach stopped running. We couldn't get any more news. There was nothing to do but wait.

Chapter Nine

BETHIE

When we got word that the Confederate Army truly had crossed the Potomac, there was quite an uproar. My parents didn't even consider skedaddling. But Teresa's flag was another matter.

We were fixing cornbread and sausage for breakfast one morning when Dr. Biggs walked in. We'd been enduring a heat wave like to fry the devil, and had a house full of travelers, so Mama and us girls had a big task in getting enough food ready. "Good morning," Mama said, and poured him a cup of coffee. Teresa was slicing some early apples to fry. None of us paid him much mind until he spoke.

"I don't mean to interrupt, Susan," he said to Mama. "But I came to talk to you and John about the flag."

Teresa put the knife aside with a frown. "What about it?"

"Margaret, go fetch your Papa," Mama said. I could tell she was smelling trouble. I smelled it too.

"I said, what about the flag?" Teresa demanded.

"Well, some folks in town have been talking," Dr. Biggs said. "People are worried. It might cause trouble if the Confederates come."

"I'm not afraid of the Confederates."

Mama frowned. "Teresa, let's listen to what Dr. Biggs has to say."

"I've been asked to speak on behalf of your neighbors," Dr. Biggs went on. "We'd like you to take the flag down until—"

Teresa stamped her foot. "I won't!" Just then Margaret came back with Papa, and Aaron too. Teresa whirled around. "Papa, they want me to take down the flag! I won't do it. I won't!"

"What's this all about?" Papa asked. He was still buttoning his shirt. "Morning, Augustin. What's the trouble?"

Dr. Biggs folded his arms, looking serious. "John, you know I'm a Union man. Most of your neighbors are too. But this town doesn't need to look for trouble. Right now the Confederate Army is east of Sharpsburg. Maybe they'll stay away. But maybe they won't! If they pass through town, they're not going to like that huge American flag hanging over Main Street. We don't need to invite trouble—"

"I am not ashamed to be for the Union!" Teresa cried. "Of all the mealy, weak-spined foolishness—"

"That's enough," Mama said, very quietly. Teresa sniffed and turned back to her apples. But instead of slicing, she began to chop the fruit into tiny pieces. Thwick! Thwick! Thwick! Her knife slammed through the apples, into the cutting block, so loud it rang in the room above the sizzle of cooking sausages.

"I can understand how you feel," Dr. Biggs said after a moment. "I don't like this either. But think about it. What will be accomplished by making the Confederate soldiers angry? Is it worth risking your home? Or your safety? I don't think so."

His words sent shivers down my spine. *Take the flag down*, I wanted to say. I was ashamed right away, and was glad for once that I couldn't voice my thoughts. But I couldn't stop worrying, either.

"We'll certainly think on it," Papa said easily. "And I thank you for speaking your mind. Now. Will you stay for breakfast?"

Dr. Biggs looked at Teresa's back. She was still pounding away at the chopping block. He smiled a little and shook his head. "I best be going. Good day to you all."

I was sorry to see him go, because once the door closed again, almost everybody started talking at once. Teresa's voice was loudest. "I will not take my flag down just because some cowards want me to! If they don't want a flag at their house, fine. But this is a Union house."

"You're acting like a child," Anne snapped. She poked at the frying sausage like it was a great annoyance.

"Don't tell me—"

"Are the Rebels really coming?" Margaret asked, as if one of us could predict the future. "When will they get here? Papa—"

"Be still!" Papa roared. Mama had her fingers pressed at her temples, and he gave her a concerned look. "You're giving your mother a headache." He folded his arms. "Now Teresa, I'm proud to fly your flag. But we need to give some thought to what Dr. Biggs had to say."

Teresa ran to him and clung to his arm. "Oh Papa, please don't ask me to take it down!" she begged. "*Please.* I'm not afraid of General Lee or the whole Rebel Army!"

"No, I don't suppose you are," he chuckled. Some of the tension eased from the room. "But there's something you're not thinking about. The flag won't just make the Confederates angry. They'll take it, sure as you're born. Is that what you want?"

"I won't let them!"

Aaron finally spoke. "You really are a child," he said. His voice was quiet. Somehow that sounded worse than Anne's preachy scorn.

Teresa glared at him. "At least *I'm* not afraid of the Confederate Army."

Mama put a hand on Aaron's arm to still him. "That may be," she said. "But if the Confederate Army comes, and they want to take the flag down, I have no doubt they will take it. Shall we fold the flag away with pride, or let them rip it down with hatred?"

For a moment no one spoke. Then Papa said, "I'll dig a hole in the garden and bury it. As soon as the threat is past we'll hang it out again."

"It's my flag," Teresa said stubbornly. "I'll be the one to hide it away. But I won't do it until tonight. I am not going to turn tail this minute just because some folks in this town got spooky. My flag is going to fly until dark tonight if I have to stand guard myself."

She turned back to her apples. I saw Mama give Papa a look; saw him shrug and nod, as if to say, It will be all right. They let Teresa be.

With some scrambling, we managed to get everyone fed before Margaret and I had to leave for school. I was looking forward to getting Timothy's opinion about the flag, about the Rebels. But Timothy didn't come. After school I asked Margaret to walk out to the McClintocks' with me.

"I don't think we have time. I promised Mama we'd be home straight away, to help with everything."

"Well, you go on then. Tell Mama I'll be along shortly. She'll understand."

I wasn't keen on walking about alone these days. The Union soldiers made me nervy enough—the thought of Confederates marching down Main Street was too much to take in! But I knew Timothy wouldn't miss school without a reason. I'd fret all night if I didn't find out why.

The McClintocks' little place looked tired, with weeds in the potato patch and a piece of fence down. Timothy met me at the door. "Elizabeth! I'm so glad to see you. I was about to set out for Dr. Biggs."

The worry in his eyes worried me. "Is it Lucilla?"

"Yes. She seems feverish. And Mama's been feeling poorly all day. Papa's out on circuit, so I stayed home to tend her and watch over Lucilla."

It was even hotter inside. Mrs. McClintock was sitting in a rocker, wrapped in a quilt. Her head rested against the chair like she didn't have the energy to hold it up. She held Lucilla.

The little girl was whimpering. Two red spots of fever burned on her cheeks.

Mrs. McClintock managed a smile. "Elizabeth, how kind of you to come."

"I'm so sorry you're feeling poorly," I said. Timothy's mother was pale as wheat flour, and I didn't like it. "Shouldn't you be in bed? Can I get you something? Fix you some tea?"

"Timothy has taken good care of me," she said, with a grateful look at her son. "I'll just sit up until he gets back with the doctor—"

"I'll go," I offered. "I can't stay long anyway, because we've got a full house and...and Mama needs my help." I didn't want to add to their troubles with my stories of flags and arguments. "So I can stop by Dr. Biggs' place on the way home. Then Timothy can stay, and you won't be left alone."

Mrs. McClintock couldn't hide a look of relief. "That would be lovely," she nodded. "You're a sweet girl."

Timothy cocked his head at me. "Would it be easier if I wrote a note?"

I was grateful. "Oh, yes, if there's time." I'd known Doctor Biggs all my life. This was an important errand. I would have done my best. But Timothy knew I'd like as not find my tongue struck dumb when I had to deliver the message.

Timothy went to his father's lap desk. I heard the pen scratching, then he blew on the paper to dry the ink. "Here."

I read the note:

Dear Sir, My mama and sister are feeling right poorly and I would consider it a kind favor if you would come. But I can only offer barter. But please come if you can. Respectfully yrs, Timothy McClintock

Timothy walked to the front gate with me. "Thank you," he said simply. "I didn't feel good about leaving them."

"It's no trouble."

"And Elizabeth...make sure Dr. Biggs will take barter. We've got lots of squash, and beans. Or eggs."

The Sharpsburg square, looking west. The prominent stone house, second from the right, belonged to Dr. Biggs and his family. This drawing was made from a period photograph.

Courtesy of Paula Stoner Reed

His face had a pinched look. "Dr. Biggs won't mind," I said, to stiff him up. "He takes barter from lots of folks." Then I hesitated. "When's your father coming home? Folks are saying the Rebel Army might come."

He nodded. "I've heard it. But my father's not due back for another ten days. We'll manage. I'll take care of them."

"Well, I'll come back when I can," I promised. "It's hard, with so much happening. We've got folks sleeping on the floor. Mama needs my help. But I'll make sure you're all right."

He nodded. I started to turn away, but he called me back. "Wait! I almost forgot...." He rummaged in his vest pocket, then pulled out a letter. "Papa left this. He said Gideon Brummer was going to come by for it straight away, but he hasn't. That was three days ago. Could you get it to him?"

I took the creased envelope. It was sealed with wax. "What is it?"

He shrugged. "I don't know. I didn't ask."

That was like Timothy. He accepted people, and their business, without prying. "I can give it to Aaron," I said. "He'll pass it on." Timothy nodded.

Dr. Biggs lived on Main Street too. I was relieved to find him at home. He scanned Timothy's note quickly. "Of course," he nodded. "I'll go at once."

But he hadn't mentioned the payment. I clenched my fists in my apron. "And the goods?" I tried. It came out a whisper.

"What's that?"

I took a deep breath. "The payment. Payment! Vegetables. Or eggs."

I'm not sure he heard it all, but he understood, and smiled kindly. "Of course. Not to worry. A doctor needs to eat, too. I'll get my bag." Then his smile faded. "Say, what is your sister doing with that flag? I see it's still flying. She's a headstrong, disrespectful girl. She'll come to woe one day."

My good feelings for him slid away. Don't you speak unkind about my sister! I wanted to shout. But the words didn't come. After a moment, so frustrated I wanted to spit, I turned and ran home.

I disappeared down to the cellar before Mama saw me. I was angry at myself for not speaking my piece to Dr. Biggs, and needed some time to stew. It was blessed cool down there too. But I could hear voices through the floor, and Mama's heels hurrying about upstairs, and before too long I went up to help.

We had so many travelers staying with us that we fed them first. Some ate in weary, worried silence. Others chattered with new-made friends, exchanging rumors like cards in a game. It was so hot we just dished up bread and cheese, cold pickled beets, and cabbage slaw. For a treat, Mama mixed a big kettle of raspberry juice and sugar, with a nice dash of cold vinegar, to make a fine fruit shrub. We collected fifty cents apiece from everyone who could afford it.

We'd done a powerful lot of kitchen chores before Papa and Stephen even got home from the blacksmith shop, and then we set the table all over again. Aaron wasn't home yet, but the rest of us dug in.

We were still passing platters when the next guest arrived, a short, sweating man powdered with street dust like he'd had a hard ride. One of the boarders must have pointed him to the kitchen. "I'm looking for John Kretzer."

"You found him," Papa said. "Pull up and rest. Margaret, get the man a plate."

"There's no time for that," he said. "I've just come from the main body of the Union Army. They're pushing west from Washington to meet the Rebels—"

"Is there going to be a fight?" Stephen asked eagerly.

The man looked at him, without smiling. "I expect so, boy. A big one. But an army needs lots of help. Right now I'm trying to round up some smiths. The army farriers can't keep up, and the cavalry rides their horses hard. Mr. Kretzer, I was told you were the best blacksmith in Washington County. Are you willing to give some time to the Union Army?"

Papa pushed to his feet. "I'll come at once. I've got a por-table forge—" Suddenly he looked at Mama. "Susan? Can you manage?"

"Of course," she said steadily.

I wasn't feeling so steady, myself. I wasn't sure I liked the idea of my papa going away with so much trouble in the town. What would we do without him if the Rebels came? But I looked at Mama, and Teresa, and knew we would manage somehow.

"I'll give you directions," the man said. "You've got to skirt around the Rebels or run the risk of losing your horse."

"I won't have any trouble," Papa said. "Stephen, I'll need you to help me load the wagon." Stephen beamed. "And... Teresa, run fetch Aaron."

"Where is he?"

"He said he wanted to help out to Brummers' after work," Mama said.

Teresa looked at me. "Come along?"

I remembered the letter in my pocket and nodded. We left the food on our plates and headed out.

I hadn't walked to the Brummer farm since I'd asked Gideon to help me fetch Teresa the year before. Teresa was evidently too excited to think on that. "Imagine! The Union Army needs Papa. Isn't it grand?"

I didn't answer. It *was* grand. But I was still a bit spooked about having him go away. I didn't want Teresa to realize how nervy I was, though, so I held my tongue.

Teresa didn't notice my mood. We hurried, and soon we were out of the village. It was so dry every step kicked up clouds of dust. We passed a boy herding cows, but no sol-diers. It made me ponder that aside from the skirmishing and scares, the real war hadn't found Washington County yet. The farm folks around were as worried about the weather as the war. We needed rain.

And with so many men off fighting, fieldhands were hard to come by. That's why Aaron was helping Gideon. We found them swinging cradle scythes in the Brummers' big rye field, with Gideon's father and brother. His sisters followed behind with rakes, and Mrs. Brummer tied double handfuls of cut grain into tidy bundles with lengths of rye straw. Later the bundles would be gathered into shocks. Not being used to the work, Aaron couldn't quite keep up with the Brummer men. But he did well enough.

They stopped when they saw us coming. Teresa delivered the news.

"I need to get home," Aaron said at once, wiping his forehead.

"Of course," Gideon agreed. "It was good of you to come."

While Aaron was saying good-bye to Mr. and Mrs. Brummer, I gave Reverend McClintock's envelope to Gideon. "Timothy's father left this for you."

"Ah, yes," he said. He didn't open it. "I expected to stop by several days ago. I've been too pressed here to get away. Thanks for bringing it." Then, with a smile, "It's good to see you. To see both of you." He looked at Teresa in particular. I noticed Teresa eyeing him, too. When Gideon shook Aaron's hand and went back to work, Teresa's gaze followed. Gideon swung the big cradle scythe easily, and the grain fell in a neat row. He looked very capable and strong. It seemed to give her pause.

Neither she nor Aaron had much to say on the way home. I left them to their thoughts. We found the wagon pulled up in front of the house. Papa's portable forge and some of his tools were already inside. Mama was tucking in a basket, probably of food, and Stephen hauled out a big jug of water. Margaret and Anne were hovering by the front step too.

"Sorry to call you in, son," Papa said to Aaron. "The girls told you?"

Aaron nodded. "I'd like to come with you."

Margaret and I exchanged surprised looks. Teresa burst out, "You? You don't smith!"

"I don't *enjoy* blacksmithing," Aaron corrected coolly. "That doesn't mean I'm not good at it."

Papa's face slowly split in a grin. "I'll be glad to have you along."

"I'll just grab a change of clothes," Aaron said, and hurried inside.

"Me too?" Stephen demanded hopefully.

"Not this time," Papa said, and when Stephen started to sulk, "You'll be the man of the house. I need you to take care of Mama and the girls."

When Aaron came back with his bundle, the good-byes were quick. "I expect to be back within a week or so," Papa said. "You all mind your mama, hear?" He and Aaron climbed to the wagon seat, and Papa snapped the lines. In a moment they were gone. I felt a strange, hollow feeling inside, and wondered if anybody else did too.

The sun was almost down. I'd plumb forgotten about the morning's fuss, but Teresa broke the silence: "Well, I guess it's time to pull in the flag."

We all trooped back inside. Mama disappeared into her bedroom, and Stephen ran off somewhere, but the rest of us followed Teresa. She was in a prickly mood. "I don't need help," she snapped at Anne and Margaret. "Just Bethie can stay."

"Fine," Anne said. "Go ahead and sulk. I've got better things to do anyway." Margaret stuck her tongue out at me before flouncing downstairs after Anne.

Teresa and I folded the huge flag tenderly. It took considerable caution to keep it off the floor. Then Teresa brought out a tin box she'd found, with a tight-fitting lid. We just managed to get all that folded silk squeezed inside.

Then we lit a lantern and went out the back door.

"Are you going to bury it?" I asked.

"In a manner of speaking." Teresa led me past the outhouse and little stable to the smokehouse. It was almost empty, empty hooks dangling from ceiling poles where we hung meat to cure over slow hickory fires after butchering time. The ashes left over got dumped in a big pile behind the smokehouse. That's where Teresa stopped.

I held the lantern high. She knelt gingerly in the mess and dug a hole with her hands. With a look like Preacher at communion time, she picked up the tin box. Then she buried it in the ashes.

"I don't think they'll find it there," she said, rising and dusting off her hands. She grimaced at the soot on her dress. "Anne will squawk. But this will wash out. What matters most is that the flag is safe. You won't tell?"

I felt surprise tears burn my eyes, and scrubbed them away. "I don't expect so," I managed. "If anybody asked, I most likely couldn't find my tongue even if I wanted it."

Teresa put her arm around my shoulders. "Poor Bethie. You mustn't mind. I'll speak up for both of us. How about that?"

I nodded. Teresa couldn't change the fact that Papa and Aaron had left, and Mrs. McClintock and Lucilla were ill, and everybody said the Confederate Army might be coming. But somehow, like always, her words made me feel better.

CHAPTER TEN

TERESA

We were all at Sunday school when some Rebel cavalry dashed through town. My stars! It caused a stampede. Preacher kept yelling "Let's keep calm!" while folks dashed back and forth, collecting children and scrambling toward the door.

"Let's go see!" I cried, and shoved outside. The riders had already disappeared in a cloud of dust.

Mama collared Stephen and steered us down the street. "Mama, we should check on the McClintocks," Bethie worried.

"I want you all home," Mama ordered, and Bethie left off. Once there, Mama herded everyone inside the parlor and asked Margaret to read aloud from the Bible.

I was excited by the commotion, and for certain too restless to sit! Instead I listened from the front door, watching and waiting.

For a long time I didn't see much but neighbors peeking out their own windows and doors. There was more to hear. The day before we'd heard the distant thunder of artillery from the south, and folks said the Confederates were shelling the Union garrison at Harpers Ferry. That Sunday we heard that same thunder, this time from the east. It was odd to hear on a sunny day.

After a time, the braver folks ventured out and flocked in the street like sparrows. "Big battle on the ridge," Dr. Biggs said. "South Mountain." We stared at the ridge. It was hard not to stamp my feet in vexation. How frustrating to not know what was happening!

About midafternoon a bunch of fellows trooped down Main Street, looking like they meant business. "Where you headed?" I yelled.

"We can't figure out what's going on," Alexander Root hollered back. He was a hired hand at Jacob Nicodemus's farm, and I didn't know him well. "So we're going to see."

"Mama, I'm going for a walk," I called over my shoulder toward the parlor, then shut the front door behind me before anyone could object. I ran after the boys. "I'll come with you."

Alexander frowned. "I don't reckon a girl—"

"She can keep up," someone else said, and Alexander shrugged. I smiled. The old stories still counted for something. I figured the bravest girl in Sharpsburg had as much right as anyone to go on a look-see.

I was wearing my Sunday best. Thanks to Anne's skill, it was a particular nuisance, with an overskirt and yards of flounces. I longed for Aaron's trousers, or even an old workdress, for once we cleared town, Alexander led us straight through the fields. But my boots were sturdy, and I held the dratted hoopskirt high and pushed on. The boys were too excited to gawk at my underpinnings.

We picked up a few more recruits on the way. By the time we reached Boonsboro, at the foot of South Mountain, I was perspiring mightily. The crash of battle from above was louder. My breath was coming a little ragged—maybe from the walk, maybe from excitement, I don't know. My frustration was gone, though. Taking action is always better than sitting and stewing, waiting for news.

We could see a haze of smoke hanging along the ridgeline. The hotelkeeper came out on his porch when we marched by. "Don't go any farther!" he cried. "There's fighting up that road!"

We held council in the street. "This is the big fight," Alexander said. "I want to nose in." No one disagreed. I tingled with excitement.

We marched on through the village. Most houses were shuttered tight. The cannon fire was so loud I felt each crash shiver down the mountain. We saw a few Rebel riders and wagons. Then more. They ignored us, so long as we kept off the road when they passed, but I stared. These were the men ripping our Union apart, and causing so much torment. *Why?* I wanted to ask them, but I couldn't find the words.

The road out of Boonsboro headed up the mountain. My heart seemed to thump in my chest. Lordy be, what were we going to see?

We hadn't gone far, though, when two Rebels limped around a bend. They leaned against each other like they couldn't walk alone. One had a bloody rag tied around his arm. The other had a big bloodstain on his shoulder.

"Y'all got any water?" one asked. He pronounced it funny: watah.

I started to say I wouldn't give water to a Rebel, but they looked so done in I held my tongue. It was harder to say such things, I was learning, when looking in a person's eyes.

"Nope," Alexander said. "What's going on up there?"

"The boys are hot at it up on that mountain," the Rebel said wearily. "I wouldn't go no farther lessen y'all want to git mixed up in it." Then they plodded on down the road.

For a moment we all looked at each other. My breath came ragged, like I'd been running. "I'm game," I said finally. My skin prickled, but I had to say it. I couldn't have these boys say later that I'd been the one to hold back.

Alexander considered. "Well...I was thinking we might just better leave well enough alone." He looked at me. If I pushed it, they'd have to go on too.

I went easy on them. "Could be you're right," I said, and we headed for home.

By the time I got there Mama was as hungry for news as she was anxious about me, and didn't say a word about me being gone for so long. I smoothed my skirt out best I could, and smacked off the worst of the dust, before finding her in the kitchen. "What did you hear?" she asked quietly. She didn't stop rolling out biscuit dough.

"Big fight on South Mountain. Along the ridge, in the passes." I paused to dip some water from the bucket, for I was parched. "Looks like some of the wounded will end up in Boonsboro." Then I paused. "The Union troops are pushing the Rebels this way." I said it low, so the younger ones, and the nervous boarders wandering about, didn't hear and get even more spooked.

"Well, I expect we should be prepared for anything."

"I expect so," I nodded. But I didn't know, then, what "anything" could mean.

Bethie was fretting about the McClintocks, so before the sun faded I walked her over to their place. Lucilla was still flushed and fussy, and Mrs. McClintock didn't look much heartier. "Doctor Biggs gave 'em medicine yesterday which helped a bit," Timothy told us. "But now Lucilla's worse again."

"Well, let's go fetch him!" I said. I hated seeing the baby so poorly.

"I already tried. He's off to Boonsboro, to see about wounded soldiers."

I hoped Dr. Biggs wasn't tending Rebel wounded while his neighbors were needing him. "Why don't you come home with us? My mama probably knows something that might help."

Mrs. McClintock shuddered as another distant boom of artillery thundered down the valley. For a moment she hesitated. Then, "No. I think we should stay. I don't want to risk taking Lucilla out."

"I'll ask Mama, then," I said. "Perhaps we can send something along."

Bethie pressed Timothy's hand. "I'll come back tomorrow," she promised. "Maybe Mama can even get away, too."

"We'd be thankful," he said earnestly. Watching them say good-bye, I felt a sudden tug at my heart. The bond between them was so strong! I wondered what it felt like to have a friend like that...then remembered that once I had. Savilla.

But there was no time to think about Savilla, no time for Mama to come back to the McClintocks', no time for anything. That afternoon the Confederate Army retreated from the bloody passes on South Mountain. They'd fought fierce, but the Union Army finally pummeled them pretty good. They tromped through Boonsboro and on to Sharpsburg.

That night we sat up behind shuttered windows and listened, expecting trouble. It didn't come until dawn. Then the Confederate Army descended on our little village like a plague of locusts.

Most everyone in our crowded house hovered at the windows, compelled to peek despite their fears. There were Rebel soldiers everywhere—in the streets, digging in folks' gardens, lazing on their porches, shoving around their pumps and wells. Compared to our Union boys, they looked like tramps, filthy and ragged.

"Those poor boys," Anne murmured. "They're whittled down to skin and bones. This is the great menacing army? Those poor boys." She turned away from the window. "I can hardly bear to look."

I looked at her, surprised. Anne sounded close to tears. I wasn't ready to feel such pity. Yes, the soldiers were hungry. But if we let them, those enemy soldiers would surely eat every bit of food we had set by. And no one in the Kretzer family was going hungry that winter if I could help it.

As the morning wore on they worried us half to death, banging on the door and asking for something to eat. Mama finally told them she'd bake cornbread if they'd wait in the yard.

"Mama!" I protested. "We're going to feed the Rebs?"

"They're starving," she said, and I didn't say any more. I figured we could spare some cornbread. That much was our

Christian duty, perhaps. I was glad she told them to wait outside, though. They smelled worse than they looked, and I expect were crawling with lice, too.

Once we started feeding the soldiers, they came like a flood washing down the Potomac. Mama and all us girls mixed and baked and sliced. Stephen begged to carry the bread to the yard, and came back with a handful of odd-looking bills. "Look, Mama! Some of them paid me."

"Confederate money," I sniffed. "Worthless."

Mama smiled. "You keep it, Stephen," she said. "Someday you'll tell your children about the day the Confederate Army came to Sharpsburg." Grinning, he stuffed it in his pocket and ran back outside, too excited to be still for more than a pop. I understood how he felt.

A little boy dashed into the kitchen, almost knocking Mama over. He was one of the refugees boarding with us. "Mrs. Kretzer! My mama asked me to come find you. My little sister just got sick all over everything, upstairs in the bedroom."

"I'm coming," Mama sighed, as he dashed away. "Girls, keep a watch on that cornbread."

Five minutes later Stephen banged back in. "Mama! There's three Rebel soldiers, coming to the front door."

"Mama's not here," I said. "Tell them they have to wait in the yard—"

"No, Teresa, I already told them! They said they weren't here to eat. They're looking for you!"

Everyone stared at me. Anne looked startled, Margaret confused, Bethie horrified. My heart seemed to beat faster. "Well, I'll go see what they're after!"

"Keep a civil tongue in your head!" Anne called after me. I was already marching to the front door.

As my hand closed on the latch I called up the memory of my papa's voice: *This family is for the Union.* Drawing a deep breath, I opened the door and faced three Rebels.

They were dressed in a dirty mix of butternut homespun and gray uniform, and one wore a bright red shirt. The tallest man had sergeant's stripes on his sleeve. "Are you Miss Teresa Kretzer?" He didn't drawl as thick as the boy I'd heard on South Mountain.

"I am."

"We've come to demand that flag you've got here."

I stuck my chin a little higher in the air. "What flag, sir?"

The one in the red shirt glared. "They said she was impertinent."

"Only with Rebels," I shot back, wondering who had told these men about me. Bobby McPherson? Savilla? The thought made me steam, and I was glad. Anger gave me sand.

"You watch yourself, Miss," the sergeant said grimly. He had black hair and bushy eyebrows that formed a V as he frowned. "You *will* hand over the Yankee flag."

I gave them a sweet smile. "Gentlemen, there is no Yankee flag in this house."

"Oh yes there is! We've heard all about the big flag you've kept strung across the street. Give it up at once, or we'll search the house."

I didn't like the sound of that. "I'll not give it up, and I guess you'll not come any farther than you are, sir."

The sergeant took a step forward. "If you don't tell me where that flag is, there will be trouble." He looked at his musket, then back at me.

Did he think I was some silly swooning maiden? I *knew* he was bluffing! The boarders were still peeking from behind the curtains, and the streets were jammed. I couldn't believe even a Rebel would shoot an unarmed young woman. "It's of no use for you to threaten," I said. "I knew somebody would tell you about that flag. Rather than have you touch a fold of that starry flag, I laid it in ashes."

The men exchanged looks. The sergeant's eyes narrowed. Red Shirt muttered, "I don't reckon she'd burn it."

"Shall I show you the ash pile? My flag is twice as sacred now."

The sergeant fixed me with a long glare. I held it steady. "I figure she's just stubborn enough to have done it," he said finally. "Let's go." He stomped down the walk. The other two followed.

I had won! I felt that glorious tingle that comes after an adventure wash over me. I'd staved off a mangy Rebel. I was doing my part! I was grinning before the door shut behind me.

CHAPTER ELEVEN

SAVILLA

When the Northern troops skeddadled from Sharpsburg, I straight off took down the American flag the provost guard had forced us to hang by our front door. Now mind, I didn't tear it down in anger. It was a sacred banner, and deserved respect. It just wasn't *our* sacred banner anymore. As I carefully folded it away, I couldn't help admiring the workmanship again. Teresa knew how to ply a needle, drat her! I tucked the flag out of sight among the winter linens.

Living through those days was like riding in a buggy with a runaway horse. First we heard that the Confederate Army was ready to storm the north and end the war! But on Monday the fifteenth we got the news about the Battle of South Mountain. It hit us hard. All our dreams for a great northern invasion seemed to die in the rocky passes of that ridge with the brave boys who fought there. The Confederate soldiers fought well, but the Union troops—we called them Yankees— finally pushed them down the steep slope. Our troops trudged south to Sharpsburg and we knew they were heading for the fords...back to Virginia.

"Never mind, the war's not over," Father consoled me, and patted my arm. "Hang out the stars and bars, and give the boys a smile. They need it."

So I pulled out the Confederate flag we'd been saving. Hanging it beside the front door heartened me immensely.

My father was in and out a lot during that time. I lost Auntie Mae's company too. Father and Samuel decided she would be better off at the farm, where her husband had been helping with the harvest as best he could. Uncle Bob was as old and wrinkled as Auntie, but would rather shuck corn or tie off grain sacks on the farm than sit idle at the village house. "It's best that they're together, and not worried about each other during this time," Samuel said. "And it may be safer there, too, away from town." If that was so, I wanted Auntie Mae there. Still, it was sad to see her go. As I watched Samuel help her gently into the wagon, I realized how dear she was to me.

I missed Auntie Mae. But for once, I had plenty of company. Clara Brining came the day after the battle on South Mountain. She lived in Boonsboro, and the town was so overrun with wounded that her mother sent her away.

"There was skirmishing right in the street," she told me, as we carried her valise upstairs. "The Confederates left a rear guard of cavalry on the east end of town when they retreated. The Yankee cavalry plunged right into them. There were wounded soldiers everywhere, and yelling and shooting...my mama and I scooted to the cellar, but Papa climbed up to the attic with his shotgun and fired at the Yankees." Her eyes mirrored fear and excitement.

I felt a pang of something inside. Envy? I wasn't sure, but it *had* been too long since I'd had a grand adventure. I almost wished the skirmish had happened in Sharpsburg, instead of Boonsboro. Nothing, I thought with regret, ever happened in Sharpsburg. I didn't know then that our time was coming.

A short while later, Jeanette arrived. Her family lived near the Potomac, and her parents were worried about being isolated when the armies passed through. Mrs. Blackford had taken the younger children to stay with kin in Pennsylvania.

"My father's at home, watching the property," she explained. "But I was afraid that if I stayed at home with Father, I'd miss seeing the Confederate Army altogether. I couldn't bear it! Father said I could visit with you while the army marches through."

I loved having Clara and Jeanette with me. It made the house seem less empty.

We stood with Father by the street when the first Confederate columns marched by, waving and cheering. But it was hard not to pity them, too. Ours was an army of scarecrows in filthy rags, many barefoot, painfully thin.

"They're like walking skeletons," Clara murmured. "Lord Almighty, it hurts to see them."

"We must have something in the house," I answered, angry at myself for not being better prepared.

We ran inside to ransack the larder. Soon we had platters of biscuits and little spice cakes to offer. The food disappeared into grasping hands quicker than I can write it. We mixed up a big tub of lemonade, and we hauled buckets out to the step. We gave out ladles-full as the boys marched by. They were so grateful for every drop, every morsel, that I felt guilty for having eaten breakfast that morning.

When the Confederate Army arrived in Sharpsburg, the Southern sympathizers weren't all of a mind regarding how to greet them. Some, happy as they were, were afraid to openly show their allegiance. "This army is in retreat," they fretted. "What happens if we hang out flags, and openly give them aid? Soon as they're gone, the Union troops will be back, and come down on us hard. There's plenty of Union folk here, and all too quick to point fingers and tell tales. We can't risk it." Those people's houses were shuttered up tight as the Unionists'.

There were others who were willing to entertain the troops, but only at night, behind their own locked doors. They were trying to walk a fence rail without falling off.

Then there were a few folks like my father. "This is a Confederate household," he declared. "I'll not pretend otherwise." I gave him a big hug, feeling immensely proud. "I'm a crotchety old man, Savilla," he said then. "And likely to bring the devil to this house. Think about it. You've plenty of other places to stay, if you've a mind."

It was true enough, with so many brothers and sisters and cousins in the county. But, "I'm not going anywhere," I said firmly, and meant it. It was too exciting! Savilla Miller was not one to skedaddle. What if Teresa heard I'd skittered out of town? She'd chuckle over that! Then I pushed that thought away like a pesky fly and imagined instead Henry Kyd Douglas, getting an hour of leave and coming to our door. Find me gone? Not likely! Come what may, I was staying.

We spent the morning baking more spice cakes and giving them away. Jeanette and Clara smiled and teased every handsome soldier, although I didn't find particular fun in that. Still, it was lovely to finally be able to do something for our army face-to-face.

Samuel showed up around noon. "What a ruckus!" he exclaimed. "There are troops everywhere. The army has splintered. The roads are jammed. Whole columns just march across fields to get where they want to go."

"Do you suppose I could get out to Ferry Hill?" I asked. Ferry Hill was the Douglas home, perched on the bluffs above the Potomac.

Samuel frowned. "Not likely. Why?"

"Well, I expect Henry Kyd is visiting his parents. I thought to say hello." I tried to keep my voice offhand.

"You'd better let go of that idea." Samuel shook his head. "There are several thousand soldiers between here and there."

"I don't care—"

"And you can't be abroad with Honey," he added firmly. "The army's desperate for horses, Savilla. Too many cavalrymen have been dismounted. Too many mules and draft horses have given out on the mountain roads. You'd run the risk of losing the mare, sure as you're born."

"But we're Confederate sympathizers!"

"And this is a war."

I frowned. I wasn't used to being thwarted. I wasn't afraid of several thousand men, but I didn't want to risk losing Honey. She was sweet and faithful and I'd miss her horribly.

I wasn't afraid of walking either, even though it was about a six-mile round trip.... Then I remembered my guests. How could I explain to Jeanette and Clara a sudden hankering to walk to Ferry Hill? And besides, what would I say to the Douglases when I arrived, uninvited?

I let go of that idea. Before I had time to brood, though, we had a visitor: Major Heros von Borcke, a huge Prussian who knocked politely at our front door. Clara came squealing to find me. "Savilla! An *officer* is here!"

I tried to wipe the worst of the flour off my hands before going to greet him. He swept his hat off with a courtly bow. "Is this the home of Squire Jacob Miller?" He spoke with a heavy German accent. "I'm told this house is loyal to the Confederacy. Yes? Then perhaps I could obtain a meal, and a quiet place to work on correspondence this afternoon?"

Samuel came up behind me while I ushered him inside. "Of course, Major," he said. "We're honored."

That we were! Samuel locked von Borcke's horse in our stable with Honey. We girls settled him in the dining room, then scurried to get a decent dinner pulled together: sausages, fried potatoes, plums, and a nice cabbage slaw. "Savilla, we're out of flour!" Jeanette hissed frantically, so we quick whipped up some cornbread. I was mortified, but the major didn't seem to mind.

Father came home while I served the meal, and was delighted to find our guest. "Sir! Please, my home is at your disposal, as long as you're here. Your reputation precedes you!"

"As does yours," the big man said. "You're known as a friend to our cause, Mr. Miller." He took a big fork full of sausage and potatoes, then beamed like it was manna from Heaven. "Oh, ladies! It has been too long since I've had such fare."

Major von Borcke told us that he was an officer in the Third Dragoon Guards of the Royal Prussian Army, but was so intrigued with reports of the Confederacy's struggle that he had left Germany. He'd run the blockade into South Carolina and made his way to Virginia, where he joined the cavalry.

"And has life with the Confederate Army met your expectations, sir?" Samuel asked. He refilled the major's wine goblet, and was rewarded with a huge smile.

"It has been a grand adventure," von Borcke said. I couldn't help smiling myself. His enthusiasm was contagious, and his choice of phrase—"grand adventure"—had meaning for me. "We try to have fun, yes?" the officer went on, as if pleased with my reaction. "In Frederick, the Southern ladies were so gracious that we staged a ball. A military band provided music and we decorated the walls with regimental flags. Perhaps we'll stay in Sharpsburg long enough to do the same."

"Oh...," Jeanette breathed. "That would be wonderful."

I couldn't even imagine such a scene. Attend a ball, hosted by Confederate cavalry officers? The past months had been so lonely, so dismal, it was hard to even hope for such. Besides, it would be hurtful to dance when so many boys in the army were hungry. "Surely, sir," I said, to steer the conversation away, "you won't be here long, will you? I mean...." My cheeks grew hot. How could I say my thoughts without sounding disrespectful? "We thought that General Lee was taking his army back across the Potomac, to Virginia. Since the big battle on South Mountain is over...." I let my voice trail away, unable to utter words like "defeat" or "loss."

Major von Borcke looked surprised. His big eyebrows lifted like tipped-over sickle moons. "But...then you don't know? You haven't heard?"

My father frowned. "Heard what?"

The Prussian put down his fork. "Have you an attic window? Facing east? I can show you better than tell."

Samuel was already on his feet. "Right this way," he said, and we all clattered up two flights of stairs after him.

The attic's heat hit me like a blow. Major von Borcke threaded his way through a dusty jumble of old trunks and discarded furniture, opened a window, and leaned out. "Yes! There. You see?"

We crowded around, following his pointing finger. I squinted, wondering what I was looking for. Suddenly I saw it: a long thin gray line, curving around Sharpsburg on a ridge east of town.

"Is that our army?" Clara asked.

"The very same."

I struggled to understand. This wasn't an army shoving toward the Potomac. This was—

"You're making a stand," Father breathed. He blotted his forehead with his handkerchief. "By God, you're making a stand."

Von Borcke laughed. "General Lee's got his back to the Potomac, but he's a fighter."

Jeanette and Clara hugged each other, squealing with excitement. I was about to join in when Samuel said in a low voice, "But the numbers...the Union Army has you outnumbered—"

"It is nothing." The major waved that worry aside like a gnat. "A Southern soldier is worth three Northern boys, that's been shown time and time again. And besides," he lowered his voice, as if someone was in the attic with us, "we just got word that General Stonewall Jackson has successfully captured Harpers Ferry. He'll bring his army here as quickly as he can to join us.

Stonewall Jackson at Harpers Ferry! My heart seemed to turn over. Henry Kyd was probably with him. Harpers Ferry was almost twenty miles away. When would Jackson's men get here?

We trooped back downstairs chewing over these new developments. Clara and Jeanette slipped back to the kitchen to clean up, but I couldn't resist following the men back to the dining room. If there was more news, I wanted to hear it.

The major resumed his meal, evidently not caring that it had grown cold. But for the first time, his face lost that laughing look. "Mr. Miller," he said between mouthfuls, "have you given thought to your family's safety?"

"My family is as safe here as anywhere," Father began, but Samuel cut him off. "What do you recommend?"

"Have you a cellar?"

Samuel nodded. "Small. But secure."

"Well, the ladies have a choice, then." He looked at me. "You can retreat away from here—at least fifteen miles or so, preferably farther. Or, be prepared to take shelter in the cellar. Have food and blankets and water ready."

Father was frowning. "Why, sir, are you singling out my daughter and her friends?"

"Because I believe they'd be relatively safe if they choose to stay. I can't say the same for you, and possibly your son. Your loyalties are well known. If the Yankees recapture Sharpsburg, it could go hard on you."

"I'm not afraid of the Yankees!" Father spouted. "I will not be run out of my own house. By God, man, it could all end here! Right here! If it does, I'm going to be here to see it."

"It could," von Borcke agreed calmly. "But the tides of war come and go. The Union Army could retake Sharpsburg. I've seen these things happen before. There's always a period when tempers are high. People are upset. Fingers are pointed, and arrests are made. In time, things usually calm down. Unless you want to see the end of the war from a prison cell, it would be safer if you go."

I couldn't bear to think of my father in prison. His spirit was stronger than his body, and I was afraid of what might happen. "Father, please," I cried. "Listen to the major."

"It's not just your safety," Samuel added. "We have things here...the gold savings. Bonds. Legal papers. I'd feel more secure if you could hide those things away. I need to keep an eye on the canalboats and the farm. I'll keep moving, stay out of sight and out of trouble. But someone needs to get our valuables away from here."

Samuel's argument had more weight than mine, I could see. I held my breath. Before agreeing, Father turned back to me. "And you girls? You want to stay?"

"It's best if someone stays," von Borcke said quietly, scooping up the last plum. "An empty house...."

"I'll stay here," I said firmly. I felt like feathers were dancing up and down my spine. "I have Jeanette and Clara for company. I'll guard the house, Father. I'm proud to do it." And I was. I was descended from patriots. Now it was my turn.

Father still hesitated, his eyes narrowed. Then he nodded, suddenly looking every one of his eighty years. "I'll gather up some things. Samuel, I'd like your assistance, if you will."

I took a deep breath. Things were happening. I had a chance to do something worthwhile.

Then I remembered my duties as hostess. "Major von Borcke, would you like some coffee?" I asked, and was rewarded with that huge grin.

Papa trotted out of town on his mare with bulging saddlebags, some legal papers sewn in the lining of his frock coat, and a pistol in his hand. I pushed away images of the Unionist mob that killed my cousin Clint. Anyone who tried to give Father trouble would only need one look at his eyes, I figured, before backing down. "Take care," I muttered fiercely, when he pressed my hand in farewell.

"I'm proud of you, Savilla," he said simply.

"Send word when you can." Suddenly, I was afraid to let him go—afraid for his sake, not for mine. "Don't worry about us." I watched him ride away with a lump in my throat.

Samuel left soon after. "I'll be back when I can," he told me. His eyes were concerned. "I don't like leaving you girls here. But I've got the business to think of, and the farm. Morgan and Andrew have their own families to take care of, so I'm spread thin."

"We'll be fine," I assured him, and didn't doubt it.

We had some excitement that afternoon when the Federals lobbed a few cannonballs at the Confederate line. They sailed right overhead and landed in the village. Major von Borcke quickly ushered Jeanette, Clara and me to the cellar. He stayed above, evidently drinking more wine and writing his report.

That annoyed me, I must admit—if it was safe enough for him to be upstairs, why were we huddled in the clammy cellar? I was just about to charge back up when he called that it was safe to return.

Major von Borcke ate supper with us before begging our leave. He kissed each of our hands before departing. His big mustache tickled, and I could tell Jeanette and Clara would have dreams of the major for quite some time.

When we cleaned up in the kitchen, I noticed that Father had left a bottle of good wine on the table. He'd probably intended it for Major von Borcke. "You know," I said thoughtfully, picking it up, "I think I'll run this over to Widow McGraw's place. I expect Joseph will be home if he can, and she probably doesn't have a drop to welcome him with." Joseph McGraw hadn't been home since joining a Virginia artillery unit. His brother Jacob kept things up best as he could, but their mother pinched pennies and barely got by.

"There's a few plums left," Jeanette said, and we ended up fixing a food basket. It held an odd mix, since we'd almost been eaten out—but I figured the McGraws would appreciate it.

Jeanette and Clara stayed behind to mind the house. The McGraws lived around the corner and down the block, just a few minutes' walk. I was glad I'd thought of it, too, because Joseph was already home. I found him sitting in his mother's kitchen while she pushed away tears and patted his hand. Jacob grinned and punched his brother's arm every few minutes. They were lingering over supper when I arrived, but I noticed their mugs held only water.

"Savilla, how thoughtful," Mrs. McGraw said gratefully. "Please, sit with us."

"When we realized one of our own heroes might be home, we had to send a token of our appreciation," I said lightly, while Jacob popped the cork. "Joseph, it's good to see you. Are you well?"

"Better now that I'm home," he grinned, although I noticed the grin didn't quite reach his eyes.

"How long can you visit?" I asked.

"Just a few hours," he said with regret. "I have to get back to my unit. And...," he looked at his mother and brother, "I don't want to risk being seen here. It could bring trouble to the house."

I felt a stab of anger. Who could be so cruel as to deprive a son a visit with his mother? I was suddenly so sad I could hardly sip my wine.

The McGraws didn't notice. Joseph told stories about his campaigns, light cheerful stories that didn't match up to the ribs showing through his faded, torn uniform—or the hollow look in his eyes.

Suddenly, there were three smart raps at the window. We all jumped like a firecracker had gone off.

Joseph was on his feet. "Don't mind," he said quickly. "It's just a friend of mine. I need to step outside. You stay here. And keep the curtains drawn." And before we could say a word he'd slipped out the back door.

"Well," Mrs. McGraw said, looking worried. "What do you think—"

"Army business, Ma," Jacob said comfortingly. "They have to be careful. And he's trying to protect us. He'll be back in soon, I'm certain."

I felt like I'd intruded long enough, and murmured my good-byes. "Give Joseph my best, will you?" Mrs. McGraw nodded.

I went out the front door, thinking about the long gray line east of town and wondering if I'd ever see Joseph McGraw alive again. I took a deep breath to steady my nerves.

I was just about to head for home when I saw Teresa Kretzer, marching down the street like the Union Army still occupied Sharpsburg and she had been proclaimed queen. I just wasn't in the mood for an exchange, right then, so without thinking I ducked around the side of the house. Afraid she might still see me, I slid toward the back of the little lot.

I heard the murmur of voices at the same instant I remembered that I was intruding. Someone gasped and I whipped

my head around. I saw Joseph standing by the grape arbor—
but he was with a young woman, not an army comrade. And
his arms were around her.

Despite the heat she was wearing a dark cape. When she
jerked her head from his shoulder the hood slipped. She
snatched at it real quick, but not before I caught a glimpse—

It was Anne Kretzer.

For just a few seconds our gazes met. Her shocked eyes
pleaded with me: *Please don't tell.*

I finally gathered my wits and turned away. I hurried back
to the street, my face hot. Teresa had disappeared. I headed
home myself, but sank on the front step before going in to my
friends. My thoughts were whirling like wagon wheels.

Joseph McGraw and Anne Kretzer! The Confederate
artillerist was courting Teresa's older sister? It wasn't
possible...yet I had seen it.

I didn't know what, if anything, to make of that information. But I did suddenly know that after everything that had
happened that day, I couldn't figure anything out. I was too
tired. Tucking the picture of Joseph and Anne away to consider later, I put a smile on my face and went inside.

CHAPTER TWELVE

BETHIE

It was a terrible time. Everyone was in a rumpus, which frayed my nerves considerable. Even Anne was agitated. She walked around with pinched lips, and sometimes seemed to be listening for something we couldn't hear. With Teresa wound up like a new clock, and Margaret pounding her melodeon night and day, and Stephen bounding about the house like a puppy, I expected better of Anne. It worried me some.

We heard much later that Confederate General Robert E. Lee planned to march his army through Sharpsburg, then cross the Potomac back into Virginia. That's what we expected. All Monday the Rebels swarmed over the village. We were so busy feeding some, and keeping others from stealing anything they could get their hands on, that I couldn't get back to Timothy's house.

Mama had rummaged in the pantry for cloves and cream of tartar and Peruvian bark, which she thought might help Lucilla's fever. "But Bethie, I simply can't get away right now," she told me Monday morning, when I managed to steal her attention for a moment. "Maybe later. If things ease a bit. I'm worried about the McClintocks, too. But with Papa gone, I have to take care of things here."

"If you give the medicine to me, do you suppose I could take it?" The thought of venturing out alone was almost more than I could countenance, so I was both relieved and disappointed when she shook her head firmly. "Absolutely not, Bethie. It's not safe for a young girl like you."

"Maybe Teresa would go with me—"

But at that moment Teresa blew past us like a winter wind. "Cursed Rebels! They're in the garden again." She stormed out on the back step and we heard her bellow, "Hey! Get out of that garden! You want food, you come to the door and ask proper. You should be ashamed. Ashamed!" Through the window we watched her charge into the garden, waving her arms at the soldiers like they were stray dogs. "Shoo! All of you! Shoo!" When one lingered, poking a potato hill with his bayonet, she actually shoved him. I held my breath, but they went.

"Oh dear, there's another group at the pump," Mama murmured. Between the dry weather and the thirsty army, we were beginning to worry that our well would go dry. "Perhaps I should just lock it...."

She hurried away, already forgetting about Timothy's family. I didn't ask again. Mama couldn't leave, and Teresa was needed at home too. I folded the powders in pieces of notepaper and slipped them in my apron pocket, so they'd be ready first chance we had to deliver them. I was terrible worried, though. I'd let Timothy down. I'd *promised* to come back. Thinking on it made me feel lower than a slug belly.

By Tuesday, we knew the Confederates weren't leaving without another fight. Excited neighbors dashed in and out of our house all day, shouting the latest reports:

"The Rebels have settled in a long line between Sharpsburg and Antietam Creek!"

"Cook at Delaney's tavern told some Rebels she'd run out of food, and one of 'em set the stable on fire!"

"McGraw climbed on his roof, and said he could see the Union troops! They're digging in east-northeast of town!

"Some Confederate officers made John Hebb and Joe Hoffmaster and Moses Cox ride out with them and give them the lay of the land! They tried to get William Logan too, but he hid beneath his wife's skirt!"

I stumbled through it all feeling like there was a chunk of ice in my stomach. I worried about Timothy's family, worried about my Papa and Aaron, worried Teresa might spark some Rebel into making real trouble, worried about a battle exploding in Sharpsburg.

On Tuesday morning another Confederate officer called. This one walked right into the kitchen. "We're advising all civilians to leave," he said. "You ladies need to find shelter."

"We certainly will not leave our home to be plundered bare by your army," Teresa retorted. "And next time, you can knock—"

"You have been advised." The man shrugged. He had dark circles under his eyes, like he hadn't slept in days.

"Where's the fighting going to be?" Stephen cried hopefully. "Can we see it?"

The man looked at Stephen so long he started to squirm. Then the Confederate turned to Mama. "Ma'am, I have a son of my own, about his age. And a daughter, too. Like her." He jerked his head toward me. "A big fight is coming. It is coming *right here*. We're warning all civilians to leave now. That's all I can do." He turned toward the door.

"Sir, wait," Mama cried. "We appreciate your kindness. But we can't leave our home. We have a cellar—"

"Then take to it. Ma'am—" He touched the brim of his hat, nodded, and slammed the door behind him.

Margaret was the first one to break the silence. "I wish Papa and Aaron were here." She was wringing her apron in her fingers like it was wet.

"Margaret, hush," Anne said quietly. "Mama, what do you want us to do?"

"We need to make some preparations in the cellar," Mama said briskly. "Come along, girls. You too, Stephen. I need your help."

The cellar—my quiet place—was suddenly abustle. A lot of the garden hadn't been harvested yet. Just a few rows of Mama's jewel-colored preserves in glass tumblers were on the shelves, and some beans and such. We carried down some chairs, and made board benches.

Our house was like a tollgate. Some of our neighbors, who'd also got the warning to leave, arrived in a fluster. They clutched babies, and portraits and heirloom candlesticks and other mementos they couldn't bear to leave. "Susan, can we stay here?" they asked Mama. Their eyes were frightened. "You've got the biggest cellar in town. And it's got the spring...."

"Of course," she nodded each time. Mostly women and children came, and some very old men. Some of the women's menfolk had skedaddled with valuables, leaving their women to defend the homeplace. Some of the men were off to war in one way or another—soldiers, or helping out like Papa and Aaron.

I kept looking for Timothy and his mama and Lucilla. I hoped Mrs. McClintock would change her mind about staying at home. But they didn't come.

With the travelers who'd ended up at our house, and the neighbors, I figured there were more than sixty people by mid-day. They milled about in the cellar, in the parlor, in the kitchen. Mostly they stood roundabout in the yard, listening and looking. Although there were still plenty of Confederate soldiers in town, most of the hungry scarecrows had left off pestering for food. Everybody seemed to be waiting.

I waited too. But as the day wore on, and nothing happened, I got more and more restless. I had promised Timothy I'd come back on Monday! And here it was Tuesday. How were they faring? What if Lucilla died? Time was slipping by....

If I'd stopped to think it through, I never would have found the sand to commence. Instead, when the idea first nibbled, I just did it. I pulled Anne's plaid shawl from the peg by the door, threw it over my head, and slipped outside. In all the fuss and commotion, no one saw me go.

I was disobeying Mama. And I was headed through Sharpsburg when it was occupied by Confederate soldiers, enemy soldiers, with a big battle coming. I didn't let myself think about it. Thinking would have scampered me home like a scared rabbit.

Instead I scurried fast as I could, zigzagging to avoid soldiers whenever they passed. I planned to deliver the medicine and hurry back home. I would bring the McClintocks with me if I could. I'd surely be back before anyone even noticed me gone. Mama would understand. Everything would be all right....

The streets were busy. Now and then some cavalry pounded through, scattering pedestrians like chickens. I also saw some townfolk who had thought better of staying. Some were heading for a big cave near the Potomac. Some were trying to scoot north. One old man walked by with a soup kettle on his head. In my mind I heard the Confederate officer's voice again: "You have been advised." It made me wish I'd brought a soup kettle too.

The walk to Timothy's house had never seemed so long. By the time I knocked on the door I was panting like I'd climbed South Mountain. I saw the front curtain move. "It's me! Elizabeth!" I cried.

Timothy jerked me inside quick. "Elizabeth! What are you doing here?" He hugged me, and I knew he was as glad to see me as I was to see him.

"I was worried about you!" I managed. "How is Lucilla?"

"Not well," Timothy whispered, looking somehow like an old man. He gestured toward a pallet of quilts and comforters on the floor. I figured Mrs. McClintock thought it safer downstairs. She was kneeling there, wiping Lucilla's face with a wet cloth. I could hear the child's breathing. At least she was still alive.

I tiptoed over and touched Mrs. McClintock on the shoulder. She looked so startled, I guessed she hadn't even heard me come in. "Ma'am? How is she?"

"Oh, Elizabeth. It's you." Mrs. McClintock pushed a straggle of hair from her face like it was lead. "She's poorly. The fever—"

"My mama sent something, ma'am." I rummaged in my pocket. "She couldn't come. But she said half an ounce of cloves and cream of tartar, and an ounce of Peruvian bark, mixed together. She said she saw her children through many a fever with that. We can give it to Lucilla in honey or molasses, if you've got some."

"I'll get it." Timothy hurried to the cupboard. Soon we had Lucilla dosed, and mixed some of the powder in tea for Mrs. McClintock. "I've been feeling better," she said. "But I've been up for two nights with Lucilla...and so worried...." She managed a little smile. "It was kind of you to come, Elizabeth."

"I'm sorry I'm so late." I stared at the floor. "I promised to be here yesterday—"

A sudden bang at the door echoed like a shot, ending my fumbled apology. Timothy stared at me with wide eyes, then darted to the window. "It's Rebel soldiers!"

"Most likely they're here to warn you to safety," I said. "One came by our place earlier."

Timothy cracked the door. "Yes?"

He stumbled backward as the door pushed open. Three soldiers walked in. The one in front was holding a pistol. That's about all I saw. I pressed flat against the far wall, wishing I could go right through it.

"Is this the home of Reverend Daniel McClintock?" he demanded. He was a spare man, not too tall, and hungered down to almost nothing. But that pistol made him seem like a giant.

Timothy sounded wary. "Yes...."

"Fetch him."

"He's not here."

"Where is he?"

"Riding rounds. He's a preacher."

"When is he due back?"

I looked at Mrs. McClintock. She was still crouched on the floor. Her hands were pressed against her mouth. Timothy hesitated.

"I said, when is he due back?" the soldier asked impatiently.

"Well, any time, I reckon," Timothy said. "I don't exactly know."

There was a pause. "What's your name, boy?"

"Timothy McClintock. Daniel McClintock is my father," he added. I was proud of him.

Suddenly Lucilla squalled a bit, weak and fretful. Mrs. McClintock pulled the little girl into her arms, and spoke for the first time. "My daughter is very ill, sir. I pray you leave us in peace."

The Confederate soldier looked around. "Is anyone else home? Upstairs?"

Timothy shook his head. "No. You can look, if you like."

The man hesitated, then slid his pistol away. "Mrs. McClintock, I was sent here to arrest your husband." I heard a gasp, and wasn't sure if it came from Mrs. McClintock or me. "We have information that he has been carrying messages to the Northern forces about our army. And providing assistance to escaped slaves. I will detach a guard around your house. You and your children will not be harmed as long as you stay inside. No one is permitted to leave."

For a moment we all gaped like dying fish. Then Timothy ran over and grabbed my arm. "This is not my sister," he cried. "She needs to go home!"

"No one is permitted to leave," the soldier repeated firmly. "Anyone who tries will be arrested as well." He turned sharply and followed the other two out the door. It seemed to slam in my very heart.

"Arrested!" Mrs. McClintock cried. "Not Daniel...not your father. Oh Timothy—"

Timothy looked bewildered. "Mama, has Papa been helping slaves escape to freedom?"

"No...that is, I don't think...." Her voice trailed away as tears spilled over.

He gave her a quick hug. "Don't cry, Mama. And don't worry. I don't understand everything that is happening, but...it will be all right."

"Those Rebel soldiers will send him to a Southern prison! We'll never see him again!"

"I won't let that happen," Timothy said stoutly. "I need to think." He looked at me. I didn't have anything to say. The lump of ice in my belly was back again, getting bigger.

It was unbearable to think of Reverend McClintock in a Southern prison. His family couldn't manage without him! They were barely scraping along as it was. Pictures darted through my head like crows, in and gone: Rebel soldiers leading him away in chains, Timothy and his family starving....

And I'm ashamed to say it, but I was scared for myself, too. I'd planned to scoot back home. Now I was under guard! Timothy had tried—he'd thought quick. But I was trapped. My mama would be so worried.

We spent probably several hours mulling it all over, peeking out the windows, pacing, sitting, pacing. "I can scarcely believe this," Mrs. McClintock said over and over. "Daniel mentioned an interest in the Underground Railroad once. But nothing more. I can scarcely believe this—"

We were talking in circles. When Lucilla finally slipped into sleep, I envied her.

Timothy went silent for a while, standing by the back window. I could tell he was pondering the situation. I tried, but couldn't come up with a solid thought. That's why my heart jumped so hopeful-like when he finally gestured me to join him.

"I've got a plan," he whispered.

I wondered why he didn't want his mama to hear. And why he looked so doubtful. "Yes?"

"I've been watching out the windows. There are two guards. The one in front is marching back and forth like he means business. Keeps his musket over his shoulder. But look at him—" He pulled the curtain aside a hair and pointed.

I looked and saw the guard slouched against the back fence. His gun was leaning against the fence beside him. "What are you thinking?"

"I think I can get past him—"

"Timothy, no!" I clutched his arm. "It's too dangerous! They'll arrest you too! I couldn't bear it!"

He patted my hand, but didn't back down. "I have to try," he said simply. "If I can get past him, I can run up into the hills and warn my father. I can't let him go to prison without trying to save him."

I took a deep breath. "At least wait until it gets dark—"

"That may be too late! Elizabeth, I keep picturing my father walking down the street. He could be coming into sight right this moment! I know he'd hurry home soon as he heard the Southern Army had come. It won't be dark for hours. I can't wait that long."

"But...how will you get by him? That guard may not be marching around, but he'll still see you."

"If I can make it through the back fence, the lilac bushes will hide me. I can't go through the underbrush on either side. They'd hear. But if I go straight back, then creep along the lilacs...I think I can get past them far enough to head out."

"But you've still got to get across the lawn and back garden to the fence," I pointed out. He seemed to be skipping the obvious. "That's where he'll spot you. He's watching the house."

Timothy hesitated. "What I need is...a distraction."

It took me a moment to seize his meaning. "You mean *me*?"

"Elizabeth, please! Just try—"

"But what kind of a distraction? What can I do?"

"Talk to him. Get him turned a bit, facing away...."

The chunk of ice was growing bigger.

"I wouldn't ask if I had any other way. I can't ask her," he nodded toward his mother, who was staring blankly at the wall. "She's had too hard a time of it lately. I don't think she could make it stick. But if you could just get me a chance—"

This was Timothy. My friend. The boy I planned to marry. I felt myself nodding.

Ten minutes later, armed with a big wedge of blackberry pie, I walked out the back door. I remembered to leave it partly open, but I had trouble drawing breath. I'd never been so scared.

The Rebel guard jumped to his feet and grabbed his gun. He looked as big as my father. I held up the pie pan and willed my feet to move me down the step, around the garden, across the grass.

"Hey, now, what're you doing there?" The guard took a step forward. "Git back in the house. You ain't supposed to be out here."

Five more steps. I was close enough now to smell him. My skin was suddenly clammy.

"I said, what you doin'?" He moved the musket from one hand to the other.

I'd rehearsed it with Timothy. It was so simple. *Would you like some pie?* My lips moved. Nothing came out. In desperation I thrust the pan toward him. When I dared look he was staring at the big wedge of blackberry pie. For a long moment we were both still.

Then, "Is that for me?" he asked suspiciously. I nodded. "Why?"

I took a deep breath. "Y-you look hungry." It came out a whisper. But it came out.

"Well, I surely am...." He debated a moment longer. I made myself look him straight on. The Rebel did look skinny as a stray dog in winter. I could see the hunger in his eyes. He didn't look quite so fierce.

Suddenly he snatched the pan, scooped some pie up with his fingers, and crammed it in his mouth. A look came over his face—almost like the look on Teresa's face when she buried her flag. A church look. "Oh, by crackers, this is fine," he sighed.

I'd almost forgotten my purpose, I'd been so nervy. Now I took a casual step to the side. Another, and another, pretending I was passing time with a friend and felt the call to lean against the fence beside him. He turned a bit my way. I didn't think it was enough. I had to try harder. "You like the pie?"

He bent his head. "Huh?"

My fingers found the fence rail and squeezed. "I said, you like the pie?"

"Well, I surely ain't tasted anything this fine since I left my mama's house." He crammed another chunk in his mouth.

I noticed he wasn't really as tall as Papa. He didn't look much older than Margaret. And with blackberry juice running down his chin, he didn't look too mean. "What's your name?"

He smacked his lips before answering. "Hiram."

Then I stole a glance at the house and saw Timothy belly-slide out the door. The ice jumped into my throat. "Where you hail from, Hiram?" I asked desperately. I took a tiny step toward him and he took one back, turning a bit farther from the house.

"Tennessee. And I surely hope I live to see it again."

"I...I hope so too." Timothy started across the lawn. He was pressed down tight. Not much moved but his toes.

Hiram was shoveling the last of the pie, but he gave me a look. "Why do you talk so low? You ain't much louder than a skeeter."

I felt my cheeks flame. "Well...I—I guess I'm shy."

"You know, you 'mind me some of my sister. Back home. She's shy too." His eyes took on a faraway look. "I miss her."

Timothy was rounding the garden corner. It was hard not to stare over the Rebel's shoulder at him. I scrambled for something to say. "Uh...what's it, uh, like? Being in a battle?"

"Well...I ain't really been in one yet. But they marched us over the field up on the mountain. The day after." Hiram shook his head, as if to clear it. "It's a sight I'll surely remember. I don't want to end up like some of those boys did up there. I ain't afeard, now," he added quickly. "But I'm all my mama's got to keep up the farm. The only son. My pa's dead. I've been thinking that maybe this soldiering wasn't the best idea after all."

Timothy had made it to the fence. I could have hit him with a stone tossed over Hiram's shoulder. But he had stopped. *Keep going*! I wanted to scream. Suddenly I figured Timothy was probably scared he'd make noise sliding through the thick lilac wall.

I had to keep the soldier talking. "Tell me about Tennessee."

He was wiping the last traces of blackberry juice from the pan with his fingers, but suddenly gave me a funny look. "Why are you so interested?"

I tried to smile. Think. Think! I felt sweaty, all over. "Well...I've never been farther than Hagerstown. I like to read, though. I read books and try to imagine what it's like in far-away places. When I meet travelers, I like to hear about it." And that, I thought, is probably the longest speech I've ever made.

It must have been convincing, too, for he sighed and leaned against the fence, facing me. "Tennessee? Well, it's a purty place. I live in a little cove in the mountains. Our place ain't so much, I guess, but with fair weather and a mule a man can get by...."

I let him talk, nodding now and then. Out of the corner of my gaze I saw Timothy slither beneath the bottom fence rail and into the lilacs. I saw the bushes heave, heard the rustle. Hiram kept right on talking and I realized he was hearing only the wind in his Tennessee cove. He was homesick and lonely and, I suspicioned, more scared than me. The ice started to melt.

I gave Timothy time enough to get a mile away, I figured, before I found the heart to interrupt. "Well, I expect I should be getting back inside."

"I reckon so." Hiram wiped sticky fingers on his filthy uniform and handed the shining pie pan back to me. He suddenly looked embarrassed. "I've talked your ear off."

"I didn't mind."

"Say, you want to see a likeness before you go?" he asked hopefully. He rummaged in a pocket and pulled out a battered tintype. A bony woman was sitting in the photographer's chair, her hair scalded back like she never wanted to close her eyes again. A girl about my age was standing with her hand on the woman's shoulder. "That's my mama and Ida, my sister."

Somehow it hurt to see those two women. "Well, they'll be powerful glad to see you home again," I said. "I hope it's soon. I hope you don't get killed in the battle."

He nodded seriously. "I'm obliged for the thought. And thanks kindly for the pie."

I was almost back to the house when I heard him shout. "Hey! What's your name?"

"Elizabeth," I called back. Hiram nodded. He'd heard. He'd heard me, all across the yard.

As I walked back into the house, I didn't know what to feel: happy, sad, worried, relieved. And I didn't have much time to figure it out. Just as I closed the door a deafening roar commenced, and shells began to fall in Sharpsburg.

CHAPTER THIRTEEN

TERESA

I was in the yard, listening and watching with some others, when the cannonading began. Everyone bolted to the cellar. I'd grown so tired of waiting I was glad the gunners had finally let loose.

The elderly folks were awarded the chairs. Some of the younger ones climbed up on potato bunks and apple bins. Anne was holding a neighbor's baby, and had her other arm around Margaret's shoulders. I saw Stephen darting back and forth among the milling people. Mama was making sure everyone was all right.

But I didn't see Bethie.

I began shoving through the mob. There were a couple of high, narrow windows in the stone walls, and one or two people had lit candles, but it was still gloomy. "Have you seen Bethie?" I asked, over and over. "Have you seen my sister?"

No one could recall. But no one seemed able to think on it either, not with the artillery booming, and the explosions from the streets above as the shells landed. The Union gunners were aiming at the Confederate line, not us, but couldn't keep some shells from landing smack dab in the village.

Finally I caught up with my mother. "Mama, I can't find Bethie."

"What?" Mama turned her head, quickly scanning the crowd. "She must be here—"

"I've looked already!" I heard my voice rising and tried to steady it. "She's not."

"But where...." Mama's eyes widened. "The McClintocks. Oh Teresa, you don't suppose—"

"She wouldn't have! Not by herself, with the Rebels...."

"I can't think where else she would be," Mama said grimly.

I couldn't either. I turned toward the stairs. "I'm going after her."

Mama grabbed my wrist. "Absolutely not!"

"Mama, I've got to! We can't leave her out there!"

"You are not leaving this house," Mama said. Her words were like iron forged on Papa's anvil. "We will pray that Bethie is safe at the McClintocks'. That's surely better than being on the streets while shells are falling."

"But...but I can't just sit here!" I cried.

"Yes you can," she said. "We both will. And as soon as the shelling stops we will go find her. But I will not have *two* daughters out in this. Is that understood?"

"Yes ma'am," I said slowly. For a wild moment I considered disobeying. Then a shell landed somewhere nearby, sending bricks flying against the walls outside. People shrieked. Mama winced, but her eyes didn't leave mine. I nodded.

So instead of charging outside I plopped on a vinegar barrel in the corner, drumming my heels. I'd never felt so trapped. Helpless. I was enraged with the Rebels for coming to Sharpsburg and bringing this fury upon us.

Anger was a feeling I knew well. But there was something else, too...an unpleasant knotty feeling in my stomach. It took a while to figure out that I was scared. All I could think about was Bethie, somewhere out in that storm.

Finally the daylight began to fade, and with it the shelling. I went rigid when I realized the booms were coming less frequently. And when two or three minutes of silence passed, I couldn't wait any longer. I grabbed up my skirt and bolted up the stairs and out the front door.

I paused on the step. The world was still whole, more or less. In the twilight I saw that the Rohrbach's chimney was gone, bricks scattered. A Confederate horseman clattered by, swerving around debris. A civilian I didn't recognize ran past, going so hard I could hear his ragged breathing. I saw a couple of lights down the street as folks dared outside, lanterns in hand. Some soldiers shouted in the distance.

Just then I heard someone calling my name. I turned and saw Bethie and Gideon Brummer hurrying toward me. Relief dropped over me like a warm quilt. Bethie looked tired, but not as scared as I'd expected, and blessedly whole. Gideon's hand was on her shoulder protectively.

"Bethie!" I cried. I ran to meet them and pulled her into my arms. "Bethie, we were scared witless! Where on earth—"

"We should talk inside," Gideon interrupted. "I don't think we'll see any more shelling tonight. But we can't be sure."

And how did *you* come to fetch her home? I wanted to ask, but he was already shepherding us back toward the house. Then Mama burst through the door and there was more commotion.

It took a while to get the story. Inside, people were drifting upstairs, chattering like old folks at a church reunion picnic. Everyone exclaimed over Bethie and Gideon, wanting to know what had happened. "I just wanted to make sure Timothy's family was all right," she said. I could tell she hated being the center of attention.

I guess Gideon could see that too, because he took over the story. "She got trapped when the shelling started. I happened by toward the end of it and brought her home. No, Mrs. McClintock wanted to stay where they were.... What? Well, we did see one Confederate soldier who got hit by some flying debris...."

I listened, trying to figure it all out. Finally Mama towed Bethie off to the kitchen. Stephen and Margaret and Anne followed, with some of the neighbors in their wake. I looked at Gideon. "Something strikes me as queer," I said. "I'm powerful obliged to you for bringing Bethie home. But I can't figure how you happened to be out at the McClintocks' in the first place."

"There's more to the story," he agreed, in a low tone. "And I'd like you to hear it. Is there somewhere we can talk privately for a bit?"

"Privacy is in short supply just now." I looked around. "Let's go outside."

He nodded, and I fetched a lantern. We walked out to the street. Darkness had masked the damage done that afternoon. I looked up at Gideon. "Well?"

"Teresa, you mustn't repeat most of what I'm going to tell you." I nodded, more curious by the minute. Gideon looked around before beginning. "Bethie walked into a mess at the McClintocks' this afternoon. Have you ever heard of the Underground Railroad?"

I nodded slowly. "I've heard of it. Not much more than that."

"Well, it's a loose trail of people who help escaped slaves north to freedom. Reverend McClintock has been involved with that for some time."

I was surprised. "He has? Bethie never mentioned—"

"His own family didn't know. He kept it from them, to protect them. It's dangerous business, so he was right to be cautious. Anyway, somehow the Confederates sniffed it out. Probably someone in town informed on him."

"I don't doubt it." I curled my fingers into a fist, remembering the Rebels who had been pointed to my door.

"While Bethie was there the Confederates arrived, looking for Daniel. They said that anyone who left would be arrested. They put guards around the house—"

"Oh! She must have been terrified." I felt a stab of angry guilt. "I should have gone with her. I knew how worried she was."

"It wouldn't have helped." In the shadows I saw Gideon smile a little. "You tangling with the Rebels likely would have done Mrs. McClintock in."

"Well, someone has to tell them what for," I muttered defensively. But I didn't want to insult him—not after what he'd done for us. "Go on."

"Timothy decided to slip out and warn his father. Somehow Bethie managed to distract one of the guards long enough—"

"*Bethie* did?"

He nodded. "Timothy got away just before the artillery started in."

I decided I'd get details on that later, from Bethie. "But how did you get there?"

He took a deep breath. "Well, I'd promised Daniel—Reverend McClintock—that I'd look in on his family. He was particularly worried about leaving on this trip, what with the Rebel Army on the move. I've had so much happening at the farm I haven't been able to get to town like I'd hoped. But I've been worried. Once my own family was settled this afternoon, I started in. I was on my way when the firing began."

My jaw dropped. "You were out in that? You could have been killed!"

He shrugged lightly. "I figured nothing would be gained by turning back. No one paid me any attention. But I was careful once I got close to the McClintocks'. I saw a guard on duty in front of the house, so I slipped around to the back—"

"Gideon!" I burst out, then couldn't find anything else to say. "Go on."

"Well, there was a soldier on duty behind the house too. I watched for a while. I didn't know what to do. He looked less threatening than the other one. In fact, he was sort of cowering by the back fence. Then a shell landed a little ways behind the house. It was deafening. Earth and branches flew everywhere. That soldier let out a howl, climbed over the fence, and took off. I waited to see if the one in front would come to check, but he didn't."

I stared at Gideon, suddenly a stranger. Everything I believed about this friend of my brother's was turning upside-down.

"So, I figured I better take advantage of the situation while I could, and headed across the yard and in the back door. I was afraid the Confederates would tighten their guard again at first chance, so soon as things seemed to be getting even a bit quieter I took Bethie out of there—"

"While the shells were still coming?" I demanded.

"Teresa, the McClintocks don't have a cellar," he said quietly, and my sudden flare of anger died. "I found all three of them huddled beneath the table. Better than nothing, but small protection if a shell hit the house. Anyway, I tried to bring Mrs. McClintock and Lucilla along. Bethie begged her. But she was afraid to leave. Afraid the Confederates would make things worse for them in the end."

For a moment we were both silent. I was still trying to take it all in. In the distance I heard some soldiers singing "Maryland, My Maryland." They sounded drunk. Then a new thought struck me. "Gideon...how are you and Reverend McClintock such friends?"

He paused before answering. "You know the Dunkers are pacifists. We also take a vow not to own slaves. I...let's say I've helped the Reverend with his work, a time or two."

My thoughts were spinning like one of Stephen's tops. "I never knew. Never suspicioned at all."

He grinned. "I hope not!" Then his smile faded. "I hope you understand how serious this is, Teresa. How important it is not to tell anyone. I'm trusting you."

I couldn't have explained why, but that pleased me. "Of course."

He nodded. "Well. I need to start back soon. My family will be worried. But how about you? How did you all fare?"

"Well enough. Just worried terrible about Bethie."

"Any word from your father and Aaron?"

"No. But we didn't expect it, not with the Rebel Army between us and them."

"I wish I was closer. I wish I could stay here and keep an eye on you all."

"We don't need you to keep an eye on us," I said, from instinct I guess, because strangely, the thought didn't bother me like it should have. "Besides, the battle's over, isn't it?"

"Over?" He looked surprised. "No! No, I don't think so. I think this was no more than the Union Army giving notice. I expect we'll see more trouble tomorrow. In fact, I think tomorrow is going to be the worst of it. The Confederates are holding Sharpsburg, and the Union boys want it real bad. You keep everyone close to the cellar, hear?"

"Yes," I said, then couldn't help adding, "But don't tell me what to do."

"Teresa, I would never dare," he said, and laughed. I wasn't sure why. "Well, I'd better head out."

I put my hand on his arm. "Gideon...I don't believe I ever thanked you proper. For bringing Bethie home." Simple words, for what he'd done.

"I was glad to do it." He thrust his hands in his pockets. Before I knew what was happening, he touched my lips with his own. Then he walked away, whistling. I was so surprised I stood in silence like some fool statue, watching him go.

The night was so quiet that most of us refused to sleep in the cellar. I snuggled next to Bethie, thankful to feel her warmth beside me, while she whispered the story again. "It was awful," she said simply.

I silently cursed all Rebeldom. "That soldier didn't hurt you, did he?"

"Hiram? No. He wasn't fierce at all, or mean. He just wanted to talk. I think he was lonely. And scared." She sighed. "And then when the cannons started firing...well, I was never so glad to see anybody as I was to see Gideon."

I let her talk. I wasn't ready to say anything about Gideon Brummer, not when all my thoughts of him were so tangled.

I was up before dawn and went downstairs, tiptoeing to keep from waking the folks curled up on quilts in the spare bedroom, the parlor, even the hall. Mama was already at work in the kitchen, and Stephen prancing about, when I snuck out to milk the cows.

The morning felt misty. I lingered in the dark, blessed cool for a moment before unlocking the stable. I hadn't quite finished with the cows when Stephen burst in. "Teresa! Mama says come quick. It looks like trouble."

"What now!" I exclaimed. We felt our way back across the yard, and Stephen steered me to the front door.

I found Mama with a lamp, arguing with several Confederate soldiers. "But surely you can find a household that sympathizes with your cause—"

"Your sympathies ain't a concern," one of them said. His voice sounded familiar. I peered, then recognized the black-haired sergeant who'd confronted me about the flag.

I pushed past Mama. "Sir, why are you bothering us again?"

He glared. "As I was saying, we're leaving this man here. He's too sick to stay with us."

I saw what I had missed in the gloom. One of the soldiers— it looked like the man in the red shirt—was supporting the third.

I felt Mama grab my hand in a way that meant, *Let me handle this.* "Sergeant, I have a house full of people," she tried again. "We have no room for a sick man, no way to care for him—"

"He's staying here!" he barked, and shoved past so rough that Mama stumbled.

Anger shot up inside. No one treated my mama that way while I stood by! "Get out of our house!"

Mama squeezed my hand so hard it hurt. The sergeant turned on me. "You, Missie, will stay quiet if you know what's good for you." His tone was full of all the frustration and fury from their earlier visit.

I didn't care. "Not when you shove ladies, and force your way into people's homes!"

I don't recall how he answered. The sick man groaned, Mama tried to calm everyone down, and I was too angry to think clear. Some of the travelers stumbled into the hall, rubbing their eyes, then set up a clamor. Someone shrieked, waking more folks and causing more of a stir.

Suddenly Red Shirt jerked his head up, listening. A moment later I heard it too—a high whistling whine. Then a deafening explosion shook the walls as a cannonball tore up the road in front of our house. Clods of earth and debris poured against the walls, shattering one window.

I thought for a moment that we were gone. My blood seemed to hammer through my veins. By the time I realized no one was hurt, our whole house was in commotion. A baby was screaming, someone was bellowing "Don't panic!" over and over, and everyone scrambled to the cellar. The sergeant and Red Shirt dragged the sick soldier to the stairs too. I pounded after them.

"Not there," I shouted, when they turned toward the main storeroom. "Bring him back this way." I could tell they thought I was being troublesome, and I stamped my foot. "He needs quiet! He'll be better off in there." And I pushed them toward the smallest room, where we kept crocks of smoked meat packed in lard. I figured the best I could do was keep the sick Rebel separated from everyone else. With folks so packed in, sickness would spread like a brushfire. The sergeant eased the sick man down.

"Here's a blanket," Mama said, appearing in the doorway. I fumbled for a candle and Lucifers. My match flared and found the wick. In the sudden candlelight, the soldiers stood back while Mama tucked the blanket around the sick boy, and pillowed another beneath his head. Then she stood and faced the other Confederates. "That's the best I can do for him right now. I'll try to find a doctor later, when I'm able."

Evidently the sergeant judged my mama an honest woman, for he nodded. Then he looked at me, real cold. "You. You remember me. You may be real sorry you didn't show more respect."

I opened my mouth but a sudden shiver down my spine stilled the words on my tongue. Red Shirt spoke instead. "Sergeant, we got to get going."

The sergeant nodded. "Good luck, Fitzgerald," he said to the sick man. Fitzgerald was too far gone to answer. The two soldiers clattered back up the stairs.

I turned to Mama. "What are we going to do with him?"

"I don't rightly know," she said slowly. "He needs a doctor, but I'm sure there's none to be found. And I've got sixty people in there," she gestured toward the main cellar, "on the edge of panic. I've got to keep everyone calmed down—"

Before we could talk things through, another shell burst somewhere nearby. Then another. It sounded like the whole world was exploding. I got the sense that Gideon had been right. It was going to be a long day.

CHAPTER FOURTEEN

SAVILLA

That day, September 17, lasted forever.

I had thought Samuel would come by that morning, but he didn't. So it was just us—me, Clara, and Jeanette—alone in the little house. When the Union artillery commenced their thunder, trying to push the Confederates out of Sharpsburg, we ran down to the cellar. "Where's the candle?" Clara asked, as we stumbled in the darkness. Our cellar was tiny, windowless—generally not a pleasant place to be.

"I'm getting it—ptew!" I had walked into a cobweb. I clawed it away from my face before finding the candles we had brought down the day before. In a moment I had one lit, stuck in a pool of hot wax I'd dripped on a cider barrel.

"Well," Jeanette said, perching gingerly on the bottom step. "This is rather miserable."

We all jumped as the shudders from another volley trembled through the cellar. I folded my arms, remembering Major von Borcke calmly working upstairs the previous afternoon, while we'd cowered in the cellar. Already, I wasn't sure how long I could last down there. The dank walls pressed in on me. With every crash, I imagined the house collapsing down, burying us—

"Girls," I said, before my imagination bolted altogether. "I'm thinking I'd rather take my chances upstairs than be trapped down here like a caged rat. What do you think?"

Jeanette cocked her head, considering. Clara bit her lip. "Oh Savilla, I don't know...."

We might have debated the merits of staying in that dubious haven for some time if a new noise hadn't snatched our attention. "Listen!" I hissed. I heard a bang from above, then the definite creak of slow footsteps.

Jeanette clutched my hand. "Somebody's up there!"

My heart was racing like a prize trotter. "Maybe it's Samuel," I whispered, although I figured Samuel would have called my name. I took a deep breath and shoved to my feet. "I'm going to see."

"Are you sure you should?" Clara's eyes were wide.

I nodded. I'd told Father I'd guard the house, hadn't I? He was counting on me. It was time to do my part. With my skirt held high, I began creeping up the stairs. I wished desperately for a pistol. Why hadn't Samuel or Father given me a pistol? How was I to defend the house without a gun?

Then I forced that notion away. The only soldiers in Sharpsburg were Confederates, weren't they? It was a sad day if the bravest girl in Sharpsburg was too spooked to greet her own army! Those thoughts stiffed my spine. I went up the stairs and opened the door.

"Hello?" I called, peering around the doorway. "Who's there?" I forced a stronger tone. "Come out!"

"In here!" someone called from the kitchen. I ran down the hall and gasped. A man in Confederate rags was standing by the dry sink, his arm around a younger soldier. That poor boy's eyes were half closed, and I could tell he would fall without his friend's support. The boy's hand was thrust beneath his ragged jacket. Both men were filthy, covered in dust.

"I'm sorry, Miss," the first man rasped. "I didn't think no one was home. We don't want no trouble. I just need some water."

That broke my freeze. "Oh, of course! Here, let me get it—" I ran for the water pail by the door, covered with a cloth to keep the flies out. The man thrust his hand into the pail and tried to scoop some up. I pushed a cup at him and he managed to give the boy a drink, then gulp some himself.

The look in their eyes—the older man desperate, the younger done in—clawed at my heart. "What else can I get for you? Some food, or—"

"Just water." The man tossed back another cupful, then helped his companion take more as well. "Here you go, lad. That's it."

"But he's hurt!" I eased the boy's jacket back and saw that the hand clenching his side was covered with blood. I took a quick breath, trying frantically to think what to do. "Does he want to rest here? Or perhaps a bandage—"

"All we want is to keep moving," the older man said. "I'm obliged for the water though, Miss. It's fierce hot out there, and being hit—" he jerked his head toward the boy, "doubles the thirst." He turned away, dragging the boy along toward the door.

I ran after them. "But why? I—this is a Confederate house! You can stay here!"

The man barely glanced back. "The Yankees are coming," he said simply. Then he was gone, the boy stumbling along beside him.

Jeanette and Clara peeked around the cellar door. "What's happening? Savilla? Are you all right?"

"I am," I answered, feeling hollow. "But our boys aren't."

That was the end of the cellar for me. I filled two buckets at our back yard well and hauled them, with a dipper, out to the street. There isn't much I can do now for our boys, I thought grimly. But if they need water, I can give them water.

Clara and Jeanette were up and down the cellar stairs a dozen times that morning. They helped as long as they could bear it, then dashed back down whenever the cannonading got too bad. Me, I seemed numb to it. Numb to it all. There was no time for fear. No time for cowering below ground like an animal, waiting to be suffocated. I couldn't go back down.

What I saw that morning is hard to even take in, much less tell. It was like the earth opened up. The artillery was deafening. A haze of smoke swirled through Sharpsburg. Shells splintered trees, shattered windows, crashed into chimneys and walls and sent bricks raining to the streets and yards below. I staggered when one landed in our orchard, shaking the very ground beneath my feet.

A dead horse was lying in the street when I came outside. I kept my eyes from it. I saw a Confederate soldier, probably sick, huddled in the Rohrbachs' doorway down the street. When I looked back he was sprawled halfway down the steps. I figured a stray bullet must have caught him. I kept my eyes away from that sight, too.

But I didn't retreat, *couldn't* retreat, because the streets were not empty. Ambulance wagons lurched by, blood dripping from the floorboards. I could hear the wounded men whimpering inside; one cried "Oh Lord! Oh Lord! Oh Lord!" But when the driver saw me he stopped and waved frantically. "Water!" he croaked, and I thrust a full pail up into his hands. He passed it back into the covered wagon before whipping his mules on again.

Couriers and officers pounded past on horseback, and few of those stopped. But soldiers stumbling by on foot did: sick, wounded, or simply exhausted, thirst fought with their urge to retreat. "Bless you, Miss," they gasped, gulping like dogs. The water washed odd tracks through the dust on their chins. They drank and splashed with something akin to reverence, as if the water was all that stood between themselves and collapse. Perhaps it was.

Where was my father, where was Samuel? How were the rest of my brothers and sisters and their families faring? Where were my friends in the army? What was happening to the Confederate line? For a time, that morning, those questions pounded in my brain. But the soldiers who clustered around for water didn't have time for questions; couldn't summon coherent answers. So I pushed the questions aside, with a promise to pursue them later.

Their faces blurred together. Then, during the heaviest barrage, I heard someone calling my name, as if from a distance. "Savilla? Savilla!"

I looked up, blinking against the dust and smoke. Henry Kyd Douglas had reined his magnificent gray in front of the porch. I felt something warm smooth out inside. I wasn't alone in the chaos after all.

He slid to the ground. "Savilla!" he hollered, trying to be heard over the din. "What are you doing? You must get to shelter at once! Get down to your cellar!"

"I will remain here as long as our army is between me and the Yankees!" I shouted back. "Henry Kyd, are you well? Do you want some of water?"

His mouth dropped open. I took that for assent. My last pitcher had just been poured dry so I scurried back to the well. A moment later I handed him a cup of water. A shell shrieked overhead while he drank, and although I couldn't keep from flinching, I waited for him to finish.

"Savilla—I can't linger, I'm on General Jackson's business—" Henry Kyd wiped an elbow across his forehead. "But you must not stay out here! I couldn't bear it if—please! Get to safety!" He pressed my hand urgently before swinging back to the saddle. "*Please!*"

I watched while he cantered away. He looked back once, gesturing, then disappeared. I couldn't move. I felt nothing but the imprint of his hand on my own. But that touch, somehow, was enough to keep me going.

I was glad Jeanette and Clara were in the cellar about midday, when I first caught sight of three soldiers walking almost leisurely down the street. As they passed our house a shell burst in front of them. The impact knocked me against the wall, but I wasn't hurt. When I looked back, I saw that the boy in the middle had been killed, horribly mangled. The other two dragged him to our orchard. They buried him there, in a shallow trench clawed out with their hands and bayonets.

I watched like it was some horrible dream, fighting off the urge to be sick. Then someone tugged my sleeve. "Miss?" It was another grimy boy. "You got any water in that pitcher?" I pushed that grave from my mind and got back to business.

But a short while later I needed reinforcements. An exploding shell set the Goods' house, kitty-corner behind our lot, on fire. I was back at the well when I noticed the first tongues of flame licking at their kitchen window.

I dropped the bucket and pounded into the house. "Jeanette! Clara!" I cried. "Come help me!" And they came, bless them. They came.

"Fire at the Goods'!" I panted. We grabbed basins and buckets and tore outside. I was so proud of those girls! Amidst flying shot and shell and whistling bullets, we carried water from a little spring in the Goods' yard and put out the fire. In a short time it caught again. We returned and this time doused it completely. I'll always remember Jeanette with her hair straggling down and a streak of black soot on her cheek...and Clara, face white and eyes wide, whimpering as she heaved a bucket of water at the smoldering curtains.

Later, folks said we were brave. Me in particular, for standing out all day with my water buckets. I'd always been happy to claim that title, and I took it then. But truth is, I don't know what kept me going that day. Maybe my need to help overcame all else, like they said. But maybe I was holding out for a sight of Henry Kyd, that needle in the army's haystack who came my way and bolstered my courage. Probably, I was simply more scared of being in the cellar than I was of being outside. It's hard to say. Courage, I was starting to learn, had different faces.

CHAPTER FIFTEEN

BETHIE

That day was so eternal I wondered if the sun was crawling backwards. I guess no one expected the siege to go on so long, because even Mama hadn't thought to carry more than a few bites to eat downstairs. We didn't have any breakfast—no dinner—no supper. A few of the women had brought some food in their baskets for the children. But most of us had to live on fear.

Someone brought Mrs. Ward down just after first light. She lived around the corner, and had a day-old baby. Some folks fretted that the cellar was too damp for them, and finally took mother and infant back up to the kitchen. Ten minutes later a shell flew into the building, nearly blinding her with dust and smoke. She was so frightened two of the men carried her back downstairs in a big armchair. I quick brought her a quilt and tucked it around her shoulders. "I'd rather take my chances on dying of cold," she quavered, trying to soothe her screaming baby, "than be killed with a shell or cannonball."

A number of babies were in the cellar, and several dogs, and every time the firing began extra hard the babies cried and the dogs howled. Often the reports were so loud they

The Kretzers and their neighbors in the cellar during the battle.
Note the Union shell exploding in the window.

Courtesy of Frank and Marie-Therese Wood Print Collections,
Alexandria, Va.

shook the walls. Occasionally a woman was quite unnerved, and sobbed uncontrollably. Some of those old men would break out in prayer.

I tried to pray: for the soldiers in battle, for Papa and Aaron, for Timothy and his family, for all of us holed up in the cellar wondering every minute if the next cannonball would crash through and kill us all. But I couldn't seem to find the right words amidst the racket.

I spent most of the day trying to be useful. I walked in endless circles with screaming babies over my shoulder. I got Margaret to sing songs with some of the little ones—hymns, mostly, that caught the old folks' ears as well. I fetched water from the spring for Mrs. Ward and anyone else who asked.

Once, during a quiet spell, I crawled onto a potato bunk and huddled there, wrapped in my cloak. It gave me time to think. I can't say I wasn't scared, because I was—head to toe. But it felt different. My insides were still. The ice in my stomach was gone. I had hours to ponder on it, and finally figured that maybe it had something to do with my talk with Hiram the day before.

I even wondered how Hiram was making on, out there in all the explosions and firing. I'd realized the Confederate soldiers were all different, just like the men in our own army—some mean, some homesick and scared. I hoped Hiram would make it home to his family and farm in Tennessee.

We saw more than a few Rebel soldiers that day. In the middle of the worst fighting half a dozen trotted down the cellar stairs. That set up a frenzy, I can say, but they stopped it quick: "We're not a-goin' to hurt you none," one cried. "We just want *in*."

"Back there," Teresa commanded, pointing to the little room where Fitzgerald lay shivering with fever. I was glad she didn't argue them into leaving. I didn't blame the men for seeking shelter. They stayed for several hours before summoning up their own courage, and heading back to the fight.

About mid-day Teresa and Mama went to check on the cows. Margaret and I held hands so tight it hurt, until they got back. "It's a mess out there," Teresa reported. "No, I didn't check all the damage! But we did see a passel of Rebels. Deserters. Found some in the haymow. I left the door unlocked this morning by mistake. Said they were hiding 'til the battle's over. Cowards! We found two more on the back porch, hiding behind sacks of seed wheat. There's probably hundreds of deserters, all over town."

I didn't blame the deserters, but most of the folks in the cellar didn't like the notion of Rebels crawling over their property. I figured that if they had a chance to talk to one quiet, like I did with Hiram, they wouldn't hate the soldiers quite so much.

The only one who wanted to talk was Stephen. Once, when the firing was terrible and Mama and Anne and Teresa had their hands full with screaming children, Mama caught my eye. "Will you check on Stephen?" she yelled, trying to be heard above the din. "I don't see him."

I found him sitting on the floor by Fitzgerald, giving the poor boy a drink. I couldn't blame Stephen either, for the sick soldier was a stick figure, in filthy rags, shivering violently. "Stephen, come away," I called. "Mama says so."

He came reluctantly. "I just wanted a souvenir. Then he asked me for a drink. I don't think he's mean."

"He's sick, Stephen. It might be catching. You have to leave him be until a doctor can take care of him." Just then a shell exploded so close the ground trembled. I grabbed Stephen's hand and hauled him out with the others.

As the day wore on some folks went silent, sitting and staring and scarcely jumping when the explosions came. Others got more angry, more shrill, more weepy, more agitated. As for me, I tried to help Mama when I could. Otherwise, I just sat. There was nothing to do but wait until the shelling stopped, and hope we'd find the world still in place when we crawled out.

CHAPTER SIXTEEN

TERESA

As the day wore on, I got more and more to feeling like a caged cat. Crimus Almighty! I got tired of the wailing, the whimpering, the praying. I couldn't bear being holed up below ground, not knowing what was going on. Slipping out to milk the cows at noontime was an adventure, but Mama made me scoot right back.

By the middle of the afternoon I couldn't bear the suspense any longer either. I crept upstairs, and when no one called after me, I dashed up to the attic.

Bullets were raining on the roof but I pushed open the shutters on one of the windows facing east. My heart thumped with excitement. What I saw made me whoop out loud.

The street below was still full of Rebels dashing about. The stink of smoke hung in the air. I could see flames from several burning buildings, and flocks of terrified pigeons circling frantic above it all. But on all the distant hills around town were the blue uniforms and shining bayonets of the Union troops. It was the prettiest sight I ever saw. Those were Union men, *our* men, advancing toward Sharpsburg.

I don't know how long I stayed at the window, watching what looked like toy soldiers. Our army advanced cautiously, driven back again and again. But they were persistent, always returning and pushing nearer. I moaned each time the gray troops shoved them back, hollered every time they rallied. "Get 'em! Keep goin'!" I yelled until I was hoarse, as if they could hear me. My! It was lovely. I was overjoyed to think the Union Army would be back in town shortly.

Finally, Bethie came to find me. "Teresa! Come back down. Mama's looking for you."

"Look, Bethie! Come see!" She hesitated near the stairs, then joined me at the window. I grabbed her hand. "Isn't it beautiful? This is a sight worth leaving the cellar for. You'll always remember what you see this afternoon."

"Yes," she began, but just then we heard the high whine of a shell sailing overhead. A moment later it exploded some-where behind the house. She pulled me toward the stairs with an iron grip. "Come down *now*," she commanded. I was so surprised that I followed without protest.

In the evening Mother and I dashed back to the stable and did the milking again. But the firing kept up until dark, so it was back to the cellar. Some of the men dared outside, and quickly reported that the Rebels still held Sharpsburg. Oh! It was frustrating to know our Union boys were so close. They might have been miles away for all the good it did us.

When night finally came we crept back up to the kitchen and snatched some bread and butter for the hungry refugees. Our neighbors didn't even think about going home. Some of the older ones we accommodated in beds, others lay on the floors with cloaks and blankets and pillows. Most sat up all night and watched.

The next day we expected the battle to begin again. I hoped it would come—hoped the Union soldiers would push the Rebels right into the Potomac! But the dawn brought silence.

I stole outside cautiously. It was unearthly quiet after all the uproar of the battle. There were several deep gullies in our yard, plowed by shells. I was confounded by the debris. A cannon and limber had crashed right in front of our house. Our street was littered with muskets, cards, Bibles, and haversacks. Our own house had been hit several times, and bricks and window glass lay scattered about. The Rohrbachs' house across the street had fared worse; their chimney was gone, and a corner of the eaves was caved in.

There was a dead horse in the street. I saw a Rebel lying on the Rohrbachs' walk, and guessed he was dead too. I stared at him for a moment. It seemed odd to see a man lying by the road. Almost like he was napping. I wondered where he'd been hit. I started to cross the street, curious to see my first dead Rebel. Then I stopped. What would he look like? Awful, or peaceful? What if he was just a boy? Suddenly I didn't want to see after all. It was disrespectful to gawk at your enemies once they were dead. With a shiver, I went back inside.

When the firing didn't commence again, our neighbors headed for home. Everybody was anxious to see what was left, afraid of what they might find. Soon only a few travelers remained, mostly women and children still afraid to dare the roads for home. Nobody knew what the day would bring, so no one blamed them for staying.

Before everyone left Mama asked a couple of the men to carry the sick Confederate boy upstairs to one of the guest bedrooms. "I will not leave any poor sick soul in that cold damp," she said firmly. "This is a Christian household." I think she half expected me to argue. But in truth, Fitzgerald looked so far gone I didn't have the heart.

And so he ended up tucked upstairs. "He's probably dying," Anne told me quietly, while Mama was tending to him. "It looks like the typhus, Mama said. He has the bloody diarrhea something awful. Poor boy—" Her voice trembled on the last word.

That caught me up short. Anne was practical, not sentimental, and not one to cave in a crisis. But she seemed about put to tears again. While I searched for something to say, she went on past.

We were surprised, soon after dawn, when Gideon showed up. He drove his big farm wagon right around the house and parked in the back yard. "I'm afraid if I leave it on the street my horse will get stolen," he explained, when we pulled him into the kitchen. Mama and us girls were fixing breakfast.

"Gideon, sit down," Mama commanded. "I'm pouring you a cup of coffee. We'll have a plate ready in a moment too."

"I'd be grateful," he admitted, sinking on a bench.

I hung back. I had thought I'd be embarrassed to see him again, after what had passed between us. After all, he'd just up and kissed me without so much as a by-your-leave! It was confusing—should I be angry with him for his sand, or take heart in it? But seeing him, all those thoughts blew away. I'd never seen him look so done in. He sagged against the wall like he couldn't sit up straight.

Mama put a steaming mug in front of him. "Here. Now, what's brought you? Is your family all right?"

He blew away the steam, dared a sip, looked appreciative. "Ah. That's good. Yes ma'am, my family's well. I'm just tired. I've been driving loads of wounded soldiers in to Hagerstown all night."

"Oh, Gideon," Anne murmured. "No wonder you're exhausted."

He rubbed his forehead with his fingers. "Our farm came under Union hands late yesterday. Every fence has been torn down for firewood. Our wheat field is trampled. The corn crop picked. All our livestock is gone. Our beehives were destroyed. Every apple picked in the orchard." Then he shook his head a little, as if to clear his thoughts. "That doesn't even bear thinking on right now. The army set up a hospital in the barn soon as the firing died down. But there's only one surgeon. We've got wounded lying in rows all over the yard. The house is overflowing. So is the stable."

I thought it took incredible sand to be out hauling wounded, unprotected, while we were sticking close to the cellar. I wanted to tell him so. But I couldn't find the words.

Just then we heard a familiar voice yelling from the front hall. "Susan? Susan!"

"It's Papa!" Margaret squealed, as he and Aaron walked through the door.

I'd never been so glad to see anyone. I was even glad to see Aaron. He was filthy and had dark rings under his eyes from more than coal dust, like he hadn't gotten near enough sleep.

My papa is not a hugging man, but he had hugs for everyone that morning. Mama got a little dewy around the eyes. Everybody was saying, "Are you all right?" and, "Yes, yes," at the same time.

"Where's my little man?" Papa asked finally. We were all in the kitchen except Stephen.

Mama looked at me. "Teresa, will you go find him? Make sure he's not in the sickroom." And to Papa, "We've got a sick Rebel upstairs, John. For some reason Stephen is fascinated with him."

I ran halfway up the stairs and hollered. Stephen poked his head around the corner. "What?"

"Come down!" I said impatiently. I wanted to be in the kitchen with everyone else, not chasing after him. "Why must you be such a pest? Mama's told you and told you to leave that Rebel be!" And before he could sulk, "Besides, Papa and Aaron are home—" I almost got trampled as Stephen shoved past.

We all had stories to tell. Papa told about working with the army smiths and farriers. "We could have used a dozen more men," he said. "I was glad to have Aaron with me, that's sure." He looked at Aaron, who nodded. "It's not just tending the animals. They've got ambulance wagons with wheels falling apart that need to be retired. Caissons that've had the hardware shaken loose. These rocky mountain roads are hard on transport."

"Are you done fixing the army?" Stephen asked.

Papa chuckled. "Well, not quite. But Aaron and I just about went mad, yesterday. We knew Sharpsburg was under fire, and they wouldn't let us through the lines to get home. We headed out first thing this morning to make sure you were all well." He looked at Mama. "But I can't stay home long."

Mama nodded, as if she had understood this all along, and began spooning scrambled eggs on plates for everyone.

Margaret and Anne told about our time in the cellar. Stephen showed off his souvenirs: a variety of Confederate notes, three buttons, and a canteen with a hole in it. He hadn't been outside yet, and I didn't tell him there was bounty for the grabbing in the street.

Instead I told Papa about the Rebels who'd come to the house looking for the flag, and how I'd tricked them. I told him about marching to Boonsboro with Alexander Root. And I told him about sneaking to the attic during the fight and spying the Union soldiers.

Papa smiled and shook his head. "My daughter, the bravest girl in Sharpsburg," he said. That was all, but I was satisfied.

"Bethie had quite an adventure too," Gideon said. Breakfast, I was glad to see, had put a bit of color back in his cheeks. He briefly told the tale, while Bethie fiddled with her food, looking embarrassed. "And if she hadn't distracted that soldier, Timothy would never have gotten away. She and Timothy probably saved Reverend McClintock from Rebel prison."

"Bethie stood up to a Rebel soldier?" Papa asked. He'd stopped eating.

"It wasn't so much," she said. "He did most of the talking. He was homesick, and lonely. And scared."

Papa squinted at her. "Yes. Well, you did a good thing—"

"Not so much," she said again. She began gathering dirty dishes.

I saw Gideon frown, but Papa pushed his empty plate away and stood. "Susan, that tasted fine. What I need to do now is see what damage has been done to our property."

"I need to be on my way too," Gideon said. "As always, Mrs. Kretzer, I thank you kindly for the food. It was just what I needed."

Aaron walked outside to see Gideon off. Mama disappeared with Papa, and Stephen tagged along like a puppy. Anne, ever dutiful, started on the dishes. I sighed. If we could just get the Union Army back in Sharpsburg, everything would be fine.

We stayed at home that day, cleaning up the damage. We had several shattered windows, several damaged spots in the walls, a yard full of bricks and debris. One shell had crashed all the way through the back wall. Papa found a dead Confederate soldier in our garden and ordered us all in the house until after he and Aaron had buried him by the back fence.

That afternoon another traveler showed up at our door. "The name's Carter," he introduced himself, shaking Papa's hand. He was a stocky man with narrow eyes that seemed to take in every detail. "I'm a reporter," he explained. "*Boston Herald*. Someone told me I could rest up here."

His "rest" consisted of a splash-off at the pump and a gulped mug of cider. Then he left, notebook in hand. But he was back for supper, and he brought the news: "Only five homes escaped damage during the shelling," he reported. "And how many people live in Sharpsburg?"

"About 1,300," Papa said.

Carter scribbled a note before continuing. "The homes of..." he squinted. "Widow Holmes and Widow Shackleford have been burned to the ground. The Confederates used the Lutheran Church's belfry as an observation station, and as a result, it drew terrible fire from Yankee gunners—oh, that's your church?" Mama nodded, her lips pressed together. "Well, ma'am, it's badly damaged. But all in all you folks fared pretty well. I talked with lots of people who came home and found smashed furniture, ransacked larders, empty root cellars and smokehouses. And many found dead soldiers in their stables and kitchens. Some were torn to pieces by shells. Some bled to death from wounds."

Hearing the tales, I figured we'd made off pretty light. I couldn't help wondering how Savilla had fared. Her house was a stone's throw from the Lutheran Church. I even thought about going to see, but just couldn't. I figured if there was any kind of bad news, I'd hear it soon enough.

The Confederates retreated that night. We listened to the shuffling tramp, the creaking and jingling and rumbling from the street. It continued for hours, and we heard later that Lee's army pushed down to the Potomac ford on the narrow country lanes. People living on the bluffs above the river could see the flicker of torches held by cavalrymen posted midstream as the Rebels crossed back to Virginia. They'd been whipped.

Next morning I was up before first light. We'd slept in our clothes again, in case of trouble, so all I had to do was pull on my shoes before racing downstairs. I opened the front door and saw Papa on the street already, talking to an army officer. The soldier was wearing *blue.* I bounded out to join them. "Sir, is it true?" I cried, interrupting. "Are the Rebels gone?"

The officer smiled only grimly. "True enough. They are safe gone, God curse them, instead of gobbled up like they should have been."

"But where is the Union Army?" I didn't see any other troops.

"Still east of town, most of 'em. I expect they'll be marching in shortly—"

Shortly! Without stopping for manners, I dashed back to rescue my flag from the ash heap. Papa laughed when he saw it, and helped me swing it back across the street where it belonged.

That officer was right. It wasn't long before the first column of Union soldiers tromped down Main Street. As the men passed under my flag they all took off their hats. Their reverence for the flag was beautiful, and so was the flag!

Lots of Sharpsburg folks came out to watch them pass. Some of them had been in their cellars for three days, and they ran into the street to shake the boys' hands. Those who could brought fruit and coffee and such refreshments as the Rebels hadn't found or couldn't carry. Every few minutes Stephen shouted "Three cheers for the Union!" and the passing Yankees responded with a will.

I was on our front step, waving and cheering our troops, when some Confederate prisoners were marched by. Bless your soul! Among them I saw the very men who had demanded the big flag that was now suspended across the street, Red Shirt and his black-haired sergeant. They looked at the flag and looked at me. "You said it was burned!" the sergeant shouted.

"I told you what was true!" I yelled back. "The flag was in ashes!"

"You're a liar!" Red Shirt bellowed, and cursed me until some of our men quieted him down.

I ran a short ways after them as they marched past. "I guess you got whipped!"

The sergeant turned his head. "We'll settle with you when we come through here again," he called, before our boys shoved him along.

Their threats didn't bother me a hair. I felt glorious! The Confederate Army was gone, and my family was safe together. Those two Rebels had tried to steal my flag, bullied my mama, and thought they were getting the last laugh by forcing their sick comrade on us. But now they were prisoners, and my flag was back safe above the street, commanding the town. Life, I felt, had never been finer.

Well, it was a good feeling while it lasted.

CHAPTER SEVENTEEN

SAVILLA

As I said, I was numb throughout that long day of battle. It didn't last, though. I wish it had. My heart didn't begin to break until the shooting faded.

The night after the battle was like a horrible dream. The smoke stained the sunset an eerie blood-red. Flames from burning buildings still danced against the sky. Hundreds of torches and lanterns bobbed through the night in every direction.

Jeanette, Clara, and I packed up baskets of wine and biscuits and quilts and anything else we could find, and hauled them to the Lutheran Church, one of the many buildings in Sharpsburg that had already been turned into a hospital. We spent the night trying to tend the most basic needs of an endless line of wounded soldiers. Clara wept quietly, all night long. Jeanette's wide eyes became frighteningly blank. My heart was wrung with every glimpse of the hospital's misery, leaving a pain in my chest that wouldn't go away. Every time I crouched beside some poor bloodied boy I was afraid I'd see Henry Kyd, or some other friend.

The Lutheran Church on Main Street. This photograph, taken some time after the battle, shows the damage done by the Union artillery. It was still in use as a hospital. The Miller and Kretzer homes may be just visible, down the hill.

Dawn broke as we trudged home. I barely paid attention as a rider threaded through the street's debris and traffic and reined to a halt in front of our house. Then, "Savilla!"

"Samuel!" I'd never been more glad to see my brother. He was dirty, in need of a shave, and had dark smudges of exhaustion beneath his eyes. But he was here.

He slid to the ground and pulled me close in a rough embrace, then took the hands of Jeanette and Clara in turn, peering at us one-by-one as if convincing himself that we were here, and whole. "Thank God," he said finally. "You're all well? Unharmed?"

"Yes," I said. Details could wait until later. "And the family? Auntie Mae and Uncle Bob? The farm?"

"Everyone's all right, as far as I know." Samuel drew a deep breath. "We've got Union troops camped around the house, and a hospital set up in the barn. We've lost almost everything. But the house didn't take any direct hits, thank God, and we saw the day safely through in the cellar."

"Have you seen anyone else?" I had so many brothers and sisters, nieces and nephews, uncles and aunts and cousins! In this chaos, who could know if everyone was safe?

"I'm making rounds to find out," Samuel said grimly. "I wanted to come here first, check on you girls."

"Everything here is fine," I said firmly, although I had to stifle a crazy urge to laugh as I said it. Fine? Would anything ever be fine again?

"Have you heard anything from Father?"

"No."

"Well, that's to be expected. The whole county's turned upside-down." An ambulance rumbled by, the cursing driver almost—but not quite—drowning out the groans coming from within. Samuel looked from it to us, biting his lip. "Savilla...I think you girls should come back to the farm with me."

For the briefest moment I considered. Then, "No. I told Father I'd keep watch on the house. I can't do that from the farm."

"I know. But this is worse than I knew to imagine." Samuel shook his head. "*Much* worse. And it's not over. Folks are saying the battle was a draw. Trouble is, the Southern Army gave it everything they had, and the Northern Army still has fresh troops in reserve. I know the Confederate Army is still here, but...I think we're whipped. The Yankees are catching their breath. They'll push on into town. There's no telling what will happen then."

I think we're whipped.... The knife twisted in my heart again. "That's why I have to stay," I said stubbornly. "I promised Father." I wasn't going to let Father down. Things were bad enough without caving in now! I wasn't going to slink out of town like a rabid dog. What would my patriot grandparents think if they were looking down from Heaven? What would Henry Kyd think, if he came back looking for me?

Samuel hesitated just a moment, then nodded. "So be it. I'll get back when I can." Then he looked at my friends. "How about you girls? You don't have to stay just because Savilla is. If either of you wants to leave, I'll take you."

I held my breath. I wanted them to stay.

"I promised my parents I'd stay put here until someone came to fetch me," Jeanette said slowly. "I don't know what's happened at my own house...I think I should wait."

Samuel nodded again. "Clara?"

Clara pinched her lips together. Suddenly tears flowed over again. "I want to go home," she managed. "I'm sorry, Savilla—"

"Nothing to be sorry about," I said fiercely, and gave her a big hug.

Ten minutes later, Clara was perched behind Samuel on his gelding. Her nightdress and toothbrush were packed in his saddlebag. "Take care," we called, and she waved. We watched until they disappeared from sight.

Jeanette's hand found mine. I squeezed it, grateful for her company, because I felt the old loneliness creeping back. I hated to see Clara go. As for Samuel, I didn't know when I'd see him again. The trip to Boonsboro, taking Clara home, added hours to his day. By the time he saw her safely with her parents, and made the rounds of our other relatives, there was no telling what might have come to pass.

"I don't think I've ever been so tired," I said finally, to fill the empty space. "My whole body aches."

Jeanette nodded. "I hate to sleep, when there's so much to be done. But if I don't get some rest...."

"You go on up," I told her. "I'm going to fetch some water and make sure the stable is still locked, then I'll join you. We can nap for a bit, then see what needs to be done."

We went inside and Jeanette plodded up the stairs. I gathered two buckets and headed out the back door. The day was already promising to be fearful hot. I wanted to get some water inside in case the well ran dry.

I'd only started those chores when I noticed a Confederate sniper in a tall tree near our orchard. Snipers, I'd learned, were crack shots who hid watchful in unexpected places, ready to pick off an unsuspecting enemy. It sounds fierce but this one was a scraggly boy, clutching his rifle like a lifeline. Pitifully, he'd pulled a cornhusk mattress among the branches for protection. Did he think it would stop a bullet?

"Come down," I called. "The fighting's over."

"No it ain't," he yelled back, ducking out of sight. "General Lee ain't beat. The Yankees will be coming again. I got to keep at my post."

"Where's your regiment? Your friends must be looking for you."

The boy-soldier poked his head back over the blue-striped mattress ticking. "I don't know where they are," he admitted. "But I cain't leave my post. Captain said so."

I didn't know how to tell him that from what I could see, the Confederate Army was broken. His captain was probably long gone. Maybe dead. "If the Union Army does come," I yelled, "they'll capture you for sure. Come down and I'll help you find your regiment."

"I'm not coming down!" His voice was an odd blend of despair and determination. "I got my duty! You just go on and leave me be. I'll keep watch, and take care of the Yankees if they come. You should go on inside, now. Ladies don't belong out in this."

For some reason it pained me particular that this poor boy might get captured, or shot, in my own back yard. There was no reason for it. It was too much. Amidst all the death and destruction, I didn't think I could bear it.

Then inspiration struck. I went inside and rummaged in the pantry. It was near-on to empty, but I managed to find a crust of bread and a little dish of peach preserves. I carried them, and a big mug of cool water, to the tree.

I heard rustling in the branches above. "What you doin' there?"

I didn't answer, just left the food and water on the ground. I hadn't gotten as far as the back porch when the tree shook and the boy slid to the ground. I figure the smell of preserves was just too much for him. I watched him wolf the food, gulp the water. Then he looked around. I could tell he didn't know what to do. Finally, still clutching his gun, he loped away.

Such was the backbone of the Confederate Army. *My* army. That poor boy knew his orders, wanted to stand up for his cause, protect the womenfolk. A Yankee bullet hadn't stopped him. Hunger had.

I hadn't wept through the long dark day of battle, or the endless, gruesome night that followed. But the sight of that poor boy, reduced to such, broke my heart all over again. I think that's when I knew, truly knew, that Samuel was right. We *were* whipped. For a long time, before finishing chores and joining Jeanette, I sat on the back porch and cried.

After getting some sleep, Jeanette and I went back to the Lutheran Church. Everything was a jumble. Exhausted surgeons shouted commands, orderlies carried wounded about, ambulances rumbled in and out of the yard. Some wounded soldiers staggered, or crawled, in on their own, looking for help. I wondered if Henry Kyd had escaped the storm unhurt, or if he was lying in another makeshift hospital like this somewhere. I couldn't let myself wonder about any worse fate. Every time my mind turned in that direction I shied away like I'd touched a hot stove.

Civilians were there too: men nailing planks over the pews to make beds, women packing away hymnals and bringing baskets of food and supplies. No one seemed to be in charge so we tried to make ourselves busy. We carried water and bound up wounds as best we knew how. And through it all my heart ached, almost choking me with the pain.

Jeanette and I were exhausted again by nightfall, and dropped into bed. But we were drawn outside an hour later, when the Confederate Army began to withdraw from Sharpsburg. Samuel had been right. The battle had been a draw, but the Southern Army couldn't stand up to another Union attack. General Lee was taking his battered, hungry soldiers back across the Potomac to Virginia. Back to Southern soil, they said, because they no longer considered Maryland to be such.

Although I heard later that cavalrymen at the river crossing had torches, lighting the way for the men plunging into the current, the army tramped through Sharpsburg in the dark. I hung a candle-lantern by the door so the troops could see a bit of our Confederate flag. It didn't give much light, though. We heard the shuffling feet and jingle of harness, smelled the dust and sweat, but could make out little in the gloom. Every footfall, every hoof clop, was painful to hear. *Don't go,* I wanted to beg as they passed. *Don't go.*

We must have watched for an hour or more before one of the riders separated from the column and eased toward our front steps. "Savilla? Savilla, is that you?"

I caught my breath. I hardly dared hope. "Henry Kyd?"

"Oh thank God." His saddle creaked as he dismounted. "I've wanted to stop ever since—I just had to make sure you were all right."

"Yes, yes, but you?" My heart was pounding and I suddenly wanted to curse at the darkness. I wanted to see Henry Kyd's face, look in his eyes and know he was truly, *truly*, unharmed. "Did you —."

"I'm well. I'd like to think I bore up under fire as well as you! You're quite a girl. I'm proud of you."

"Oh Henry Kyd...."

"Savilla, I can't stay." He found my hand and pressed it, as he had in the street during the barrage. "Take care of yourself. Be sensible when the Yankees come."

"But—" I felt his fingers slip from mine, heard him remount. Thoughts were suddenly shooting through my head: questions unasked, wishes unspoken. He was leaving! When would I see him again? The Southern Army might never come back across the Potomac! It was almost unbearable. "Henry Kyd!"

My voice, louder than I'd intended, caught him. "Yes?"

"Will you write?"

I sensed his smile. "Of course!" Then he turned his horse's head back toward the street. In a moment he was gone, hidden among the other shadows of the Confederate Army.

We heard some gunfire from the river toward dawn, but the Union Army took control of Sharpsburg again without a shot. Jeanette and I watched from the window as Union soldiers poured down the street.

Within minutes one was banging at the door. "Open up!"

I didn't feel a lick of fear. I was too hurt, too dazed by all I'd seen, to be afraid. I jerked the door open and saw a Union soldier with my Confederate flag crumpled in his hands.

"Get this inside," he ordered coldly. "I'm with the provost guard. If it's hanging next time I come by, I'll put the house under arrest."

I snatched the flag from his hands and slammed the door. The man had been a stranger. At least, I thought, he hadn't—yet—forced me to hang a Union flag. Not yet, anyway.

Jeanette and I were folding the flag reverently away when we heard another pounding at the door. "Oh stars!" I snapped. "If it's that blasted provost officer—"

But it was only Mr. Blackford. "Jeanette!" he cried, and she flew into her father's arms. "Oh Lordy, we've been so worried—"

I watched the reunion with, I'll admit, some envy. I hated to see Jeanette go! Her father tried to talk me into coming with them. Mr. Blackford was concerned when he heard my father wasn't home.

"He left with some valuables," I explained. "A Confederate officer said he'd likely be arrested, if the Union Army won back the town." I swallowed hard, tasting bitterness. "*When* the Union Army won back the town." That I realized that sounded mewly. Not like me at all! I stood up straight. "I'll be staying. But I thank you, sir, for the kind offer."

"You call on us if you're in need."

"Yes, sir. I will." I shook his hand, then turned to Jeanette, who had fetched her things, and gave her a fierce hug. "Jeanette," I whispered, "thank you so much for being here. It meant a lot."

"To me, too." But I saw the look in her eyes. She'd had enough. She was ready to go home.

When they'd gone I wandered around the house for a few minutes. The emptiness rang with every step. Finally I drifted into the kitchen. I found some old dried apples and a tin of tea leaves. They would do for breakfast.

I had lit a fire in the cook stove and was waiting for the water to heat when someone else knocked on the door. What now? I wondered, and finished chewing an apple slice before answering it.

Another Union officer stood on the front step. He held a piece of paper in his hand. If he tells me to hang a Union flag, I thought, I'm going to scream at him—

"Is this the home of Jacob Miller?"

I felt something grow cold inside. Major von Borcke had been right! The Union Army had wasted no time in coming for my father. I pushed my chin in the air. "It is. He's not here."

"Where is he?"

"He left home before the battle. He took some valuables to safety."

"Who are you?" Bright blue eyes pierced into mine.

He didn't know? I wasn't even tempted to lie. "I am Savilla Miller. Jacob Miller's daughter."

The man looked at the piece of paper in his hand. Then, "When do you expect him home?"

"I don't know."

The man gave me a curt nod and, to my utter surprise, turned and marched away. I realized, though, that he wasn't going for good. He'd be back.

Somehow, I had never quite believed it could come to this. Would they truly arrest my father? What about Samuel? What about me?

For about two shakes I panicked. Then, it was gone. I wasn't going to sit and stew about things that couldn't be helped. I wasn't ashamed of my family, or my cause. *My cause.* The battle was lost, but the war wasn't over yet.

I went upstairs straight off and closed the curtains in Father's bedroom, the signal we'd arranged to warn him of trouble. By that time the kettle was steaming and I made myself a nice cup of tea. When I'd finished, I braided my hair and coiled it tightly behind my head. I had no intention of cowering at home when there was work to do.

I gathered what clean bedding was left in our linen cupboard before heading up to the Lutheran Church. I could tell, as I approached, that some order had been gained since I'd last left. A new surgeon, in Union blue, was in the yard giving instructions to several orderlies.

Women were tending several big iron kettles over fire pits beyond the church. Several were strangers but I saw a couple of Sharpsburg women among them—Mrs. Collins, and Mrs. Rohrbach. I walked over and saw laundry being boiled in one, soup simmering in another. Thank God, I thought. The poor wounded men were getting better care now.

"Good morning," I said, and held out my bounty. "I brought some fresh linens. They can be used for bedding or ripped into bandages, whatever need is greatest. How can I help?"

"Bless you, dear," one of the newcomers smiled, and took them from me.

But Mrs. Collins bore down on us like a steam engine. "Off with you! Your services aren't needed here." She took the linens from the other woman's arms and shoved them back at me. "And take your Rebel rags with you. We don't want them."

"But surely—" the other woman protested. Mrs. Collins whispered something in her ear. The woman looked at me, then turned away.

I felt anger boil up inside. "You refuse bandages for wounded men? You have so much help you refuse a willing pair of hands?"

"There is no room at this hospital for a Confederate sympathizer!" Mrs. Collins snapped.

"But there are both Union and Confederate soldiers here! I'm not particular! I'll help any soldier who needs it—"

"Not at this hospital."

I stamped my foot. "I served all day yesterday! And I did a good job! No one found fault!"

Mrs. Collins did not back down. "Yesterday, the Union Army was not in control of this hospital. Today it is."

That rendered me speechless. Among the other women's faces I saw a mixture: some angry, some sheepish, one or two downright embarrassed. But no one was willing to speak up for me. "It's the rule," someone finally said, when the silence got awkward.

"Well, shame on you." I shoved the linens back at one of the women. "Don't make the soldiers suffer for your ignorance."

I marched back across the yard to the surgeon. He was still talking to an orderly, but I interrupted like I was Mrs. Lincoln or somebody. "Excuse me, sir, but I'm here to offer my services. How can I help?"

The surgeon was a tall skinny man, with a straggly beard and dark pouches under his eyes. "You've got to speak with the other women," he said. "They'll put you to work."

I grabbed his sleeve. "No sir, I already tried. They turned me away."

Those tired eyes bored into mine. "Why?"

I didn't look away. "Because my family is known to have Confederate sympathies. But I truly came to help—"

"Not here."

"But...." Stunned, I watched him walk away.

The orderly took my arm and firmly propelled me toward the street. "Let's go, Miss. You have to leave."

I wrenched my arm free. "Let go of me!" Under my own steam, I walked away with all the dignity I could muster.

There was nothing to do but go back home. I walked slowly, still smarting with anger and humiliation. How could they turn me away? The need was so great! I would have been content to boil laundry all day, or make bandages! Why could Union women nurse Confederate men, but not the other way around?

As I reached my house, I glanced up and saw what had been missing through the glorious days when the Confederates held Sharpsburg: Teresa's big Union flag, hanging back over Main Street. I stared at it for a moment. It hurt to breathe.

Then I ran inside and slammed the door behind me. The noise echoed through the painfully empty house. I'd never felt so alone.

CHAPTER EIGHTEEN

BETHIE

Fitzgerald, the sick Rebel forced on us, died while the Union troops were tromping back into Sharpsburg. Perhaps he gave up when he heard the Union cheers. Papa tried to find a coffin, but there were so many dead soldiers in and around Sharpsburg that none were available. Finally he and Aaron wrapped him in a blanket and buried him with the other dead Confederate, by the back fence. "Don't forget his name," Papa said. "Someone will want to know." I wondered when Fitzgerald's family, wherever they were, would learn he was dead. I thought about Hiram, and wondered if he had found his way into some lonely grave too. It all made me powerful sad.

And it made me lonely for Timothy. I was aching inside with the worry of wondering where he was. Was he safe? Had he found his father? We'd have a lot to talk over when we got the chance.

Then Papa and Aaron left for the shop. With the Union troops back in control, Papa and Aaron were able to do their army work there. I was glad they were close to home.

The Confederates had eaten lots of folks out of house and home. We fared some better, since we'd stayed to defend our garden and pantry. The day after the Union troops began marching back into Sharpsburg, the last of our refugee boarders left for home. Mama packed up two big baskets of bedding and wine and fruit and such. Then she and Anne hauled it all up to the Lutheran Church.

After several hours they came home with empty baskets and grim eyes and pinched lips. "Would you like some tea, Mama?" I asked, and she nodded gratefully. Quick as I could I fired up the kitchen stove. Mama and Anne sank down on the bench. No one had much to say until I set steaming mugs of mint tea before them. "Thank you," Mama murmured, and patted my hand. "Call Teresa and Margaret and Stephen, will you dear?"

I found them in the front yard, still waving at the Union boys. "Mama wants you."

Teresa looked at me quick. "Is there trouble?"

"I don't know."

We all trooped back inside. Mama had already finished her tea, and was packing more supplies. "Are you going back to the church, Mama?" Margaret asked.

"No." She paused, a crock of honey in her hand. "It's awful there. So much suffering...." She shuddered, then looked back at us. "But plenty of women are there already. Things are in hand."

Stephen frowned. "Then where you going?"

"We've been told the largest hospital has been established at Smoketown—"

"Smoketown!" Teresa interrupted. "Why on earth there?" Smoketown was a tiny settlement north of Sharpsburg, not much more than three houses and a pigpen.

"Well, I don't know," she said. "But we've been told there's hundreds of men there. Anne and I are going to help." She looked at Teresa. "We may be gone for a long time. Perhaps several days, even, before we can come home. Your papa is nearby, but he's very busy at the shop. I don't want to trouble him. Can you manage here?"

"Of course," Teresa said. "The worst is past."

"I don't think that's true," Anne said quietly. It was the first thing she'd said since they'd gotten home. She was wearing a dirty old workdress. Her hair was pulled back in a tight knot and covered with a kerchief. I hardly recognized her.

We all stood on the front step to watch them go. "Mind Teresa, now," Mama said to me and Margaret and Stephen. "And stay at home, all of you. There are sights about that weren't meant for young eyes." She kissed us all. They trudged away, lugging their baskets. I watched until they were out of sight.

That day, the four of us rattled around a suddenly empty house, too restless to sit still. The silence seemed strange, after the din and commotion.

Teresa set out a cold noon meal of cornbread and cheese. Mr. Carter clomped in just as we were sitting down. "I'll give you two dollars for a plate," he offered.

"Sold!" Teresa said quickly, before anyone else could speak up. She fixed him a plate with heaping portions, and pocketed the coins the reporter pulled from his pocket.

Mr. Carter began to eat quickly, like a starving man. "That's good," he managed finally, wiping his mouth.

"We would have given it to you for fifty cents," Stephen informed him.

I thought Mr. Carter might get angry, but he only shrugged. "Well, I'll tell you, son. Most folks have bare pantries. You've got thousands of wounded and sick in the army hospitals around town. Food prices are only going to climb. I'm an honest man, and I'll pay you what it's worth."

That made me think again about Mama and Anne. I hoped they would get enough to eat, and not give it all away. And the McClintocks? Did they have enough to eat? I wished I dared go see. But Mama had made it clear we were all to stay put.

"What's the news?" Teresa asked. "Are you getting what you need to send to the newspaper? I hope you wrote that the Confederate Army was whipped."

"I could fill three newspapers," Mr. Carter said around a bite of cornbread. He fished out his notebook and flipped through the pages. "Some folks are calling the battle a draw, since the Confederates got away across the Potomac River, instead of surrendering or getting captured. But the Federal government is calling it a Union victory—"

"Of course it's a Union victory!" Teresa blazed.

Mr. Carter eyed her. "Well, yes, whatever," he said. "Anyway, the folks at home want more than battle numbers. I've got some great stories. Your flag, for instance. My readers will love hearing about you and your flag. I've got it all down." He tapped his notebook.

"Well, that flag will fly over Sharpsburg until the war is won," Teresa said. Margaret gave me a look, obviously hoping Mr. Carter wouldn't get Teresa fired up about her flag. I just smiled. So much of the world had turned upside-down. Most everyone was in a fettle. But not Teresa. Never Teresa.

"My readers like hearing about young people," Mr. Carter said. "It's a wonderful story. And I've got so many more of them, I may do a whole series. One of your neighbors, now...let me find the name...." He squinted at his penciled scrawl. "Miller. That's it, Savilla Miller. Down the street. You must know her?"

I froze in my chair. I wanted to stop him, but didn't know how. Teresa's voice was clipped. "We know her."

Mr. Carter didn't notice the change in her tone. "Well, she's the other heroine of Sharpsburg, it seems. I've heard from three different people that she stood out in the street during the worst of the bombardment, giving water to soldiers. And sometime...about noon...an exploding shell set—" he squinted— "Mr. Good's house on fire. Oh—I didn't write down the address. Is that on Main Street?"

"East Antietam."

I could hear the anger in Teresa's voice. How could Mr. Carter miss it? "I don't want to talk about the battle any more," I tried.

But Teresa wouldn't let me dam that spring of information. "No, Bethie, let him finish," she said. "I want to hear."

"Well, Miss Miller and a couple of other girls staying at the house—I have their names somewhere—rushed to the scene. With shells and bullets flying all around, they carried buckets and basins from a spring and put out the fire. In a short time it caught again. These young ladies again returned to the scene and this time were successful in thoroughly extinguishing it."

"That's quite a story." Teresa's hands were clenched into fists.

Mr. Carter paused long enough to eat his last wedge of cheese. "Indeed. It's already inspired a local bard. Look what I found." After rummaging in another pocket he pulled out a crumpled piece of paper. He carefully smoothed it flat on the table. It was a crudely-lettered handbill, and he read aloud:

> "If deeds of daring should win renown
> Let us honor these ladies of Sharpsburg town;
> Who, while the battle was raging hot
> 'Midst whistling bullets, and flying shot
> They braved the danger, then let their names,
> Be inscribed in gold on the scroll of fame."

"Hey, that's first rate!" Stephen said. "I wish I could have—"

Teresa slammed her fist into the table so hard the dishes rattled. "It is not first rate! You ignorant little jacknapes!" She snatched the handbill and ripped it in two.

Stephen, who obviously hadn't paid mind to Teresa's feud with Savilla, was so surprised his mouth dropped open. Mr. Carter sputtered, but didn't seem able to find words.

"Teresa!" Margaret began to scold, but Teresa put her arm on the table and with a mighty sweep, sent dishes flying to the floor. That silenced us all.

Mr. Carter bolted like a spooked stallion. At the same time we heard someone calling, "Mrs. Kretzer? Good afternoon!" A moment later Gideon walked in the kitchen door.

"*Gott in Himmel*, what is this?" he asked, surveying the mess. Most of the dishware was tin, thankfully, but a little crockery pitcher of cream had shattered amidst the plates and cornbread crumbs. "Where is your mother?"

"She and Anne went to Smoketown, to work in a hospital there," I said. Teresa still hadn't said anything, and Margaret and Stephen still looked bewildered, so I took charge. "Margaret, will you and Stephen please unlock the well and draw up some water? Let's get the woodbox filled too."

Stephen grabbed two buckets and retreated gratefully outside. Margaret followed more slowly, but she went. I waited until they had disappeared before turning back to Gideon. "How are you faring?"

Gideon squeezed my shoulder. "Well enough. I came by to tell you that last time I headed back through town for another load of wounded, I stopped to see how Mrs. McClintock was faring. There's been no word from Timothy or the Reverend, I'm afraid."

I nodded, not giving voice to my own gnawing worry about Timothy. "Thank you for letting me know." Teresa hadn't made a move to clean up the mess, so I knelt down and began collecting shards of broken crockery.

Gideon sat down beside Teresa. I noticed the dark stains on his shirt, his trousers. "Now. What happened here?"

"You wouldn't understand."

"Let me try."

She hesitated. Sighed heavily. Then, "It was the consarned reporter. Mr. Carter. I'm just so frustrated! Look!" She snatched the torn broadside pieces and slapped them down on the table in front of him. "It's about Savilla Miller!"

Gideon's shoulders sagged as he read. "Oh Teresa. This is what has you so angry?"

"They've turned her into a heroine!"

"What does it matter?"

His question obviously confounded her. "What does it matter? She—why she—well, for one thing, she's a Rebel!"

"Teresa, she put out a fire. She helped save a family's home from destruction."

I was getting a damp rag to wipe up the cream. Something about Gideon's tone sent a warning through my brain. Like he didn't want to talk about it any more. For the first time, Teresa's headstrong will embarrassed me. I didn't like that feeling. *Let it go*, I silently willed her.

She wouldn't...or perhaps couldn't, I don't know. "I should have known you wouldn't understand."

"What's to understand?"

"They're saying she didn't just put out that fire! They're saying she stood out on the street during the bombardment! She was giving water to the soldiers!"

"So?" His tone was even more impatient. "I'm sure it was well intended, even if foolish—"

"Foolish!" Teresa cried, shoving to her feet. "It took sand! Don't you see? She was outdoors under fire, while I was huddled in the cellar! Everyone will think I'm a coward!"

"Everyone will think...." Gideon shook his head in disbelief. Slowly he stood up to face her. "That's all you're concerned about? At such a time as this?"

"I'm the bravest girl in Sharpsburg!" Teresa cried, stamping her foot. "What would you know about it? You're a—"

"*That's enough*!" Gideon bellowed. I backed against the dry sink, my heart hammering like Papa at the anvil—and Gideon's anger wasn't even directed at me! "You are a silly, selfish girl."

Teresa looked like he'd slapped her. "How dare you!" she steamed. "Get out."

"I'm not leaving until I speak my piece." Gideon's words came like water over a dam. "I've had all I can swallow about your definition of bravery, Teresa Kretzer. You don't know anything about courage. Not real courage! Courage can take different shapes. You're too headstrong to know the difference."

"What do you know about courage? You wouldn't even enlist!"

"And that makes me a coward in your eyes. Well, you're wrong. Do you think my stand has been easy? You think it didn't take courage to stand by my beliefs, even though it brought nothing but scorn from the girl I—from you? It's been the hardest thing I've ever done. Much harder than enlisting would have been."

"Well," Teresa began, but then didn't seem able to finish the sentence.

"Same thing for Aaron." Gideon's voice was a little quieter now. "It took courage for him to choose his own path, in the face of your contempt. Even Bethie—"

Teresa's head snapped my direction. "Bethie? What about Bethie?"

"What Bethie did at the McClintocks' took enormous courage. Yet you don't treat her like a heroine, far as I can see."

I wished he hadn't dragged me into the middle of this. "I didn't do so much," I said.

Teresa planted her hands on her hips. "Bethie did a wonderful thing," she admitted, "but after all, it was just one soldier. She said he was young. And scared. And all she did was talk to him—"

"No! Listen to what you're saying! Bethie is terrified of talking to any stranger, much less a—" He broke off abruptly, a look of sudden understanding chasing the anger. "That's it, isn't it? You've never been afraid of anything in your life. It's all a lark to you. A game."

"That's not true," Teresa began, I think more out of ornery habit than anything else. Heaven knew *I'd* never seen her afraid of anything or anyone.

I guess Gideon hadn't either, because he grabbed her arm. "Come with me." He headed for the back door, dragging her along.

She didn't go easy. "Let go of me! Stop it! Let go!"

But he didn't, despite her screeching and fighting. I followed, almost against my own will—I hated to see, but I had to.

It happened so fast that Stephen, lurking near the back door, stumbled backwards and sloshed water all over himself.

"Jiggers!" he began, but I silenced him with a look. Margaret, crouched by the woodbox, looked at me. I shook my head at her: *Be still.* I realized, with a hurtful twist inside, that I trusted Gideon more than Teresa. Whatever he was doing, I'd let him do without comment.

Gideon hauled Teresa off the back porch and over to his wagon, parked in the yard. The draft horse stood in its traces, head drooping. The poor beast was exhausted.

Gideon pointed Teresa toward the seat. "Get in."

"I won't! Mama left me in charge, and I can't leave—"

"Get in."

"And I don't take orders from you, Gideon Brummer—"

"*Get—in—the—wagon!*"

I think Teresa must have realized that he would throw her in if she didn't go herself. Boiling mad, she hitched up her skirt and scrambled over the wheel to the wagon seat. Gideon climbed up beside her.

They didn't look at each other, or at Stephen and me. Gideon picked up the lines and clucked to the tired horse. "Get up! Let's go." Then the wagon rumbled around the corner of the house and out of sight.

CHAPTER NINETEEN

TERESA

I don't know that I've ever been more angry than I was when we drove out of the yard in Gideon's wagon. That's saying a lot! I was determined to vex whatever plan he had by not speaking, and staring straight ahead.

But as we rumbled down Main Street, it was hard to keep eyes front. The road was still littered with debris, and that morning clogged with traffic: troops, an artillery train, wagons, ambulances. I saw lots of civilians I didn't know—come to help, maybe, or search for wounded kin. It was noisy, with teamsters, officers, and a few quick peddlers all hollering over the tramp and rumble. The press was something to behold. Our little village was overflowing.

It also stank of smoke. I hadn't been out of my yard since the battle. From my perch on Gideon's wagon, I saw the blackened ruins of Widow Shackleford's house, and the charred remains of Delaney's stable. The stone and brick houses fared some better—just crumbled spots where the shells had hit. Millwood wasn't to be found, and folks had nailed quilts and bedsheets over broken windows.

I caught my first look at our church. It had taken a pounding, and I recalled Mr. Carter saying it had been a particular target for Union cannoneers. Rows of wounded men were lying on the ground outside, where we'd spread picnics and cheered new-marrieds. The look in my mama's eyes when she'd come back from tending the wounded came to my mind. I tried to shove it away.

Gideon wove through the street and headed east. I couldn't hold my tongue any longer. "Where are you taking me?"

His gaze didn't leave the road ahead. "Home."

His home, now a Union hospital. I felt a new flame of anger. Unlike Mama and Anne, I had no particular skill in a sickroom. Who was Gideon Brummer to order me about? Why, even my own father had never treated me with force! "Stop this wagon," I cried. "Stop it right now or I'll jump off. I swear I will."

He stopped immediately. I began climbing down. For the first time, he turned to look at me. "What's wrong?" he asked quietly. "Are you afraid?"

I stopped with one foot on the wheel, glaring. In his eyes I saw exhaustion, something like despair—but still shreds of anger, too. At that moment I think I hated him. I wondered if he hated me, too. But I climbed back in the wagon. What else could I do?

We rumbled on. I wished I'd grabbed a bonnet. I didn't care a fig about my complexion, but the sun beat down like a hammer. I wished I'd grabbed a handkerchief, too, for a powerful stench was reaching my nose. The farther we got from town the worse it got. I'd never smelled the like. Gideon didn't say anything, so I tried to ignore it too. Finally I pinched my nose.

Gideon pulled a man's big handkerchief from his vest pocket and handed it to me. It didn't look too clean but I couldn't refuse. "Put it over your nose," he said, "and breath through your mouth."

It helped a little. "What is it?" I finally asked.

"Dead men."

A Union burial detail photographed two days after the battle.

Something sour pushed from my stomach up my throat. I pressed the handkerchief against my mouth. *I will not throw up, I will not throw up....*

"The burial crews can't keep up. There's probably a thousand bodies still waiting. And horses too. They're trying to burn the dead horses, since they can't bury them all, but that just adds to the stink. And the heat doesn't help. We're in the heart of the battlefield. All the farms hereabouts were fighting ground."

*A thousand dead bodies...*still waiting two days after the battle? Heavens above. I closed my eyes for a moment, still fighting with my stomach. I refused, absolutely refused, to be sick in front of Gideon Brummer.

"Here we are," Gideon said a moment later, coaxing his tired horse into the driveway. "Come on, girl. Get up."

I stared. The Brummer farm was almost unrecognizable. The lovely, fertile farm had disappeared, its fields churned under by artillery and cavalry. Saddled horses were tied to the porch railing, the laundry poles, a reaper. Gideon's mother emerged from the house with an armload of soiled sheets and dumped them on the ground, in the dust, as if she didn't have the energy to take them any farther.

In back, hospital tents stretched in rows beyond the yard. The doors of the big thatched grain barn were open, and I could see surgeons at work on the threshing floor. Gideon carefully drove through the commotion and parked near the barn. He jumped to the ground and ran to the well, where he fetched a bucket of water for his horse. I stayed put. Truth is, I was still feeling rocky.

Then I saw something that hit even worse. One of the attendants left the surgeon's table and came outside. He was carrying an *arm.* He walked to the corner of the barn and tossed it on a pile of what my shocked senses realized were other severed limbs: legs, hands, feet.

I felt a drumming in my ears. The edges of my vision got blurry. I leaned over, dropping my head down for a moment, terrified—yes, terrified!—that I was about to faint. Heavens! I'd never felt so before. I gripped the edge of the wagon seat so hard it hurt. A splinter dug into my palm. Good. The pain seemed to bring me back to the moment. With an effort, I sat back up.

A man in blue army trousers and filthy white shirt, with a blood-smeared apron tied over, hurried to greet Gideon. "Brummer! Thank God you're back. We've got another load waiting. There's never enough transport, blast it all to—"

"I'll be ready in a moment, doctor," Gideon said. He was rubbing sweat from the mare with a rag, while she gulped water from the bucket. "In to Hagerstown?"

"No, just to Smoketown," the doctor said. "They've got better facilities there, we've been told." Then he turned his head. "Curtis! Murphy! Give me a hand here."

Two orderlies hurried from the barn. The doctor gave directions and soon half a dozen wounded men were being loaded into the wagon. Best I could tell it was a mix of Union and Confederate, but that didn't seem to matter anyway.

Suddenly the surgeon looked at me. "You there! If you came to help, get inside!"

"Uh, I'm helping him," I said quickly, pointing at Gideon. I did not think I could walk into the shadows of that barn.

"Then help," Gideon said curtly. "You can ride with them."

I stared at him. He didn't even give me a glance. What did he expect?

When his horse had been cared for he helped with the wounded. He lifted them with ease, at once strong and gentle. There was some straw in the wagon bed and he cushioned it beneath the soldiers.

Well, that much I could do. Drawing a deep breath, I lifted my skirts and clambered over the seat to the wagon bed. Crouching in one corner, I tried to keep out of the way as the orderlies slid a young Union soldier in beside me. He'd lost an arm, just above the elbow, and had a new bandage wrapped tightly around his chest. One side of his face was terribly bruised. He looked about sixteen.

This photograph of a farm near Sharpsburg, taken a few days after the Battle of Antietam, is indicative of what the Brummer farm looked like in this story. Note the makeshift hospital tents, some made with blankets, some with brush. The barn roof visible on the right appears to be thatched.

"Keep his arm raised," one of the orderlies told me. He showed me how, mounding some straw beneath it. "It helps. And keep an eye on his chest wound. We think we got the bleeding stopped, but you never know."

"But—" I began, but the man was already gone.

The loading took but a minute. They packed the wagon bed tight, and three men in somewhat better condition perched on the back, their legs dangling. Most of the men lying in the straw were unconscious, and for that I was grateful. Those who weren't groaned when Gideon called "Giddap!" and the wagon lurched forward.

I thought the boy beside me was out too, but as we rumbled down the drive he murmured something. His head tossed back and forth. His face was twisted in pain.

I had never felt so helpless. *Mama, what do I do?* I begged silently, but my mother was far away, helping other shattered soldiers. The boy muttered again, louder. In desperation I put a hand on his forehead, a gesture I'd seen my mother make, and smoothed a sweaty lock of dark hair away from his face.

The boy opened his eyes. "Ruth? Ruth, is that you?"

"My name is Teresa," I began, but the boy interrupted me. "Ruth! I knew you'd come!"

An older man lying beyond looked our way. "His name is Billy," he told me, in an Irish brogue. "He—Mother of God!" He groaned as the wagon wheel lurched into a rut. "He's been calling for his Ruth since they brought him in."

I hesitated a moment longer. Then, "Yes, Billy," I said clearly. "It's Ruth. I'm here."

Billy's face relaxed at once. "Oh, Ruth. I've been waiting ever so long. I knew you'd come."

"Well, it, uh...took me a while to get here. But I'm here now. I came to be with you." His remaining hand moved, and I took it in my own. "Can you feel me holding your hand?"

"Yes, Ruth. It's good. But it still hurts, Ruth. It hurts so bad—"

"I know, Billy. I know. We're getting you to another hospital. They'll take good care of you there."

I forgot about the sickening stench. I forgot about Savilla Miller. I forgot about my anger. All I could think about was trying to ease the journey for Billy, and the other men tossing restlessly, or lying death-still, in the bloody wagon bed.

Gideon, I could see, was picking his path with care, trying to give the men the easiest ride possible. But the road was rocky, riddled with puddle holes and wheel ruts left from the last rain. And twice he had to pull off the road altogether, once to make way for an artillery crew thundering by, and once to make way for a general and his staff who pounded down upon us.

"You should make way for us!" I couldn't help yelling as they passed. Forcing their own wounded out of the way! Shameful.

Then I felt a faint pressure on my fingers. "Don't fret, Ruth," Billy murmured. "It will all be all right. Now that you're here, it's all right."

He was comforting *me.* It was almost more than I could bear. "Yes, Billy," I promised recklessly. "I'll see to it. Everything will be all right."

We were about halfway to Smoketown when another lurch threw me against the sideboard. It cracked against my ribs and I almost yelped in pain. Several men moaned, and the Irishman cried "Mother of God!" again.

"We're getting there," I said helplessly. Then I noticed something new: a bright spot of blood on the clean bandage wrapping Billy's chest. While I watched it grew, spreading like a glass of spilled wine.

"Gideon, he's started bleeding!" I cried.

Gideon craned his head to snatch a look before turning back to the road. "Try to stop it."

Panic ripped at my chest. "I don't know how! Drive faster! We have to get there—"

"Apply pressure. There's nothing else to do. I can't drive any faster or I'll kill them all."

"Ruth!" Billy's voice was breathless. "Ruth, it hurts! Make it stop hurting...."

The bloodstain was still spreading. I bunched my skirt in my hands and pressed it against the stain.

The trip took an eternity. The only thing that hurried was the blood: rushing, gushing, soaking Billy's bandage and my skirt. My hands were covered with blood. Blood pooled in the straw. I'd never seen so much blood.

"Ruth—"

"I'm here."

"I can't see you anymore."

"I'm still with you, Billy. Can you feel my hand?" I squeezed his, hard.

"Yes," he sighed. "Thank you, Ruth. Bless you for coming...."

I didn't know I was crying until a tear dripped onto his cheek.

Finally, finally, we arrived in Smoketown. The hospital tents had been arranged to catch any cooling breezes, in neat rows on a rise. They stretched into the horizon, far as I could see. But despite the overwhelming numbers, there was a sense of order about the place. Several men ran to meet us before Gideon had even stopped the wagon.

"Take this one first," I cried. My tone must have been commanding, for one of the orderlies crawled in the wagon to look. "His name is Billy, he needs help—"

"He's dead," the orderly said, and as quickly went on to the Irishman. "All right! Get this one into that first tent—"

They moved with practiced haste. Gideon helped, and soon the wagon was empty. Billy was taken aside, laid on the ground, and covered with a blanket. He joined a long line of other blanketed boys.

My heart felt like a stone. I crawled dully to the ground and stared at the row of dead soldiers. Now one of them had a face, a name: Billy. I had stopped crying, but I wanted to wail, to scream, to run home and be comforted by my mother.

Suddenly another thought struck like a thunderbolt. His Ruth!

I snatched up my skirt and ran into the first tent. There were four men inside, on the ground. A woman was crouching beside the Irishman, offering him a cup of water.

"Excuse me, ma'am," I said, kneeling beside them. I looked at the soldier. "I'm so sorry to bother you, but that boy...Billy...he died. I want to write to Ruth...and I don't even know his full name."

"I don't either, lass," the man said. "He wasn't in my regiment. We just ended up together in the field hospital. And he didn't have any papers on him. They checked. They thought he was from Wisconsin, though. They found him among some boys from the...the Seventh Wisconsin, I think they said."

"Thank you. And—good luck." I pressed his hand before leaving him. The Seventh Wisconsin. I repeated it in my brain several times. It would have to be enough. I *had* to find Ruth.... Who was she, anyway? A sister? A young sweetheart? It didn't matter. I couldn't bear to think that she would never know how her loved one died. I wanted to tell her that he hadn't died alone. *I* had been there.

As I emerged from the tent, I heard someone yelling. "Gideon Brummer!" It was another doctor, by the look of him.

"Here!" Gideon had been helping with one of the wounded, but he hurried over.

"We just got word that a special train is running from Hagerstown to Chambersburg. We've been sorting out a crew that can stand the journey, and needs the care. If you hurry, you can get them to the depot on time. It just might save some lives. Can you make the trip?"

"Of course," Gideon said, although I knew he was bone-weary. He took another moment to care for his horse while more orderlies quickly loaded his wagon with a fresh load of wounded. When he climbed back to the seat I realized he had forgotten me...or perhaps he just didn't know where I was, and had no time to look. He carefully backed the mare, turned around, and rattled away. *He's gone*, I thought, and somehow realized that those words referred to more than just the moment.

For a few moments I stood, just stood, trying to think. I felt numb inside. What to do? My mother was here, somewhere, at Smoketown...but there were hundreds of tents, stretching in every direction. The wounded needed her care more than I did. And she had told me to stay at home, anyway. The younger ones needed me. No telling what trouble Stephen was getting into....

I looked at the row of dead, at the still form that had been Billy. And I was suddenly frightened again—not for me, but for all the young men. I was afraid that the war would not soon end. I was afraid that more boys would go the way of Billy. The fear tied my stomach in knots, threatened to choke my breath away, made it hard to think clearly. It was a horrible feeling, and I couldn't shake it.

It was hard to walk away...but I suddenly realized I was afraid of something else. I'd had my fill. Others could have done better, I know, but I was at the end. If I didn't leave, and quick, I was afraid I just might break down and shame myself good.

So I trudged off toward home, staying off the road, hardly noticing the sun surely burning me fierce. When another wagon pulled up, it took me a moment to realize the driver was waiting for me.

"You want a ride?"

I squinted. It was Bobby McPherson, driving an old delivery wagon scrounged up from somewhere. Bobby McPherson: for so long my enemy, who had tried to shame me and Savilla all those years ago, who had torn down my flag, and pelted Bethie with eggs. We'd always hated each other, but I couldn't find any hate just then; and when I looked at Bobby, his eyes were empty of it too. I nodded, and climbed wearily up beside him.

For a moment no one spoke. Then, "You headed home?" he asked. His voice sounded strange.

"Yes." I turned my head and saw the telltale piles of bloody straw. "You been hauling wounded?"

He nodded. "From the Lutheran Church. They—they keep bringing more in from the field fast as we can get 'em in to Smoketown. I...." His voice faded away.

We rattled on in silence for another minute or so. Dully, I heard Bobby making funny noises. It took a while to realize he was crying. He sniffed and snuffled and finally wiped his nose on his sleeve. Every few minutes he scrubbed his eyes with the back of his hand. I'd lost Gideon's handkerchief, so I had nothing to offer.

Then he pulled to a stop in front of my house. "Here you go."

"Thanks." I climbed down to the street, feeling hollow. I started to turn in, then looked back up at Bobby. "You going back to the church for another load?"

"Yes." Tears welled in his eyes again. He wiped them away.

I nodded. "You're very brave," I said, and walked in the house.

If I'd hoped for a few minutes of calm, I didn't get it. The moment I shut the door I heard footsteps pounding down the stairs. It was Margaret. "Teresa? Is that you? Thank God you're home!"

Margaret was excitable, but this was no tantrum. The look in her eyes sent a new stab of fear through my heart. "What is it?"

She grabbed my hand, tugging me up the stairs. "It's Stephen," she cried. "Bethie's up with him. He's powerful sick, Teresa. We didn't know what to do."

"Sick? But he was fine!"

"It came on fast! And he's real bad off. Real bad."

I was taking the stairs fast as I could. "Go get Papa!"

"I tried! There was a note on the shop door saying he'd been called out to one of the army camps. No telling where. Mama's gone, and there's no doctor to be had, and we've been so scared! It looks like the typhus, Teresa. Just like that Rebel soldier."

Fitzgerald. The Confederate boy who had been forced on our home after I tangled with his comrades over my flag. The Rebel sergeant's words rang in my head: *You. You remember me. You may be real sorry you didn't show more respect.*

The roaring noise was back in my head, louder than before. It took every bit of sand I had left to not cave altogether. I clutched the banister, trying desperately to think. But all I could do was look backwards: *I* was responsible for bringing Fitzgerald to this house. Stephen had befriended him.

And Fitzgerald had died.

CHAPTER TWENTY

SAVILLA

The hours ticked by like days. I hoped Samuel would come, but he didn't. Had he been arrested? Was he busy with other family? How had the rest of my family fared during the battle? Was my father all right? The not-knowing was enough to make me insane.

I spent the morning pacing. I didn't know what else to do. Besides being worried about my family, I was still furious about the treatment I'd received at the Lutheran Church. "How could they be so arrogant?" I steamed, stalking back and forth. The empty rooms rang with their silence.

Oddly, I thought suddenly of Teresa. If the situation were reversed, she wouldn't stand being turned away. She'd storm in and make herself heard! I almost smiled, picturing the scene.

Then I had an idea. Dr. Biggs! He must be working in one of the hospitals. He'd vouch for me, I was sure. Quick as that, I snatched a bonnet and my basket and headed out the door.

The doctor's house was abustle, the door standing ajar. I pushed it open and saw that the house itself had become a hospital. Soldiers were lying on the floor in the parlor, in the doctor's office across the hall. I saw Darcy, the elderly Negro housekeeper, spooning broth for one of the wounded.

"Darcy? Excuse me. Is the doctor here? I came to help."

Darcy shrugged. She looked exhausted. "I think he may be on the back porch, Miss Savilla. But he was gettin' set to head out. He may be gone."

I threaded my way through the crowded house. Half a dozen more wounded soldiers were lying on the back porch, and I tiptoed around them. Dr. Biggs was in the back yard, talking to a Union soldier. "Yes, tell him I'm coming," he said as I approached.

"I was to fetch you, actually, sir. You can take my horse."

"Doesn't he know I've got my own house full of—" The doctor cut himself off, raising his hands in a gesture of defeat. "Of course."

I was afraid he'd ride off before I could speak with him. "Dr. Biggs?" I called. He turned his head, and I hurried to greet him. "Just a moment, sir. I came to help."

"Savilla." He regarded me with something less than enthusiasm. His face was haggard.

I was determined to stall any objections. "Look, I know the rules. I was turned away from the hospital at the Lutheran Church. But Dr. Biggs, you know me! I swear I only want to help. I swear it! I'll do anything you say. But please, *please*, don't send me away." I stopped just short of saying I couldn't bear to go back to my own empty house.

Dr. Biggs stared at me. The dark circles under his eyes looked like bruises. For a moment I thought he was going to refuse. Then he shook his head. "Go on inside," he said. "There will be the devil to pay, no doubt. But this is a private home. Commandeered, but not yet under the direction of an army surgeon. I can't be everywhere at once. They want me at Smoketown when I've got a house full of my own to worry about. Lord knows we could use another pair of hands."

I felt a rush of relief. "Oh, thank you!"

The hint of a smile twitched at his mouth. "Besides, you're not the first who's come with the same argument. You'll find Mrs. McGraw inside, and Mrs. Douglas—"

Mrs. Douglas. Henry Kyd's mother? I had to stifle a smile of delight.

"—and Mrs. Grove just left an hour ago to get some sleep. I can't stand up to all of you. And I need the help."

The waiting soldier coughed. "Ah, Dr. Biggs...."

"Yes, yes. I'm coming." With a sigh the doctor slowly swung to the saddle. I caught the soldier's eye, daring him to say something. He was the first to look away.

I hurried inside. Darcy had slumped down on the floor in a corner, leaning against the wall, asleep. I wondered if it was the first sleep she'd had since the battle. I found Mrs. McGraw in the kitchen, unpacking a hamper. She gave me a big hug. "Oh, Savilla! It's good to see you."

"I couldn't bear being cooped up. Have you had any word of Joseph?"

Her face clouded, and she turned back to her chores. "No. Nothing. I needed to keep busy too. I tried the hospital at the school, but...I ended up here."

"How can I help?"

"Some ladies from Funkstown sent these supplies, bless them. Dr. Biggs said any of the boys who want it can have a sip or two of wine. Most of those with desperate wounds have already been taken off. We've got a lot of men who just need rest and care. We've got a few cases of typhus upstairs, in the back room. Dr. Biggs said with so many farm boys packed in close quarters, in this heat, it's bound to be trouble. I'll check on them in a few minutes."

I took the wine and started from the room, then turned back. "Is Mrs. Douglas here? From Ferry Hill?"

"Why, yes, she is. She's upstairs, I believe."

Mrs. Douglas was in the master bedrooom. She was sitting by a soldier, reading aloud from the Bible, and I could tell that all four men in the room were listening intently. She smiled when she noticed me in the doorway, and nodded.

I wanted to hug her. Seeing her brought Henry Kyd back to me. She turned a page and I felt his hand pressing mine. I looked forward to speaking with her later.

I moved on to the next room, where two men were resting in bed and three more were lying on blankets on the floor. "Would anyone like some wine?"

They were glad to see me. I gave them each some wine and they thanked me like it was manna from Heaven. I was going to move on, but they seemed so glad of my company I decided I could linger for a bit. "We need a pretty lady to tend us more than any other medicine," a young redhead said, as gallant as if he was on a dance floor, instead of the bedroom floor.

Truth is, they cheered me about as much as I cheered them. I didn't care whether they were Confederate or Yankee. After so much gloom and despair and death, it was good just to behold these men, hear them actually laugh and joke with each other. They were bandaged, and probably in some pain. But they weren't cast in doom.

"It's good to see you so hale," I said finally. I was sitting in a chair by the bed. "I didn't expect to find such, in a sickroom."

"We're all on the mend," the redhead answered. "So many aren't...we're grateful."

I understood. "Well. So am I."

"And we have even more to be grateful for," another man said. He was older than the others, a thin man with dark hair and eyes. He spoke with a funny accent, even for a Yankee. "When I was carried from the field, I thought the day was lost. Now, we know the Rebels have retreated back across the Potomac. God has granted us victory."

Words stuck in my throat. "The war's not won yet," I said. I tried to make it sound light. Dr. Biggs hadn't let me in here to stir up trouble.

The man folded his hands on his chest, looking very peaceful. "Oh, but we have struck the final blow. Maryland is liberated once again. And President Lincoln is going to use our victory to strike the chains of slavery down. Have you heard?"

I didn't know what he was talking about. I twisted the wine bottle in my hands, groping for words.

My silence must have become awkward, for another man, his bandaged leg propped on pillows, spoke from across the room. "Ease off, Tippet. You're still in Maryland, not back home in Boston. Don't assume you know this lady's sympathies."

Tippet, the one with the funny accent, looked at me. "Miss? Have I presumed? Are your sympathies with the Union?"

I drew a deep breath. The last thing I wanted was trouble, but I could not defy my family, my friends, my cause. "No," I said. "My heart is with the Confederacy."

Silence draped the room like a blanket. Every bit of cheer had disappeared. Tippet's gaze didn't change. "I see," he said calmly. "And do you own slaves?"

The question was so abrupt I stumbled over my answer. "My father...well, yes. Two." And I set my jaw, staring back at him. I'd heard about Northern abolitionists, who worked to free slaves. Right or wrong, I didn't want this stranger to criticize my father.

But his next question was even more unexpected. "What are their names?"

"Their names? Why...Auntie Mae, and Uncle Bob."

"What are their last names?"

I squirmed in my chair, wanting to leave but not knowing how to get out of the conversation, short of walking away and admitting defeat. "They don't have last names, I guess. I've always just known them as Auntie Mae and Uncle. They're very old." I realized even as I said that last that it sounded like a feeble excuse.

"Ah. So very old people don't deserve a name of their own? I see."

"It's not like that," I snapped, then clamped my mouth shut. Who was this stranger to say "I see," like he knew my family?

Like he knew our situation? It wasn't what he thought. No one else in my family owned slaves. We would never buy another. Samuel and I had discussed it, and agreed it was wrong. The rest of my brothers and sisters felt the same way. Auntie Mae and Uncle Bob were part of our family. Who would take care of them if we didn't? To free them, now that they were old and unwell, would be cruel. Wouldn't it?

"Well, soon it won't matter," Tippet said. "President Lincoln is going to issue an Emancipation Proclamation, proclaiming all slaves to be free. We've heard rumors for a long time. He was just waiting for a strong Union victory to do it. Now he has it, right here at Sharpsburg. Because of what happened here, the Union Army will now fight on for a more glorious cause."

Was this true? I tried to take in what he was saying. Of course, I had always known that some people in the North wanted the Union Army to fight against slavery. But that had never been official and here in Maryland, where everything was so mixed up, it was almost never mentioned. "This war isn't about slavery," I said finally, and it came out sharp. "This war is about states' rights."

"It's about slavery now," Tippet told me. "The Union will fight on to free the slaves. That means the Confederacy will be fighting for their right to own them."

I looked around the room at the other men. No one spoke up in defense of Tippet. But no one spoke against him either. It must be true.

"Not *my* Confederacy," I said, and pushed to my feet. "Excuse me." I hurried from the room before anyone could argue.

In the hall I paused, leaning against the wall. My heart was hammering. My face felt hot. Tippet's words tumbled about my head like dice in a game of chance. Everything I believed in seemed to be crashing down around me.

When Mrs. McGraw came out of one of the other rooms I straightened up, trying to compose myself. But Mrs. McGraw was a mother, and her gaze was sharp. "Savilla, dear, are you well?"

"Fine," I mumbled.

She wasn't convinced. "You must take care of yourself. We can't help these poor men if we let ourselves get worn down. Why don't you take a rest? I believe Mrs. Douglas went down to the yard for a spell. She'd welcome your company, I'm sure."

Henry's mother. The thought was a comfort. "Yes," I said, and managed a little smile. "I believe I'll do that."

Downstairs, Darcy was on her feet again, changing the bandage on a soldier's arm. "There, now, that's better," she crooned. *Darcy is a slave*, I thought, *and yet Dr. Biggs is one of the biggest pro-Union men in Sharpsburg.* It was all so confusing.

I found Mrs. Douglas sitting on a garden bench, under the shade of an elm tree. "Savilla, do join me. It's good to see you, my dear." She patted the bench, and I sank down gratefully.

I didn't know if I wanted to bring up my conversation with Tippet or not, so for a few minutes we talked of other things. I told her about seeing Henry Kyd during the barrage, and the night the army left. She told me about his visit home to Ferry Hill, just before the battle. "We were entertaining several officers when Henry Kyd walked into the room. One of the officers, who didn't know him, ordered him rather curtly to rejoin his unit. Just then my daughter came back in the room with refreshments, and almost dropped the tray in order to give Henry a hug. The poor officer was mortified." Mrs. Douglas chuckled at the memory. "Oh, it was good to see Henry Kyd, even if for such a brief time."

It eased my heart so to talk with her! It made me realize how much I missed having a mother of my own. It also made me realize how much I liked Mrs. Douglas. "I felt that way too," I said. "I would have liked a longer visit. But it was good to see him."

Mrs. Douglas pressed my hand. "My dear, Henry Kyd told me how good you've been at writing. Letters mean everything to him, when he's so far away. He was so upset about your cousin Clint's murder...they were such good friends. I think it's eased his grief, a bit, to correspond with you."

"It's meant just as much to me," I said, straight from the heart. "I wish I knew where he was headed. I'm never sure where to send my letters. The army moves around so quickly...."

"It's troublesome. If you're ever in doubt, though, you could just send it to Miss Conrad. I know Henry Kyd manages to see her with as much frequency as the war allows. I'm sure she'd hold your letter until his next visit."

"Miss Conrad...."

"In Winchester. We haven't met her yet, but I'm looking forward to it. She's written me, several times, and seems very sweet."

The blood seemed to pound in my temples. My skin was prickling. No. *No.*

"The war makes things difficult, of course. I'm sure you know, a pretty girl like you! But she seems willing to wait. They have an understanding."

I don't recall the rest of our conversation. Words she'd already spoken echoed like thunder through my head: *Miss Conrad...in Winchester...seems very sweet...willing to wait...they have an understanding....*

I take immense pride in the fact that I didn't bolt. I spent most of the afternoon at Dr. Biggs' house, holding tumblers of wine, spooning broth, sponging fevered foreheads. The older ladies didn't allow me to change the men's bandages, or their nightshirts, but I fed them all supper. Even Tippet. I didn't spill a drop.

And finally, later that afternoon, when several other women arrived and Mrs. McGraw suggested I go home and get some rest, I nodded. "Yes, thank you, Mrs. McGraw. I believe I will."

I'm lucky I didn't get run over on the short walk home, I suppose. The army traffic was still heavy. Strangers were pouring into town too—soldiers' mothers and wives, looking for their loved ones among the hurt and missing. I didn't see a thing. My mind was too full. My heart was too heavy.

How could I have misunderstood Henry Kyd's intentions? I went back over every word, every gesture, every letter. And to be honest, he'd never led me false. He'd treated me like a treasured friend. But nothing more. I'd read more into it, built dreams around it. And now they were gone.

Just as my cause was gone. I didn't want to believe it, but Tippet's words had come with too much sincerity to doubt. The war for states' rights had become a war about slavery. The South, *my* South, was fighting against those who wanted to end slavery. And I couldn't countenance that fight.

Everything was in ruins. My dreams of a future with Henry Kyd, the Confederacy—everything.

At home, there was no sign of Father or Samuel. I shut the front door and wandered back to the kitchen. It was empty. Empty like my heart. Empty like my life.

I sank in a chair, because I didn't know what else to do. My chest ached. I tried to collect my thoughts, and couldn't. There wasn't anything left to cook for supper, so I couldn't even busy myself. Just as well, perhaps. The thought of eating turned my stomach.

I might have sat so for hours if it hadn't been for an urgent pounding on the front door. "What now?" I said aloud. Trouble, no doubt—and yet what more could come my way? The battle had been lost. The war, from my point of view, had been lost. My heart's desire had been lost.

The pounding sounded again. "I'm coming!" I said, and shoved to my feet. I was bone-weary. The walk to the front door seemed eternal.

I took a deep breath, trying to stiff myself up for anything. But I opened the door to a surprise.

"Savilla, I'm most sorry to disturb you," Bethie Kretzer cried. I could see fear in her eyes. "But everything's gone wrong. Will you help us?"

"Of course," I said, and suddenly, I felt a little flicker of—of *life* inside. There was something left after all.

CHAPTER TWENTY-ONE

BETHIE

I didn't think of Savilla straight off. When Stephen came down sick, we tried to fetch someone to help. No one could come. After that, I had all I could do to keep Margaret calm.

"Margaret, hush!" I finally said, and she swallowed hard. "You sit with Stephen. And, uh...give him sips of water." It was all I could think to do for someone with fever. "Teresa will be home soon. She'll know what to do."

And I tried to believe it. I was worried sick—and sick of worry! Worry for Timothy was a blanket I never shook off. Now Stephen. It was almost too much to abide. All I could think to do was wait until Teresa got back from her ride with Gideon. Teresa would know what to do. Teresa always knew what to do.

But the Teresa who came home was like a stranger. I didn't know what frightened me more, the blood on her skirt or the shadows in her eyes.

And Teresa *didn't* know what to do. "It's all my fault," she whispered. I saw the telltale shine of tears in her eyes, and that struck the fear of God into me like nothing else.

"But what should we *do*?" Margaret asked. The three of us were huddled in the hall after Teresa had seen Stephen for herself. Margaret was teary too. "I think we need to fetch Mama—"

"Mama's too far away. And the hospital at Smoketown is huge. I was just there." Teresa's eyes were wide. "Hundreds of tents. It could take hours to find her."

"Well, Mama's got all kinds of medicines in the pantry," I said. "What do we need? What did she use with that Rebel soldier?"

"I don't know! She and Anne—I didn't help, I should have helped—" Teresa took a deep breath. "I didn't pay any attention. We have to find someone who can help—"

"I've already been to Dr. Biggs' house, and he's gone," Margaret interrupted, her voice rising. "And I went to all the neighbors. They're either gone to one of the hospitals too, or have a house full of sick or wounded themselves. Teresa, do something!"

"I don't *know* what to do!" Teresa rubbed her forehead with her knuckles. "I—I...just don't know...."

I couldn't bear it a minute longer. "I'm going for help," I said, and turned away. I'm not sure they even heard me until I clattered down the stairs.

It was a fine idea, but once outside, I wasn't sure where to turn. Dr. Biggs was gone, and it was window-glass clear that doctors wouldn't leave their army wounded to care for a sick civilian. The women hereabouts with any doctoring experience, like Mama, already had their hands full. The only ones left were the young ones like us, girls who hadn't yet started families of their own and so didn't know beans about nursing a disease like typhus—

I was about to head for Smoketown and Mama after all when the solution came to me. *Books.* Books had answers to everything! I needed a book about doctoring and such. And I only knew one person who owned a lot of books: Savilla Miller.

When I knocked, it took her so long to answer I was afraid she wasn't home. I was about to march in anyway when she opened the door.

"Savilla, I'm most sorry to disturb you," I cried. "But everything's gone wrong. Will you help us?"

"Of course," she said, and I could have hugged her for not hesitating. "What do you need?"

"Can we look in your father's library? It's Stephen, you see. He's come down with typhus. We had a sick soldier, and Stephen caught it from him. There's no doctor about, and all the women are busy with the wounded, and—"

"Come on." Savilla pulled me inside. "I know just where to look."

In the past, I'd read books for pleasure. Now, they seemed like the ropes thrown to people who fell off canalboats. All that stood between them and disaster.

Savilla ran her fingers along a row of leather-bound books. "Let's see.... Let's try this one." She grabbed a large volume from the shelf and leafed through it. "I looked in here once when Auntie Mae came down with a fever, and Dr. Biggs was off delivering a baby.... Here. 'Typhus Fever'. What are Stephen's symptoms?"

"He was complaining of being tired. And Stephen's *never* tired." I bit my lip, forcing down my own choking worry. "He started having pains, and his breathing got heavy. He had a spell of bilious vomiting. It came on so fast—"

"Bloody diarrhea?" Savilla was reading ahead.

"Yes. Savilla, Fitzgerald—that's the Confederate soldier we tended—he died—"

"Well, I don't expect Stephen is going to die," she said briskly. "The Confederate soldiers were half-starved, which makes everything worse. This books tells what to do. We just need castor oil. And Virginia snakeroot—"

"Mama keeps a lot of such things in her pantry—"

"Then let's go." She headed toward the door, then stopped, looking uncomfortable for the first time. "That is...well, I've been at Dr. Biggs' house. Nursing. We had a few cases of typhus there, and I thought—"

"Please come." My whole heart was behind those words. I hadn't dared hope she'd come back with me, but I was immensely grateful. Savilla knew how to keep her head in an emergency.

We hurried down the street. "Savilla, thank you," I said earnestly. "We were terrible worried. Mama and Anne are off to the hospital at Smoketown, and Papa and Aaron are off smithing for the army, and—"

"Is Teresa home?" Savilla's voice was a bit wary.

"Yes, but in honest truth...well, we need your help." I wasn't sure what else to say.

We found Margaret and Teresa sitting with Stephen, who was clutching his belly and moaning. His nightshirt was soaked in sweat. The room smelled foul. Margaret was weeping. Teresa held Stephen's hand. I saw the panic in her eyes, then surprise when she saw Savilla. I thought I saw a flash of relief, too.

"How is he?" Savilla put a hand on Stephen's forehead. "Poor thing. I brought a book. It has some directions. Here's what we need...."

She was a wonder. Soon Stephen was dosed with the castor oil. He threw most of it up at first, so we just gave him a few drops at a time. "I'm so hot!" he muttered over and over, so we bathed his skin with cold water and vinegar.

He managed to get a little potato broth down. An hour later we gave him Virginia snakeroot and chamomile tea to strengthen his system, and water with a few drops of oil of vitriol mixed in. The book also suggested some yeast, given in wine, but Stephen pitched a tantrum. "No more!" he ordered peevishly, shoving the glass aside. I figured his irritation was a good sign.

Between the four of us, Stephen got constant nursing. At first, we all hovered at once. As time wore on, we took turns. Margaret went to bed when it got dark. When the hour stretched late, Teresa told me to get some rest too. "Go on, Bethie. We'll wake you if we need to, I promise."

I hesitated. Stephen had finally fallen asleep. The only lamp was turned down low, so the room was dim. Savilla and Teresa didn't need my help with nursing, right that minute. Did they need me to help mend other fences? I glanced again at Teresa, and saw her nod. *Go on*, her eyes said. *It's all right. It's time.*

I went.

CHAPTER TWENTY-TWO

TERESA

After Bethie tiptoed out, the only sound was Stephen's raspy breathing. Savilla kept her gaze on him. I wondered if she felt as uncomfortable as me. I tried to find some words. Jiggers, it was hard! Finally I just came out with it. "Savilla...I don't believe I've thanked you yet for coming."

"I was glad to. Truly. Poor Stephen."

"I keep thinking about all the times I called him a worm." I stared at my little brother. Guilt and remorse were heavy in my heart. "And if I hadn't been so stubborn, well...." I was about to mention the brawl I'd had with the Confederate soldiers which led to Fitzgerald being forced on us, exposing Stephen to typhus. It was all my fault! But I didn't quite dare bring that part of it up. Not yet. Not to Savilla. "I just wish I'd been more patient with Stephen."

"That's what all sisters and brothers are like. Don't think on it now."

Her voice was even. Was she still angry at me? Did she want to be friends again, or was she just helping out? I side-stepped that whole question. "I was so...scared. I didn't know what to do." I dared a glance at her, ready to bring the conversation up short if she jumped on the word "scared."

But she didn't. "Good thing Bethie thought of our library. There's not much other help to be found in town, just now."

I sighed. My brain felt like a shell about to explode. "Everything's gone all wrong, hasn't it." It was not a question.

"Yes. Everything." For the first time, I thought I heard a tremble in Savilla's voice.

"It was my fault. Well, a lot of it, anyway." I didn't quite have it in me to shoulder all of the blame.

And Savilla met me halfway. "Mine too. Just as much."

I plucked up every grain of sand I had and risked it all. "Savilla...I've missed you ever so much. I tried to make friends with some of the Union girls, but...they're not much fun." I hesitated. Savilla wrung a cloth out in the basin and dabbed at Stephen's forehead. I could tell she was listening, though. "Do you think we could...try to be friends again? Only if you want to," I added, and made a big show of smoothing a wrinkle out of the quilt.

"I don't know," Savilla said slowly. Then she looked me square in the eye. "But I'd surely like to try."

Aaron and Papa came home at first light the next morning, just when I'd gone down to put the coffeepot on. I was never so glad to see one of my parents! I didn't want to be in charge any more. Worry for Stephen—and guilt about my role in his illness—gnawed at me.

When Papa heard about Stephen he took the stairs two at a time. "He's still feverish," Savilla said. "But we think he's holding his own. No worse."

Papa touched Stephen's cheek with a big dirty finger. "Hang on, son," he whispered. Then to us, "I'm fetching your mother."

I nodded, wanting nothing more. Bethie was hovering in the doorway, and I saw the relief in her eyes. We'd done our best. We all had. But at such times, a sick boy needs his mother.

By mid-day, Mama and Anne were back. They looked white, exhausted. Their eyes were haunted. I understood that look, now.

But Mama wasn't too tired to catch all of us in her arms for a big hug before hurrying upstairs to tend Stephen. "You did well, girls," she told us, after taking everything in. I'd never been so glad to see her, and I don't figure Margaret or Bethie felt any different.

As for Savilla, all Mama said was "It's good to see you, dear. Thank you so much for helping. Did your family fare well during the battle?"

"As far as I know, Mrs. Kretzer. No one else is in Sharpsburg just now. My father's gone to Pennsylvania. I'm waiting for news."

"You're home alone? Why not stay with us, then, until he gets back?"

I caught her eye, hoping she would agree. Savilla hesitated only a pop before nodding. "I'll just fetch some things, and leave a note so my brother and father know where to find me." She looked grateful.

We tiptoed through the next day or so. Mama took over Stephen's care, but we all took turns spelling her. In between there were mountains of nasty laundry to do, cups of broth to prepare, meals for the rest of us. Anne made a few short visits to the hospital at the Lutheran Church, and once or twice I went with her. It broke my heart, but I went. I thought I might see Gideon there, but I never did. I didn't know if I was glad about that or sorry. I didn't seem clear on much, any more. It wasn't a feeling I relished.

Savilla brought some things and settled into our house. She went back to Dr. Biggs' house every day too, to help with the nursing, until an army surgeon took charge there. Then she was no longer welcome. So she just stayed close by and helped Mama. There was a terrible sad look in her eyes sometimes, but she never complained. I didn't ask her questions. I figured that little by little, it would all come out. Just as I'd find a way, in time, to tell her everything that had happened to me.

It was good to have Savilla around. She was a little bit of something getting better in the midst of so much gone wrong. Lord knows everything else was still a mess. Aaron was broody, like something was on his mind. Anne was too, it seemed to me. She was jumpy as a spooked cat. She didn't have two words to say to anybody.

Poor Bethie snatched time to hurry over to the McClintocks' house every day. Mrs. McClintock and Lucilla were fine, but they'd still had no word from the Reverend or Timothy. "Mrs. McClintock is worried sick," Bethie told me. "And so am I. Between worry about Timothy and worry about Stephen, it's hard to breathe sometimes."

I gave her a big hug. I hated the desolate look in her eyes. I ached to ease her burden, to tell her I would take care of everything, like I used to. But I knew neither of us would believe it anymore.

CHAPTER TWENTY-THREE

SAVILLA

It was both strange and not strange to be at the Kretzer house. Sometimes I'd think of the war, of the people I cared about in the Confederate Army, and was ready to bolt home. But no one spoke much on it, and most of the time, I was thankful to be back in a house with other people, with voices and slamming doors and the smell of food drifting from the kitchen.

My brother Samuel found me a day or so later. "Savilla—are you well? I saw the curtains."

It seemed like a month had passed since I closed those curtains as warning! "I'm fine," I assured him, and told him about the provost guard.

"I'll get word to Father," Samuel said grimly.

"And you be safe too!" I added, squeezing his hand. "I couldn't bear it if you were arrested."

"I'll be careful. I'll just visit at night. You're keeping an eye on the house?"

"I check every day."

"I didn't expect to find you here." He peered at me closely. "Are you comfortable with this arrangement?"

"Yes," I nodded, more sure than ever when Samuel said he had to leave. The old aching loneliness loomed. I was grateful to the Kretzers for taking me in. I made myself busy and helpful and, like everyone else, let my world turn around Stephen.

Finally Mrs. Kretzer announced what we'd been waiting to hear. "I think Stephen's turned the corner," she told us one morning. "He's still very sick. But I think he's going to get well."

Mr. Kretzer put his hand over his eyes. "Thank the Lord," Teresa said, and Margaret clapped her hands. I felt a weight— no less than Mr. Kretzer's anvil—slide from my shoulders. The family had come to me for help. I had done my best, in a time when everything seemed to spin beyond my helpless grasp. And I had desperately longed to see Stephen get well.

That evening Teresa fixed a supper of cornsticks and cheese and cider. It wasn't much, but nobody thought to complain. Mr. Kretzer had gone back to his shop to catch up on his army business. I took a tray upstairs, where Mrs. Kretzer and Margaret were sitting with Stephen.

When I came back down, I noticed a dirty envelope lying on the floor in front of the door. I picked it up and saw Anne's name on it. Figuring she'd dropped it, I carried it into the kitchen. Anne, Teresa, Aaron, and Bethie were sitting at the table, picking at the food. Everyone was tired, and there wasn't much talk.

"Margaret and Stephen are eating," I reported. "We talked your mother into lying down for a bit. And oh, I found this on the floor." I held the envelope out to Anne.

"Oh," Anne said, staring at it. The envelope was battered, like it had been crammed in somebody's pocket. She took it very slowly. "Where did you say you found this?"

"In the front hall. Right in front of the door. I figured you dropped it. Or maybe it got slid under."

Anne turned the envelope over. There was a stain on the back, but the sealing wax had long since cracked away. The envelope flap was loose. Suddenly she stood up. "I'll take this upstairs—"

"You will not!" Teresa said. I almost smiled, because it was the first time she'd sounded like herself in days. "Jiggers, Anne, you get a mysterious envelope and you want to sneak away? It could be all kinds of news! Open it, quick."

"Well, I...."

"Do, Anne," Aaron added, more quietly. I could tell he was worried it was bad news.

And suddenly I was too. *How could I have forgotten?* I had plumb forgotten what I had seen at the McGraw house. This was probably a letter from Joseph! Or worse, *about* Joseph. Not a letter intended for public reading. I wanted to snatch the envelope back.

Slowly, Anne slid a single piece of paper out of the envelope. It was folded once, and she hesitated before unfolding it. While we all held our breaths, she quickly read the page— and burst into tears.

Oh Lordy be, I thought. A ball of dread knotted in my stomach.

Aaron's voice cracked through her sobs. "Anne? What is it?"

She let the paper drift to the table. "He's all right!" she wept, and buried her face in her hands. "Oh, he's all right."

"*Who's* all right?" Teresa demanded. She snatched the letter and read aloud:

> "Anne, I have just the briefest moment to scribble a line. I came through the battle unharmed, although many comrades did not, and I saw scenes too terrible to believe. I have found a courier heading to Sharpsburg, and he promises to try to get this into your hands somehow. But he is leaving at once, so I must stop. Never fear, dearest. I'll write again when I can. J."

Teresa put the letter down and stared at Anne with disbelief. "Anne, who is 'J'?"

I couldn't hold my tongue any longer. "Oh stars, Anne," I interrupted. I balled my hand over my mouth. "If I'd known—if I'd thought—I'd have waited until later—"

"What is going on!" Teresa demanded. "Who is that letter from?' "

"Give her a moment!" Aaron snapped at Teresa, but even he looked at Anne expectantly.

Anne wiped her eyes, groped for a handkerchief, then blew her nose on a dish rag. Then she looked around the table at her brother and sisters. "The letter is from Joseph McGraw," she said. "And Teresa, if you say one unkind thing, you'll hear words from me like you've never heard."

I saw Bethie's jaw drop open. I knew they were all thinking, *Anne?*

Teresa stammered for words. "But...but Joseph McGraw is in...." Her voice trailed away, like she couldn't even say the words.

"He is lieutenant of the Purcell Battery, in the Confederate Artillery, under General John Pegram." Anne recited the list proudly. "And if this horrid war ever ends, he is going to come home and marry me."

It was so quiet I suddenly became aware of the crickets, starting their night song out in the back yard. My thoughts were in a tumble. Poor Anne! What kind of load had she carried in silence all these months? I'd been so lost in my own misery I'd forgotten hers.

Teresa was still staring. "He's in the Confederate Army," she said slowly.

"Yes he is." Anne's voice was strong.

"Do you...are you...a Confederate?"

Anne's face softened, just a bit. "No. But I don't fault Joseph because he is. A man has to follow his own conscience."

Teresa's expression was something to behold. I think a civil war was raging inside her. *Don't say anything mean,* I willed her silently. *Please. No more anger.* It suddenly seemed as important to me as it must to Anne. Teresa and I had reached a tentative truce. I didn't want it shattered now. If we couldn't find a way, what hope was left?

Perhaps she heard me. Or perhaps, more likely, she just found her own tongue. "I don't hold with the Confederate cause," she said slowly. "But I hope your Joseph comes home safe, and soon. When he does, I'll wish you both well." Then she clamped her mouth shut tight, like she was afraid something else would pop out.

Anne let out all the breath she'd been storing. "Thank you," she whispered. Then she took the letter upstairs. I figured she wanted to be alone for a while. We all let her go.

CHAPTER TWENTY-FOUR

BETHIE

I didn't even think to ask Teresa about her trip with Gideon for several days. "Where did he take you?" I finally asked. We were hanging new-washed sheets on the line.

"First to his farm." She was hidden behind a flapping sheet, and her voice was muffled. Or had it just taken on a strange tone? I wasn't sure. "We picked up a load of wounded and carted them to Smoketown."

Standing on tiptoe, I shoved a clothespin firmly down on the line. "Was it...awful?" I knew it had been, but I had to ask.

"It was horrible." She paused. "I need to visit someone in Wisconsin, when the war is over."

That was all she said. I didn't ask any other questions.

We didn't see Gideon for several more days. Then one afternoon Papa came home from the shop and stopped in the kitchen, where we were fixing supper. "Got any wash water warm? Good. Pour it in that basin, Bethie, I'm coal dust from head to toe." He splashed noisily for a few moments. "Oh, by the way. Gideon came by just before I closed. He and Aaron were going to stop for a drink, if Delaney's back in business, and then come by the house. Set an extra place, Margaret."

I glanced at Teresa. I thought I saw her cheeks go pink, but she bent her head over the biscuit dough she was rolling. It was hard to tell.

Aaron and Gideon arrived just as we were setting out the plates. Savilla volunteered to sit with Stephen, so for the first time in too long, we had Mama and Papa at the table with the rest of us. It's almost back as it should be, I thought. If we can get Stephen well enough to come downstairs, and Timothy home safe, and everything sorted out between Teresa and Gideon.... The two of them, I noticed, didn't once look at each other, all through the meal.

Still, it was pleasant enough until we'd almost finished. Then, Aaron cleared his throat. "I have something to say."

"Well, say it, boy," Papa said, scooping up the last apple fritter.

But Teresa, who'd gotten up to fetch the coffeepot, set it down with a clatter before dropping back in her chair. And I noticed that Mama's eyes were wary. I sniffed trouble.

Aaron took a deep breath. "I...Gideon and I, actually...we're going to enlist."

Oh no.... I caught my breath. I didn't want Aaron—didn't want either of them—to go! But there it was. Aaron had always known his own mind, even if nobody else did. He wasn't one to be talked around to anything.

There was a long moment of silence. Then Papa put his fork down. "I'm proud of you, son," he said. "You've got sand."

Mama's eyes were brimming with tears, and she had a little red spot in each cheek. Her lips were pressed together tight, so she couldn't speak. But when Aaron looked at her, she nodded.

Then Teresa banged her fist on the table so hard the dishes rattled. "No!" Everyone jumped and stared. Her face had gone white. "You can't go," she said to Aaron. "I mean...you always said you wouldn't go."

"No," Aaron said gently. "I always said I didn't believe the Confederate Army would cross the Potomac and invade the North. I was wrong. They did."

"But—"

"And I was doing...service here. Things have changed now. Everyone's saying President Lincoln is going to issue an Emancipation Proclamation, freeing the slaves. I wasn't willing to invade the South over economic principles. I *am* willing to defend my home, and to fight for emancipation."

"But..." Teresa tried again, then floundered. She turned on Gideon instead. "And you! You're a Dunker! You said Dunkers are pacifists and don't believe in fighting!"

"I'm not enlisting to fight," Gideon said. "I'm enlisting in the medical corps. This campaign has shown me how much good I can do."

"But...I don't want you to go!" Teresa's voice was bewildered, like a lost child's. She looked from Aaron to Gideon and back again. I knew just how she felt.

Mama had collected herself, and took charge. "It seems they've made up their minds," she said, and began clearing the table. "When are you off, boys?"

Aaron hesitated. "Tomorrow morning, we thought. No sense in waiting."

"No, I suppose not." Mama began scraping crumbs into the slop pail for the chickens. She clutched the plate with white-knuckled fingers, but her voice was level. "Well, you must let us know what we can do to get you ready. Send you off proper."

Margaret was starting to sniffle. Anne reached across the table and squeezed her hand. "Margaret, why don't you and I make a plum cake this evening." It was one of Aaron's favorites. "Teresa, Bethie? Would you like to help?"

Teresa was not in the mood to bake. "I'm going to milk the cows," she announced, and shoved away from the table. A moment later the door slammed.

She sounded angry, but I knew better. I threw Anne a look of apology and hurried after Teresa. I wanted to make sure she was all right.

I found Teresa in the stable, plopped on the milking stool by Bess. But her pail was empty, and her face was pressed against the cow's flank. She looked up when I came in. "Oh Bethie. I keep thinking things can't get any worse. Then they do."

I groped for an answer. Before I found one, someone cleared his throat behind us. "Forgive me for interrupting," Gideon said.

He looked embarrassed. I noticed Teresa's cheeks flame too. These two obviously had some talking to do. "I think I'll go back into the house," I said, and turned away.

But Gideon stopped me. "No, stay. I wanted to talk to both of you." He took a deep breath. "You both deserve an apology."

"Me?" I didn't know what he was talking about.

"Yes," he said firmly. He slid his hands in his pockets. "Because of me, Teresa wasn't home when Stephen took sick. It was awful for you. And for Margaret. I'm so sorry."

I felt squirmy. Gideon was one of the finest people I knew. "It turned out all right," I said, and hoped it would be left at that.

He turned to Teresa. Just then Bess got impatient and switched Teresa with her tail. My sister stood up slowly and faced him. "Teresa," Gideon said slowly, in a voice tight as a fiddle string, " I don't know what came over me the other day. I was tired, I guess. Worn thin. And I let myself get angry. I dragged you away from home when your mother had told you to stay, and took you to a place no young woman should ever have to see. And then, on top of it all, I abandoned you there! When they asked me to go I just jumped into action. You'd wandered away and I...I just drove off. It's unforgivable. All of it. Just unforgivable."

Teresa dug a hole in the straw with her shoe. "No it's not," she said slowly. "It was a horrible thing to do. But I reckon...I reckon I needed to see it. I'm not sorry I went."

"You don't hate me?"

"I thought you hated me, that day!"

Gideon looked as if he was in pain. "No, Teresa. I was just...just angry."

"Are you still?"

"No. I—no."

"Neither am I." Teresa twiddled the bucket handle in her fingers. "This is a bold thing for me to say, but..." the faintest smile twitched at her lips, "I was once known as the bravest girl in Sharpsburg, so I figure bold is expected." Then the smile was gone. "Gideon...don't you think we should talk about us? You and me?"

Heavens, I wished I was anywhere else! I didn't know whether to scoot back outside, or stay still as a fence post.

It took Gideon a moment to find words. "Teresa, I don't think that's a conversation we should have just now."

I could tell that's not what Teresa wanted to hear. I couldn't have moved then if I wanted to.

Gideon spread his hands. "Now...the war...everything that's happened, is happening...I'm too tired to think straight. I think we should wait until...later. After. See where we are then."

Teresa's chin came up in the air. She didn't argue. I figure for her, that took a passel of sand. "Well. Yes. All right." Then a terrible sad look came into her eyes. "And now you're leaving. You and Aaron. Going off to war."

"Yes."

A pause, long enough to hear a mouse skittering through the straw. Then, "I don't know if I can bear it."

And finally, *finally*, Gideon took those three long steps that separated the two of them. He put his hands on her shoulders. "Watching someone march away to war takes uncommon courage. I think you can muster it up. Am I right?"

Teresa nodded. Gideon slid his hands down and suddenly he was holding her in his arms. After a bit Teresa put her head on his shoulder.

I chose that minute to slip away. I don't think either one even heard me go.

The next morning, Aaron and Gideon went to war. Gideon had spent the night with his own family, but he was back before first light to collect Aaron.

They took a moment to say good-bye to each of us, one by one. Aaron gave me a fierce hug. "Take care of yourself, Bethie."

Something had been nagging at my mind. "Aaron...have you been helping Gideon and Reverend McClintock with their work? Helping slaves to freedom?"

"When I could."

I nodded, remembering the little Negro boy I had once seen hiding in the cellar. I was proud of Aaron, that was sure.

He squeezed my shoulder. "I know you're worried about Timothy and his father. Try to keep the faith. There's a dozen reasons why there's been no news. No reason to believe they won't yet be safe home." I nodded gratefully.

Gideon gave me a hug too. "Say hello to Reverend McClintock and Timothy for me, when they get home." When I nodded, he leaned over and whispered in my ear. "Thanks for everything, Bethie. I've always known who the bravest girl in Sharpsburg really is. No contest." Before I could blink he moved on to Margaret. I watched him say a word to cheer her up, too. I'll miss Gideon as much as Teresa will, I thought. Well, almost.

We loaded them down with spare shirts and testaments and plum cakes and anything else we could think of. Teresa had stayed up all night sewing, and presented them each with a little American flag. They both got more hugs, and orders to write often, and pleas to be safe. Then they walked away, down Main Street, headed for the recruiting office at Hagerstown.

We all stood in the street, beneath Teresa's big flag, and watched until they were swallowed up in the traffic. The town was still jammed. Visitors were sleeping in the village square. As soon as Stephen was past contagion, we'd have a house full again.

Mama was the first to turn away, and the rest followed. Something kept me standing on the edge of the street. I looked at the crowds, so many strangers, and felt lost. I'd miss Aaron and Gideon something terrible.

Then I heard someone calling my name. It was faint at first, then louder: "Elizabeth!"

I looked, and saw Timothy running, shoving through the people best he could. "Timothy!" I hollered. I figure it was the loudest thing I'd ever voiced, because people turned and stared. I didn't even care. Next thing I knew Timothy was grabbing me up in a hug of his own. I started to cry.

"Oh Elizabeth, are you all right?"

"Yes—I've just been worn to a fray, worrying for you—"

"I got away safe, and managed to find my father, but he fell the day after the battle. It was a runaway horse. He twisted his ankle, and couldn't travel for a bit —"

"Let's go inside." I wanted to hear the whole story, and tell him mine, but in the relative quiet of our big kitchen. I wiped away my tears and took his hand.

"Yes, but Elizabeth—wait." Timothy's dear face had a look of wonder on it. "Lordy be, it fills my heart to see you. I never stopped thinking about you. I think—yes. Yes, it's time."

I wasn't sure what he meant. I didn't even care. All that mattered was that he was home, and safe.

Inside the whole family clustered around, I think grateful to have a happy story to cling to after watching Aaron and Gideon walk away. Timothy retold his tale, starting from the time he'd slipped from the garden while I talked to Hiram, the Rebel guard. Timothy made it sound so dramatic, and my role so important, that even though they'd heard that part of the tale, the family stared at me like I was a stranger.

"So we got home late last night," Timothy finished a few minutes later. "Mama and Lucilla are fine. Ever so glad to see my father, you can imagine. I waited just until first light before running over here to let you know."

"We're so glad you did," Mama said. "We've been worried."

Papa shoved to his feet. "Well, I need to get back to the shop," he said. "It's good to see you, Timothy. Send my regards to your father. Susan, if you could send one of the girls 'round with a lunch basket—"

"Just a moment, Mr. Krezter." Timothy stood up. "If I may. I'd like to speak with you."

Papa stopped and stared, looking very surprised. Then, "All right. What is it?"

I suspect Timothy meant it to be a private conversation, but I could see from the looks on everyone's face that they weren't going anywhere. Timothy must have figured so too, for he looked my father in the eye and got straight on with it. "Well sir, Elizabeth and I want to get engaged. I'd like your permission."

I gasped. Margaret started to say something and was quickly hushed by Anne. Papa's jaw dropped open. For a moment he just stared. "You're too young to get married," he said finally, and started to turn away.

But Timothy did not back down. "No sir," he said firmly, louder than before. "I didn't say we wanted to get married right now. But we do want to get married. Soon as the right day comes. And we want to be engaged now. So things are final. All decided. And we can make plans."

I looked at his familiar wild red hair and freckled face, and felt more love and pride than I'd ever known. My heart seemed to be overflowing.

Then I looked back to Papa. He was staring at Mama, his mouth still open, his eyes still wide. I watched my parents and had a sudden flash that Timothy and I would be like this one day, communicating without words as people do when they're married. And I knew I wanted that more than anything.

And somehow Mama told all that to Papa with her eyes. Finally he looked next at me. "Bethie? Is this what you want?"

"Yes," I said, and my voice was as clear and loud as Timothy's.

"Well then. I guess it's settled. You have my permission, young man. But the details have to wait. At least two years."

"Yes sir!" Timothy grabbed Papa's hand and pumped it joyfully. "Yes sir. We'll wait."

Mama had tears in her eyes. Margaret was bouncing up and down. Anne and Teresa and Savilla were all looking at me with a mix of happiness and envy in their eyes. I nodded at them, trying to say I understood.

Papa reached for his hat. "Now, I must get back. I've got a month's work waiting, and without Aaron...well, anyway. I need to get going." He planted his hat on his head. "I'm pleased for you, Bethie. I am."

"Papa." For the first time I stood up, too. So far Timothy had done all the talking. I needed to square something on my own. "Papa, I prefer *Elizabeth*. I'd like to be called Elizabeth."

Once again I saw surprise in his eyes. For a moment I felt a bit sorry. Maybe it was too many changes, too fast. But I couldn't back down now. I stood my ground—

And he nodded. "Very well, Elizabeth. We'll talk more about this when I can get back home. All right?"

"Yes, Papa," I said, and ran to give him a big hug.

So, that's where it all stands. Stephen's on the mend. As for Aaron and Gideon, we can only hope for the best, and pray.

Savilla's still staying with us. She checks on her house every day, and once Papa had to go with her, and talk to some army officers who wanted to use it for storage. Her brother Samuel stops by from time to time with news. Some of her family had a hard time of it during the battle, and lost so much livestock and crops that they may have to move. And her father is still away.

There's moments when I think things between Teresa and Savilla are still a bit on the delicate side. But they've talked through most of their troubles. And I think they were both so lonely for each other that they were grateful when the war threw them back together, even if they didn't admit it out loud. Last I heard, they were concocting some wild scheme to get them both admitted as nurses in one of the Hagerstown military hospitals. They both want to help, and they both want to pull a trick on the ornery Union surgeons who made the silly rules.

Savilla has changed. There's a sad look in her eyes I never knew before. Teresa told me her heart got broken over an unrequited love. And although Savilla hasn't changed colors, become a Unionist, her heart doesn't seem in the battle anymore.

As for Teresa, she's worried she lost Gideon for good. And she bears a powerful guilt about the way some things turned out. "I was so hard on Aaron," she said to me. "I'd give a lot to take back some of the mean things I said. And the whole time Stephen was so sick, I kept thinking about all the names I'd called him. How short-tempered I used to get with him. Never again."

After Stephen began to get well she was all kinds of nice to him, playing with him and fixing special treats. But it didn't last forever. Stephen went through a spell where he felt good enough to be up and about, but Mama wouldn't let him go outside. He pitched his energy all over the house, and when he used one of Teresa's bonnets as a stable for his toy soldiers on the floor, she whaled into him. "I didn't give you permission to touch that bonnet! You little pest—"

Stephen howled, and Anne scolded, and Margaret, who was at the melodeon, played louder than ever.

And truth be known, I didn't mind the clamor a bit.

Author's Note

This is a work of fiction. It was based, however, on the lives of real people, so it is especially important to explain what is known and what is made up.

The historical context for the story is accurate. The troop movement through the area, the Battle of South Mountain, and the Battle of Antietam Creek (also called the Battle of Sharpsburg) all took place as described. When Confederate General Robert E. Lee brought his hungry army across the Potomac in 1862, panic spread throughout the Northern states. The Union Army stopped the Confederate advance at the Battle of South Mountain, but even then, most people expected Lee to retreat back across the Potomac, not make a stand. The people of Sharpsburg were horrified to find the Southern soldiers settling in for another battle in their farmfields and village streets. The battle which took place on September 17, 1862, has been called the bloodiest day in American history. No other single day, before or since, has produced so many casualties. By best counts, about 23,000 men were dead, wounded, or missing by nightfall—one of every four soldiers engaged in the battle.

A variety of sources provided information about the Kretzer family. The Kretzer children were known by their middle names,

219

which were listed in the 1860 Federal Population Census. In that record, Anne was listed as a dressmaker; Teresa, a milliner; and Aaron, a clerk. The younger children were still in school. Mr. Kretzer was listed as a "master blacksmith," in a village with several other "blacksmiths"; and the property value listed for the Kretzers' home indicates that they were better off than most of their neighbors. Mr. Kretzer's death record (1901) lists the children as Anna Mary, Maria Theresa, Margaret Savilla, Malinda Elizabeth, and Stephen Philip. (Aaron was not listed.) Different sources note different spellings for some of the names (Anna/Anne, Theresa/Teresa, etc.). I used Margaret Savilla's first name to avoid confusion with Savilla Miller. Savilla/Civilla was not an uncommon name in Sharpsburg.

The story of Teresa and her flag has become legend in Sharpsburg. The entire family was for the Union, but one account refers to Teresa as "more fiery and impulsive than the rest." She did make a huge flag, and hang it over Main Street at the beginning of the war; and she did tangle with the Confederate soldiers when they arrived in 1862. Several accounts have survived, including Teresa's own account of the flag and battle, which was published in a book called *Battleground Adventures in the Civil War* (Boston: Houghton Mifflin, 1915). Although some details are not consistent, each story talks about the huge flag hanging over Main Street and Teresa's reluctance to take it down. The flag was buried in the ash pile, Teresa argued with the Confederate soldiers, and they were later marched by as prisoners. Teresa also describes the crowd in the cellar during the battle, and of going to the attic with a friend and spotting the line of Union soldiers trying to push into town. "Although the bullets were raining on the roof," she wrote, "we threw open the shutter and looked out toward the battleground. We were curious to know what was going on. The bullets could have struck us just as easy, but we didn't seem to fear them. On all the distant hills around were the blue uniforms and shining bayonets of our men, and I thought it was the prettiest sight I ever saw in my life."

In this story, the girls' trip to the haunted house is fictional. The request that Teresa make flags for the provost guard is fictional. I based it on an account from nearby Funkstown, in which a resident noted that the provost guard "amused themselves" by forcing Confederate sympathizers to hang American flags from their homes. Teresa's attempt to enlist is entirely fictional. Her trip to Boonsboro, during the battle at South Mountain, is also fictional. It was based on the account of Alexander Root, who was real and did lead the hike as described, out of curiosity.

Most Kretzer anecdotes from the war years do not mention Teresa's siblings. I made up actions and feelings for them, including Elizabeth.

It was difficult to verify many details about Savilla Miller's life. I do not have genealogical records for the family, and a biographical sketch of Jacob Miller mentions Savilla only once. The best known anecdote—about Savilla dispensing water during the battle—comes from Henry Kyd Douglas, who wrote a book about his war experience called *I Rode with Stonewall* (Chapel Hill: The University of North Carolina Press, 1940). "(Savilla was) standing in the porch of her father's house, as if unconscious of the danger she was in," he wrote. "At that time the firing was very heavy, and ever and anon a shell would explode over the town or in the streets, breaking windows, knocking down chimneys, perforating houses and roofs. Otherwise the village was quiet and deserted, as if it was given up to ruin. ...Knowing the great danger to which Miss Savilla was exposed, I rode up to protest and ask her to leave. 'I will remain here as long as our army is between me and the Yankees,' she replied with a calm voice, although there was excitement in her face. 'Won't you have a glass of water?'" Douglas noted that "when the battle ended, she was still holding the fort."

Douglas also described his friend Clinton Rench's death, which happened just as it was described in the story.

Between 1851 and 1901, Savilla's sister Amelia, who had moved to Iowa, received a number of letters from home. Most

were written by Jacob, who mentioned Savilla only occasionally. For example, a letter dated December 29, 1851, reveals,
"Mother, Savilla, and I was out at S. Mumma's yesterday in a
sleigh.... Savilla is going to school at Hagerstown to Elizabeth
Carney('s), but came home to spend the holidays, (and) will go
up the last of this week again."

Those letters were almost miraculously saved, and kindly
loaned to the Antietam National Battlefield just as I was writing this book. They provided insight into the family and their
politics. The family remained pro-Confederate throughout the
war. One unidentified family member, wrote, "I did not know I
had so much gall in my nature until this war question was
brought up, and when one of these Union shirkers murdered
our dear cousin. Dear sister, I shudder now at my feelings. I
hated my most intimate friends because they were in favor of
the Union, right or wrong." This letter is almost illegible, but
the sentiments expressed suggested some of the issues I ex-
plored in this story.

During the battle, several girls were evidently staying at
the Miller home. Douglas refers only to Savilla, but a newspaper article refers to four girls—Jeanette Blackford, Clara Brining, Maggie Hart, and Jennie Mumma—putting out the neighbors' fire and inspiring the local bard to his verse. Savilla was
not mentioned, but the article says the four girls were staying
at the home of Jacob Miller.

Gideon Brummer's character was not based on any single
real person. Timothy McClintock's character was based on a
story preserved in the Antietam National Battlefield archives.
Years after the war, a woman described her home being surrounded by Confederate soldiers who had come to arrest her
father, a "circuit-riding preacher." Her mother was a cousin of
Confederate General Robert E. Lee, so the family was shocked
when the soldiers placed a guard around their home. "They
had information that he had been carrying messages to the
Northern forces," the daughter recalled. "Mother could scarcely
believe this, but knew he had mentioned an interest in the
'Underground Railroad.'" The guard remained throughout the

battle, but a young son managed to slip past them, and warn his father of impending arrest.

Many of the minor characters in the story were based on real people. For example, Heros von Borcke did spend the afternoon working in a Sharpsburg Confederate sympathizer's home, although it was not the Millers'. One branch of the Rohrbach family did live across the street from the Kretzers. The story about Mrs. Ward and her infant being carried down to the cellar, the day of the battle, is true. Dr. Biggs was a well-known community physician, slaveowner, and strong Union man.

I relied on many stories to paint a picture of Sharpsburg during and after the battle. The rural village and farm valley were overwhelmed with the sick, wounded, and dead. Only one account mentions a civilian—a little girl—being killed during the actual battle. But a number of townspeople became ill when sick soldiers were boarded in their homes. Typhoid fever spread quickly, at times with fatal results.

Armies passed through Sharpsburg again in 1863 and in 1864. I don't have any accounts that discuss the Kretzer family during the final two years of the war. The Miller family experienced difficult times. In 1864, Jacob Miller, his sons Morgan, Andrew Rench, and Samuel, and Savilla were arrested by the Union Army. They were transported to Harpers Ferry and incarcerated for several weeks. Finally, with no formal charges brought against them, they were released. However, their troubles were not over: "We got home on Thursday," Jacob wrote, "and on Friday...some fiendish rascal set fire to our barn, and burned it to the ground...."

Savilla Miller apparently never married. The only postwar clue I have is a 1917 cemetery record for Savilla Susan Miller. Henry Kyd Douglas remained single as well. He was involved in a wartime romance with Sallie Conrad, of Winchester, Virginia, but Sallie married someone else.

Teresa Kretzer also never married. She lived in the big stone house on Main Street until her death in 1931. Anne married Jacob McGraw (not his brother Joseph, as in this story). I believe

Jacob's brother Joseph was the Confederate artillerist, but because of duplicate names in many extended families in the area, it is difficult to know for sure. If so, Teresa Kretzer acquired a Confederate veteran for a brother-in-law.

Aaron Kretzer died in 1867; his tombstone lists him as a doctor. Elizabeth married Joseph W. Seiss. Margaret Kretzer married Charles Wesley Adams, who later served as superintendent for the national cemetery established in Sharpsburg.

In the limited accounts left by each family, there is no reference to the other. And yet, they were neighbors in a small village. Teresa and Savilla were similar in age, and must have been at the least acquaintances. It seems likely that Teresa's big flag, hanging over Main Street, was a source of irritation for the Confederate sympathizers in town. We can, of course, never truly understand these people, or their experience. Was Teresa, who risked an army's anger to protect her flag, patriotic and brave, or stubborn and unreasonable? Were the Southern sympathizers in Sharpsburg patriots in the tradition of the American Revolution, or outlaws? These questions have no answer, but it is my hope that Teresa Kretzer, Savilla Miller, and their families would have understood my wish to use their stories to illustrate the painful choices confronting so many Maryland families and communities during the Civil War. The situation in Sharpsburg mirrored that in all border states. *The Bravest Girl in Sharpsburg* grew out of my respect for all those who faced such extraordinarily painful choices.

Today, a visit to the Antietam National Battlefield and Sharpsburg provides a glimpse back in time. A number of beautifully restored homes can be seen in Sharpsburg. If you walk down Main Street, look for plaques that denote buildings standing during the battle. Several still bear the scars of shell damage. The Kretzer home and smokehouse are still standing. Dr. Biggs' home is identified with a small sign.

Unfortunately, the Miller home is gone. It stood where the gas station is now.

Many people have been involved with the efforts to preserve Sharpsburg's heritage. For more information, contact Antietam National Battlefield (Box 158, Sharpsburg, MD 21782) or Save Historic Antietam Foundation (Box 550, Sharpsburg, MD 21782).